Praise for *Outrageous Fortune*

"*Outrageous Fortune* is captivating, absorbing, infuriating and disturbingly funny; it takes you hostage on the very first page and refuses to let you go until all its demands have been met."
—Tom Holt, author of *In Your Dreams*

"Rarely does a first SF novel have as much energy and creativity as Scott's madcap, mischievously irreverent depiction of a definitely post-postmodern future. Consider this the opening salvo of one of the genre's most promising and original new voices in years."

—*Booklist*

"Diverting . . . a zany tale of a slippery future shaped by bogus reality and prefab memories . . . Delightfully droll."
—*Publishers Weekly*

"A crazy world with a rich tapestry of concepts and characters that will most likely make you laugh out loud . . . even if you happen to be in a doctor's office and that sort of thing is frowned upon."

—*SFRevu.com*

also by tim scott

Outrageous Fortune

LOVE IN THE TIME OF FRIDGES

OF FRIDGES

TIM SCOTT

BANTAM SPECTRA

LOVE IN THE TIME OF FRIDGES
A Bantam Spectra Book/August 2008

Published by Bantam Dell
A Division of Random House, Inc.
New York, New York

Book design by Catherine Leonardo

Library of Congress Cataloging-in-Publication Data
Scott, Tim, 1962–
Love in the time of fridges / Tim Scott.
p.   cm.
ISBN 978-0-553-38441-3 (trade pbk.)
1. Seattle (Wash.)—Fiction. I. Title.
PS3619.C6855L68 2008
813'.6—dc22
2008019830

Printed in the United States of America
Published simultaneously in Canada

www.bantamdell.com

BVG   10 9 8 7 6 5 4 3 2 1

To all those who are coming home.

acknowledgments

A huge thanks to Anne Groell, Josh Pasternak, and everyone who has worked on this book for their enormous patience, dedication, and boundless enthusiasm.

And to fridges everywhere for their inspiration, and for keeping the beers cold.

"Tribe follows tribe, and nation follows nation, like the waves of the sea. It is the order of nature, and regret is useless."

"Quoth the raven, 'Nevermore.'"

LOVE IN THE TIME OF FRIDGES

PROLOGUE

The drone carried on the breeze.

She scanned the top of the hill and just made out the slits of light as they huddled together.

The rest of the park seemed deserted, nestled in this forgotten backwater, still clinging desperately to the idea it *was* a park rather than a derelict piece of waste ground. But she sensed it would lose that battle soon. New Seattle had other things on its mind.

She quickened her pace. It wasn't a safe place to be after dark.

Or probably before dark.

Or even at a time between the two, when it seemed light enough to see, but you kept tripping over things. Or banging your knee on carelessly dumped bed frames and other bits of shapeless metal. She hurried across the long uncared-for grass as a thick, dewdrop-sweet smell of rain brought the brooding promise of an approaching storm. And the wind herded the litter in circles.

Now she heard them more clearly, speaking in their own

language, which consisted entirely of humming. And she could see they looked battered, as though they had seen their fair share of lettuces, mayonnaise, and cartons of milk. As though they had each been through the ceremony of having the remnants of a meal carefully sealed in plastic wrap and placed neatly on their top shelves, and then, inevitably, tossed in the garbage a week later when it had gone bad.

A snap of lightning shattered the horizon and silhouetted their awkward, bulky shapes. Ravens were gathered in a leafless tree above them, perhaps hoping for scraps if they opened their doors too far, but she guessed they would barely have any food between them.

Now they saw her, and they all closed their doors so that their lights went out, and hunkered together trying to blend in. As much as six-foot-tall white objects can blend in against a grassy hill.

Which, actually, is not at all.

When she was close enough to almost touch them, she knelt down and began talking, still half expecting them to bolt with their trademark shuffle, pedaling their little feet and waving their tiny arms. But she was pleased to see that they gradually opened their doors, just a little—throwing out a slit of light—and she knew she was winning their confidence.

Not because she had a pint of milk—although now she wished she had brought them something—but because she offered freedom. They were all desperate to avoid the Fridge Details that roamed the city hunting them down, sending them to compounds in the desert. They longed to go to a place where electrical goods had certain rights, such as complimentary yogurt.

That's why they dreamed of going to Mexico.

And now, she was giving them a chance.

Lightning snapped and the storm prepared to engulf the city.

PART ONE

chapter one
ONE DAY LATER

I didn't know her then.

Not when she stepped into the tiny drongle and sat down, soaked through, her slim lips mouthing a faint curse, her brown eyes a stark echo of someone I had once known.

The drongle had just clattered under the concrete snarl of New Seattle's main gate, carrying me back into a city that I had not seen for eight years.

My life had gone missing since I had last been here, mislaid among too many motels, too many bad memories, and a never-ending succession of nights fogged with the bittersweet taste of mojitos. I stared out at the gleaming city lights star-bursting through the rain.

I had tried to close the door on all that had happened here. But that door had never quite shut, and the past had seeped out in a deathly trickle, contaminating my life.

And now I was back, watching the city slump by, pretending these awkward, unfamiliar buildings were my home. We passed a new city sign that shone with garish insincerity in the rain:

WELCOME!
New Seattle Welcomes Visitors*
*See exclusions

A billboard with a huge list of exclusions rose up behind it and I caught the words *real estate agents* somewhere near the bottom. They were resented in a lot of places now, and actually hunted down in Texas by bounty hunters, because the residents had lost patience after being randomly sent inappropriate house details time after time.

The drongle juddered to a halt and the sign loomed over us. It seemed unlikely anyone had ever actually read all that small print, however much it constituted part of the legal agreement to enter this city. It would have probably ranked as the dullest half hour of my life, and I had once talked to a man at a party who was a real fan of scat singing.

I tilted my head as we passed by and saw a bird sitting on the top, motionless, staring down, and the image sat frozen in my mind as we shuddered on through the streets. When it faded I saw the girl was wrapped in her own thoughts, and her deep brown eyes appeared lost in an alleyway of her past.

A Health and Safety sign rose up behind her, filling the drongle dome with a screaming green light.

"New Seattle Health and Safety asks you to stay safe! Be careful of apple pie filling! It's absurdly hot! A strong Health and Safety Department means a strong city!"

I had seen a handful of these signs already and I had read somewhere that the H and S Department wielded the political power behind the machinations of the west coast of America now, and especially in New Seattle. The department had become so powerful it even had an army and had invaded Denmark a few years before. It claimed the war was neces-

sary to settle an international disagreement over the use
of hard hats. Eventually, after it had taken over most of
Copenhagen, a protracted truce was agreed. Health and Safety
published several Venn diagrams to prove that more people
wore bright reflective clothing in Denmark than they had pre-
viously and this, they claimed, meant victory. So they left.

Although two thousand people died in the fighting, nobody cared too much. It was a long way away, and wars in
other people's countries don't really count. Except to some
life-shattered veterans who probably walked through the
crowds in the mall on a Saturday afternoon drunkenly telling
a story in snatches that no one wanted to hear.

The drongle rattled to a halt behind a line of others in the
splattering rain, and I felt a prick of frustration. I had been in
this city less than fifteen minutes and I was already about to
be hassled at a police checkpoint.

The girl's eyes came back and looked around.

"Thank you for traveling today," said the drongle. "Your
lucky color is blue. Your lucky artist who died miserably is
Toulouse-Lautrec. Please take the receipt that is being
printed. It may contain traces of nuts, so if you are allergic to
nuts, use the gloves provided." A sheaf of paper spewed out,
along with some gloves, from a small slot, but neither the girl
nor myself made any move for them.

We just sat with leashed-up frustration without exchanging a word as the rain teemed down, smattering the
roof with a heavy thumping cry, as though the gods were not
just angry, but insane.

Welcome home, I thought, trying to believe the cops
would just wave us through with a glare. The minutes passed
until finally they crisscrossed the translucent dome with flashlights before hauling open the door, their black ponchos reflecting silver streaks in the lights.

"Out of the car, please," said a voice.

"What's the problem, Officer?" I said, really not in the mood to be hassled by a bunch of rookies.

"No problem. Just step out of the drongle, please, both of you."

So we got out and stood waiting in the teeming rain as they hassled the people in the drongle ahead amid a flurry of don't-fuck-with-me faces. It seemed some hoods had pulled off a downtown robbery and these cops were trawling for evidence from anyone they could find. And right now, that was me.

The rain pattered and slapped on everything it could find, and above us another huge New Seattle Health and Safety sign flashed in the wet. "Beware! Treading on small toy building blocks when only wearing socks really hurts."

"You just in?" said a different cop with a flashlight walking over.

"Yeah, that's right." I tried to sound polite, but the brightness in my voice got lost in the storm.

Eventually, another cop trudged over with the rain sliding off his poncho in rivulets and gathering on the peak of his cap in a long line of playful drops.

I had a feed on the back of my neck like everyone else. He plugged in, and a twist of looping wire spooled from the jack plug to his Handheld Feed Reader.

I felt a cold jolt in my neck.

"You showed up as only just in. We tracked your drongle. We like to check out strangers," said the first cop.

"I'm not a stranger. I was born here. I lived here until eight years ago."

"Registered in New York State," said the cop scrolling through my details on his handheld. The system saved cutting through a lot of crap. Sometimes people had their profiles altered on their feed, but if you knew what you were looking for, you could usually tell.

"What's your business?" The first cop shone the flashlight in my face, and I squinted into the glare.

"I'm looking up an old friend, Gabe Numan."

"Old friend, huh?"

"Yeah."

"Hey! He's an ex–New Seattle cop," said the one still scrolling through my details on the screen. "Huckleberry Lindbergh."

"That right?"

"Yeah. Once upon a time," I confirmed.

"Kicked out?"

"I left for my own reasons."

"Couldn't hack it?"

"No, I just left."

"Sure. You left. Let's hear his mood."

The mood program played a few bars of music that was meant to represent your mood. For some reason mine played something classical—a heavy, brooding piece that might have been banged out by a Russian composer after a night on the vodka. It sounded melancholy in the rain.

"I don't like that. That doesn't sound right. What kind of mood is that?" said the cop with the flashlight. "Take him off to Head Hack Central—and the girl, too. If there's one group of people you can't trust, it's cops who got kicked out. They hold a grudge."

"Hey!" cried the woman. "We're not together. I'm not with this guy!"

That was the first time I noticed the fire in her eyes. Even through the snapping drops of rain, I could see it burn.

"Hey, calm down, lady," said the cop, pocketing his flashlight. "If you've nothing to hide, you'll be out within the hour. Just routine. Normally we use the street booths, but they're all broken around here. Now get a red tag and some cuffs on these two and get them in a drongle."

Welcome home, Huck, I thought. *Welcome home.*

My hands were cuffed and a thin red collar snapped onto my neck. They did the same to the girl. It wasn't comfortable. Then we were herded into a four-man cop drongle and, after I kicked up a commotion, they retrieved my bag and threw it in after me.

An officer stooped inside, pulled the hood shut with a grinding crack, and sat with his legs apart, chewing gum and treating the world with enough disinterest to power a small country.

As the drongle rattled away into the night, the hard, wet seats felt cold and soulless. Several tiny screens flickered into life, and the image of a small man with short, neat hair and overlarge eyebrows appeared. For a moment, his words ran out of sync with his mouth, and then the two fused together.

"Hi, I'm Dan Cicero, mayor of New Seattle. You might have heard of me. People call me the Mayor of Safety." He pulled an overly serious expression that played havoc with his eyebrows. Neither seemed to know which way to go. "We have a zero-tolerance policy on danger in this city. If you feel scared—or even nervous about anything—call our slightly-on-edge help line, where a counselor will be happy to talk to you about nice things like pet rabbits." His eyebrows returned to their default setting, then the left one began to head off. "New Seattle Health and Safety is the finest in the world. And certainly a lot better than anything they have in Chicago. Their safety mascot is a piece of crap. An absolute piece of high-end crap. So enjoy your visit."

"New Seattle Health and Safety," sang a close harmony group as pictures of the city were splayed across the screen. "Stay safe! Watch out! Stay safe! Watch out for that—"

Then the drawn-out sound of a long, tortuous crash.

And the mayor's face again.

"And remember, please don't die for no reason. I mean, what's the point? Right?" Then the screen flickered, went black, and those last words hung in the air mocking me, daring me to stir up my anger.

"Don't die for no reason? Why does he say that?"

"It's just a slogan," said the cop.

"A slogan? Sometimes people do die for no reason. Isn't that obvious?"

"If you say so."

The noise of the drongle wheels crunched over the conversation.

I closed my eyes trying to breathe away the anger provoked by that absurd slogan. But the more I pushed it away the more it came back. And the more the memories waited in line in my head.

Another back-wrenching jolt and I looked up.

The woman was quiet. Her features had a soft warmth, but her dark eyes were wrapped up with thoughts I couldn't begin to read. Maybe she saw bad memories running like reels of film in her mind. Maybe she was a prisoner of the past as well.

She barely saw the streets slip by; barely saw the crowds on the drenched sidewalks, the posters, the hawkers and sellers, the bedraggled skyline of skyscrapers, each with tethered advertising balloons bobbing in the wind and their sides a maelstrom of pinprick-white lights star-bursting through the evening gloom, proclaiming the merits of some must-have, must-buy, must-show-off item.

Her eyes remained lost in another place and I wondered why.

Another H and S sign limped past. "Do not open beer bottles with your teeth when you are drunk. You will only realize this is a bad idea the next morning." Who were they kidding?

I recognized the building near it. It was by the Business Center for Not Answering Questions. I remembered how, at one time, it had been a popular institution, giving high-profile talks on the importance of not answering too many questions in business because it had been proven to cut into profits. It was rumored that if anyone ever tried to clarify anything they said, they simply ignored them.

Or sometimes they all put on hats and pretended to be French.

More buildings passed by, but the new architecture just looked like secondhand ideas served up cold, seeping disdain into the city. I didn't like it.

Finally we thumped through a gate and into a massive lot heaving with police drongles—some empty, and others disgorging people into the night.

The cop chewing gum opened the hood with a grunt, shoved my bag into my cuffed hands, and nodded. It was pouring rain as we climbed out and wove our way through the puddles and across the drenched lot that sparkled with reflected lights.

Head Hack Central was lit up with glowing red columns of light. The building was meant to look like it came from classical Greece, but the facade was more like a cross between a wedding cake and a nativity display.

I had been here as a cop.

As we walked through the massive worn doors and into a lobby, memories came at me, one after the other, like stones dropped in a still pool. But I ignored them all. There would be plenty of time to trawl the memories of this place and I wasn't interested in doing that yet. I had been traveling for what seemed like a decade, and right now I just needed to get out of here and find a bed.

We were led down a corridor lined with offices. The woman was taking it all in. It occurred to me she was looking for a way out, and I suddenly felt a frisson of pity for her. Now I understood why she had been caught up in her thoughts in the drongle.

She had something to hide.

THREE

The use of the color red was restricted in New Seattle, because the cops held the franchise. That's why they carried small red truncheons and guns, because it was a marketing thing. I learned all this from a chubby cop who chattered good-naturedly as he left the two of us in a small temporary holding area, composed of a dozen seats enclosed by a small cage. He kept my bag, saying I could pick it up on the way out.

A few other people were already waiting under the glare of a harsh fluorescent light that doused the area with a particularly soulless sense of inhumanity. Across from me was a gaunt man, staring off at things only he could see. His limp-waisted appearance made it appear as though his body had been blown up without quite enough air, and his thin lips didn't seem as if they would have any words behind them. He saw me and smiled, and it creased up more of his face than expected. The girl paced slowly around, still taking in the layout, and I wondered if she would make a bolt for it when they took off our cuffs.

Then someone else was brought in, remonstrating fiercely with a cop. "But I have a license to drop melons," he was saying. His voice was thick with phlegm, and he dripped water from a blotchy raincoat.

"Sure you do," said the cop, shoving him through the gate and leaning his bulging shopping bag up against the desk.

"I do. I have it here. You want to see it?"

"There's no such thing as a license to drop ripe melons from the roofs of very high buildings," said the cop. "Make yourself comfortable. We'll call you."

"But I have license. Where's the thing?" He began to thumb through his raincoat pockets, pulling out a variety of dirty objects. "I got it from the State Department. It cost me fifty dollars. Hey—you see? Here!" He flourished a piece of paper and shoved it through the bars.

"You write this yourself?" said the cop, handing it back.

"No! It's a genuine license to drop ripe melons from the roof of tall buildings. Genuine! You haven't read it, have you? An official melon license. Ah, goddamn it. Cops!" He took the thing back, rammed it into his pocket, and sat down grouchily across from us. I could see a melon protruding from the top of his shopping bag by the main desk.

I sat back and closed my eyes, and realized the smell of disinfectant in this place hadn't changed at all. Another cascade of memories came at me, bright and clear.

Then a tiny voice filled me with a shiver, and it took me a moment to realize that it was someone whispering in my ear.

"They say there's another city like this one, but it is empty," it said, and I opened my eyes and turned.

It was an old man.

"What?" His deep blue eyes sparkled and then he leaned close to my ear again and whispered, "A place where there are no people. And you walk through and there's not a sound. Just the empty buildings. I've dreamed of it."

His delicate words slid through me and I felt them resonate.

"About an empty city?"

"Shh! Not so loud. Shh!" He pulled a wilted smile so fragile it was touching. "Secret," he said gently, drawing away from me and making a wide welcoming gesture with his hands.

Then a cop grabbed him by the arm and hauled him through the gate and off down the corridor like he was a small child. "Mr. Zargowski, they're all waiting for you." The man held my gaze as he stumbled backward until the reality of his situation broke over him and he collapsed in a tantrum.

"Don't do this to me!" he cried. "Please. Don't do this. For the love of God!" Another cop went over to help the first as he began to kick and scream, lying like a child on the floor.

"I don't want to live a waking death!"

"This is a routine head hack. You'll be fine, like everyone else. I promise you, you won't feel anything. I promise."

And they dragged him away. As his shouts receded I thought, *but that's what the guy is scared of, that he won't feel anything. That he'll come out from that room numb and senseless to whoever the hell he was when he went in.* The girl was still pacing and I closed my eyes.

"This is a genuine melon-dropping license, isn't it?" said the man, nudging me back to the present again. He thrust the crumpled sheet toward me.

"Looks like it," I said.

"You see?" he said walking back to the bars. "You see? This guy knows!"

But the cop behind the desk ignored him. And then another came and led away the limp-waisted man opposite, and

I saw his eyes were sunken dark things, as though the pools that had once been there had been drained.

He had the kind of history you don't sit down next to in a bar, and yet I had deliberately sat down to talk to too many people like him over the past eight years.

They had been a distraction. A way of filling time without being left to the mercy of my memories. So those last years had become a vast wasteland in my life, and I did not want to acknowledge they had taken place. For most of them I had worked in a Memory Print store in a mall in Saratoga Springs. I'd printed out people's memories. Twenty-four pictures from the last twenty-four hours for ten dollars, glossy or matte. I hadn't been there because I got some job satisfaction printing out pictures for people so they could go away happy, or because I had enjoyed operating the cumbersome, ammonia-reeking machines. I worked there to pilfer other pasts, immersing myself in other people's lives so I could avoid my own. At Memory Print, there was always a fresh supply of someone else's life to live inside for a while.

But I had never had my memories printed out, even though the company allowed employees free access. They would have been proof that all I experienced from day to day was my life, and if it was on paper it would be harder to disown.

Another cop headed over, his huge feet landing on the floor in untidy steps. He beckoned to the girl and me. "You two. This way."

The girl stared at me, and I saw her brown eyes burn with adrenaline.

But there was no way out for her.

chapter

FOUR

A grimy corridor.

The cop tapped a framed certificate. It said: "New Seattle Police are congratulated on being second in the interstate police awards for the most doughnuts eaten on a stakeout." He'd done a stint for a couple of hours as part of the team, he said, and didn't eat another thing for the next twenty-four hours. Then he got to talking about how the red smoke they used when they went in had stained his hair. We passed offices with the doors ajar, stacked with files and people lazing behind desks letting the time wander past until their shift was done. And ultimately, I guess, until their life was done, too.

"You're in here, lady," said the cop, opening a door marked: Head Hack 4. "And you're next door, in five." He nodded to me. His eyebrows had been stained a faint shade of red, too. He undid the cuffs. "We remove the red-tag collars when you're done."

I wondered if the girl would try and run, but she turned and was gone.

A nurse appeared through the door to Head Hack 4. She

had a smile that was so full of lipstick and insincerity that it made unusual demands on her face.

"I'm Francine, your nurse today. This way." Her heels fiercely clipped on the linoleum. "Can I get you a cup of coffee?" she said over her shoulder as she led me through a small white room that was surprisingly ordered and clean—totally at odds with the paper-filled chaos of the offices we had passed.

"No thanks," I said.

"Or a glass of wonker?" She turned and smiled again but the expression never reached her eyes.

"Wonker? What is that?"

"It's like water, but not as good."

"Okay. No thanks, then," I repeated. She opened the door. It was a small operating room, and I was hit with the rich smell of ammonia—the same smell that had infected the Memory Print store in Saratoga. It caught at the back of the throat and drove my mind to reach back and touch the raw ends of my past.

"So you said no to the wonker?" asked the woman.

"That's it."

"Then please take a seat in the chair and we'll see if we can find anything useful."

"A lot of pictures of the small bar I was in last night outside of Portland, is my guess, or maybe the diner where I ate chop suey that contained more MSG than actual food," I said as I sat down. The room had no windows, but one of the walls was glazed and looked into a viewing booth.

"Yes, I'm sure. But it's amazing what people store away, isn't it? Sometimes without knowing."

"Yeah," I said. "It's amazing what you can store away."

"Everyone has a past," she said. "I'll get you your wonker."

"Everyone has a past," I repeated.

And that's the problem isn't it? I thought. It would be easier if we just didn't. Or if we could erase the bits we didn't like, or could just choose someone else's.

That's all I had been trying to do in Memory Print. Thumbing through everyone else's past so I didn't have to recall my own. The past was not my friend, and I'd tried to avoid it. I'd pushed it away. But the more I'd pushed it away, the more it came at me, like a rabid dog straining and straining on a chain, getting closer to the moment when it could bite.

chapter

FIVE

Mendes had been sent from Washington to oversee Porlock, Inc. It was a new department whose function was to stop people from doing stupid things.

The government was unleashing massive state funding into the area, after research at MIT reported that people doing stupid things was costing the country billions every year.

DST, as they called it, was one of the biggest waste areas of the country's entire economy. The president himself had said in a confidential memo that this was the new frontier; the war on people doing stupid things could affect the position of the U.S. as a world leader.

Even just that morning at Porlock, an agent had interrupted a man intent on driving a golf cart as fast as possible into a swimming pool, and another had rescued a gamekeeper who had just been zipped up in a giant pheasant costume and set loose during a shoot by some animal activists to see how he liked it. They had also interrupted a man who had taken the cover off the main computer at air traffic control and was about to try and fix it with a spoon.

But in his heart Mendes didn't like overprotecting people like this.

He stared down at the city lights sprawled out below, and saw the glow of the brightly colored musical finger-print and head hack booths. As he followed the streets, they wandered their way up the coast and crawled into the shad-owy, undulating hills that once the coyotes had called their own.

Hadn't he been a Harvard high flyer? Hadn't he gone to work in Washington with high ideals of making the world a better place? And now, here he was in charge of some satel-lite project that seemed sordid and sad.

But if he made a good job of this, then he'd be promoted when he got back to Washington. He just had to make sure it all ran smoothly. But babysitting the operation didn't inspire him, however cutting edge the technology.

He tried to pick out the lights of the main gate of the new city wall, tracing the roads that were flecked with orange lights. And that's when it struck him that the maple and myr-tle trees were nearly gone from this city, and the few that he could see looked bedraggled and sad. They were going through the motions of doing all that photosynthesis stuff everyone always gave them so much credit for, but their heart clearly wasn't in it.

Nature hardly had a toehold here.

His office door burst open. It was Kahill.

"We've got a virus," Kahill said. "The system is entirely infected. The mainframe is locked up."

"Locked up? All of it?"

"Yeah. The sensors are jammed and the screens are down."

"How could we have caught a virus? This is a closed system."

"Yeah. That's the mystery. I still think it's probably just something random thought up by a kid in his bedroom."

"A kid?"

"Yeah. There's a message on all the screens that says: 'Can someone please remind me how to do long division?' But we'll sort it. Don't you worry, sir."

Kahill fumbled with the door as he made his way out.

chapter

SIX

S o, if you sit up for me and pop on the bib," said the
nurse, bringing out her dead smile again, "and also
pop on the safety goggles for me as well?"

I hadn't been patronized this much since I was five.

"And I've put your wonker there," she said, indicating a
glass.

She fixed up the bib and plugged a lead into my feed as a
balding man with a ring of neatly trimmed hair at the level of
his ears hit the room rapidly, carrying a file.

"So, I'm Dr. Johansson, and this will only take a few seconds. We're going to get a few images from your head." He
looked through some notes. "This is a routine, twenty-four
hour memory hack."

He tactfully didn't mention that long-term hacks, which
were classed as anything beyond twenty-four hours, still had
a better-than-even chance of leaving the patient a vegetable.

"So, okay. Good, that all looks good. Have you been
hacked in the last two weeks?" He perched on the desk, staring at me. He was wearing a white coat. I sensed his mind

was partially burned away by the stress of his responsibility, but that had given him even more leeway to be smug. It was as though he felt that his job gave him a reason to feel he had a valid role on the earth, and nobody else's did.

"No," I said.

"Owkaaaay. Are you on any medication?"

"No."

"Any problems with headaches?"

"No."

"Any allergic reactions to alfalfa?"

"No."

"You're certain about that? No swelling? What about sneezing? Anything like that?"

"No."

"Doesn't make you feel hunched? So you walk like this?" He lifted his shoulders into his neck, bent forward, and walked a couple of steps.

"No. Definitely doesn't do that. It gets stuck between my teeth, but that's about it."

"Good, okay. That makes things simpler. Shall I check the box for adverts? We insert them perfectly painlessly and they'll play across your memory randomly once a day, maybe twice, for about a month, and then fade away. You'll get paid a small sum. It's easy money."

"No adverts, thanks."

"You're certain? We have one about cookies at the moment. It's very unobtrusive. It lasts only about fifteen seconds, and is quite funny."

"No way," I said. "I do not want adverts."

"As you wish. So, sign here and here. And fingerprint there. And kiss the paper there."

He shoved a pen in my hand and held the form for me.

"And kiss there, please," he said, pushing it to my face.

"Kiss. Harder—and again. Right. This is your copy and your spare, which you send to the ombudsman. Though the last ombudsman was sacked for not knowing what the word *ombudsman* actually meant. He thought it was to do with gardening. Can you believe that?"

His words rattled out quickly, as though by cutting out the pauses from his life, he thought he might gain an extra ten minutes in the day.

"Really?" I said.

"Yes, so . . . Look directly forward and hold your head nice and still for me. That's it. Fire the Head Torsion, please, Francine."

Two flat boards on the end of some kind of hydraulic arms squeezed onto my cheeks, clamping my head into a vice and forcing my mouth open until I was doing a bad impression of a fish.

"That looks fine. Comfortable?" I made a stab at some words, but they came out garbled.

"Good. Francine is going to put some gel on your head. It may feel a tiny bit cold. Gel 3-B, please, Francine. With alfalfa extract."

I felt the cold slop of gunge over my head.

"It can discolor the hair," she said, sweeping it around with her rubber gloves until I could feel it dripping down the sides of my face and onto the bib.

"This will take only a second or two. Francine has a card of some poetry, which you can read to help keep you calm," he said. "Prepare the Vault for the images, please, Francine. And I'd like a hard copy as well."

They exchanged a few other words behind me, and Francine gave me a card. It had some lines of a poem on it, under the heading Government Approved Poetry. "This poem has been approved by Health and Safety to promote calm. It can be read in an emergency to patients who are in shock. Alternatively, show them the picture of the puppy on reverse and encourage them to imagine they are stroking it."

Then the doctor's voice was much louder. "Head hack in five, four—nice and relaxed for me—read the poetry to yourself, that helps—two—keep reading the poetry—one...

"Fire!"

A t Porlock, Inc., they had now induced an error code onto the screens. It read: "The system cannot perform that operation due to error 3.87."

But when Kahill looked that up in a manual, it said: "Error 3.87. A bad error. Actually, that's astonishingly bad. What did you do to get that? Please let us know."

Kahill knocked over his coffee.

Mendes shook his head.

The banks of mutimillion-dollar consoles should have been displaying all the most recent instances of people about to do stupid things, but instead the computer was asking how many bytes there were in a gigabyte. And was it more than forty-seven?

Mendes went back to his office, feeling unease break through him. No one was supposed to know they were here, and the computer wasn't linked to any outside system. So how had they picked up a virus? Maybe it was a programming glitch. He looked out at the city below.

People would be doing stupid things down there.

If it was only small stupid things, the Pentagon would never hear about it and he could bury the whole episode. As long as no one down there did anything really stupid. As long as no one in this city suddenly decided to do something so utterly stupid that the consequences reverberated all the way to Washington.

He felt a chill.

chapter

EIGHT

Fire!" the doctor cried.

My mind tingled and flamed as though it was filled with fireflies.

Then images ran amok as if disturbed by a soft breeze. Pictures of New Seattle fluttering one after the other. The hood of the drongle. The bird sitting on the city sign. The brown eyes of the girl. A Health and Safety sign. More and more shots getting quicker and quicker. Vibrant and sharp, running through my consciousness too fast to comprehend. And then they echoed away into a tumbling dark void.

"All done," said the nurse, and I realized I was breathing hard and my vision was a splintered blur of colors. "Your eyes will adjust in a minute as your brain settles itself."

A crash.

And a scream. I couldn't make out what was happening. For a second I saw the doctor held under the jaw, his tired, smug expression replaced with a panic that stretched his skin taut and infected his eyes.

He was flung across the room, and his head smashed a

console. Smoke erupted from the thing and the plates holding my head kicked like a mule.

A firestorm of pain ran through my head. My eyes stung and it felt like I was swimming about in my own mind. Memories from years before were ripped out and splayed open in a riot of semiconsciousness. I struggled to breathe.

The machine was clawing at my mind with a vicious squeeze, collapsing who I was into a crow-black sea of half-consciousness.

Images boiled. Memories fused together before burning in a great pyre. A man sang Mozart opera. Then another louder voice was suddenly singing about cookies. "Cookies!" The voice sang happily. "They're lovely! Cookies!" It rang on, and my whole self was nothing but this voice going on about cookies. From somewhere, a tiny insignificant part of me wondered if I was dying.

Wondered if this was death—a confusing jumble of memories and voices running around and out of control like they had finally been let off the leash.

But I didn't want to die.

I had done too little of the things that mattered. And too much of those that didn't.

The voice sang aggressively one last time before it swam away.

Then hordes of memories bathed in the spotlight of my mind for tiny fleeting moments. Green fields rolling with wild-flowers.

A swirl of off-blue incandescence.

Abigail smiling on a beach as we ran with our dog, Rufus.

Sitting at a desk in school.

Abigail's hands, playing the piano.

The swirling rocks of Bryce Canyon.

Then I sank into myself. Deeper and deeper until I was in a place where living had stopped. Where something else took place.

Far away, I heard the distant calling of a voice, singing opera again but this time as calm and clear as a child's breath on a still winter morning, each note casting a forest of light.

And then it melted into a furious dark energy that strove to burn away the soul of who I was. I stood my ground as it rose up, screaming with a power that was beyond anything I could understand. I was dying. This was death.

And then, darkness.

The noise of the machine snapped away.

I forced my eyes open. For a moment I could not focus but I sensed someone was there with me.

"Abigail?" I said.

And then I saw the gun.

chapter

NINE

I stared, frozen, as my eyes fought to contend with the white light. Silence scuttled about the room. I slumped forward, the jack plug ripping from the back of my neck as my head released from the boards. It was the girl from the drongle.

"What the hell are you doing?" I said. "You nearly killed me. That machine was searching my long-term memory." She held the gun at my head. On the floor, the doctor and nurse were out cold. The silence settled amid the raw glare of the lights.

"We're getting out of here," she said.

"You're out of your mind."

"You're Huckleberry Lindbergh, an ex-cop, so you know this place. Get up."

Her eyes shone with the passion I had seen before in the drongle, but now it was mixed through with adrenaline.

"I can't help you," I said.

"Yes, you can."

She kicked away the boards that had clasped my head

and pulled me up. I felt remnants of pain snake through my spine and go to ground through my legs, leaving a numb trail in my lungs. The world was still there, but it all seemed slightly farther away, as though all the fittings had inched back slightly and were eyeing me with suspicion.

"You're struggling to keep your own past in check, aren't you? It's in your eyes. I've seen that look before," she said.

"You're making a mistake."

"I don't think so." And then she shot the wall near me and the sound reverberated. "Move."

I stumbled toward the door. She grabbed the images that had been printed from my head and stuffed them in my pocket. I locked eyes with two cops who appeared behind the glass partition with stony faces, each displaying a dish-scourer of a mustache. Their sense of humor looked as though it had been drained away by a machine, leaving their faces empty of a whole range of basic emotions. They stared at the two bodies on the floor.

Then the woman lugged me out of the room, and I stumbled along behind as she gripped my arm, like a favorite toy being dragged by a child.

chapter

TEN

M addox couldn't see his face.

But he knew unmistakeably that it was the man in black.

He had an emptiness about him, an absence. He didn't fit in here, but he didn't entirely fit in anywhere. There would always be a slight gap between him and the rest of the world. Maddox scooted down the bench seat, making his stomach fold around the table edge, and sat opposite. Cathy had been insistent that he lose weight, but doughnuts were too easy to come by in the force.

"You're late and I can't stay long here. Do you have it?" The man spoke from behind black sunglasses. Maddox tensed, and the man seemed almost to fade away before his eyes.

"My eyes are going," Maddox said. "There was a complication. I got the fridge out with the whole batch, but it escaped."

"Escaped?"

"Yeah. I've put out feelers, but I have to be careful. I don't know where it is."

"Find it, and before they do," said the man in black. "I have to go. I have been here too long."

chapter
ELEVEN

The head hack gel stung my eyes.

"Grab those smoke canisters. Grab them," cried the woman as we passed a stack of boxes. I managed to get hold of one and crammed it under my arm. "Which way to the roof?" she cried.

"The roof?"

"Yeah. The roof." She looked at me and I felt the energy in her deep brown eyes slip from her and resonate through me.

"Left," I said. "Stairwell ahead. But you'll be trapped."

She pushed me forward, and I felt the muscles in my legs react like they were strung as tightly as piano wire. An alarm screamed and I tried to wipe the gel from my face as she pulled me along. Even if we got out of here, the cops would hunt us down with their zealous brand of dull efficiency for as long as it took.

Even if it took until after we were dead.

They would probably come along to our graves just to heckle us.

She dragged me toward the stairwell and forced me up-ward. The echoes of our steps came back in empty snaps.

I was breathing hard, my chest virtually exploding with the effort. Too many mojitos over too many years. Christ, I needed to cut back, or maybe I just needed to have more. Maybe that would nullify the pain.

She hauled me up five flights and then we stumbled out through the fire escape door and onto the rain-drenched roof. She let go of my arm and headed to the parapet, jinking easily through the air-con units and aerials. The gel had stung away my vision and I stopped to wipe it away with my sleeve as the rain teemed down in the darkness. The situation was hopeless.

She was up shit creek without a paddle.

Or a boat.

Or a hotel where she could call the travel agent and complain about the whole way the creek had been misrepre-sented generally.

chapter
TWELVE

I stumbled toward where she had stopped, still retching for breath, but I caught my arm on an air-conditioning unit so that the smoke canisters spilled from the box and scattered across the roof. One exploded in a scream of smoke. I left them lying there. When I reached her, she was standing by the parapet looking at the fire escape.

Or more precisely, where it should have been.

There were the rusted remains of fixings and a sign that had been posted. It read: "In case of emergency, break the glass and pull out the picture of the puppy. Then stare at it until calm."

The other buildings on the block were too far away to access. "We have very little time," she said. "Can you think of a plan?"

"No. And I don't make plans."

"What?"

"I don't make plans." I leaned against one of the large stone birds that adorned the parapet, still trying to get my heart rate down to something less than several hundred. The bird toppled from the roof. I watched it loop end-over-end until it blew apart into shards on the steps below, amid hordes of people.

"But it looks like jumping is out," I said.

"Set off all the smoke canisters, then find me. I'm not shooting cops, no matter how annoying their mustaches are."

I nodded and headed back through the night rain to where I had dropped the canisters. I fumbled with the wet tags and let them off one after the other so they formed a massive, impenetrable red cloud. I thought about giving myself up to the cops. There was no sense staying here, but I felt some misguided loyalty to this woman. She understood what was behind my eyes, and that seemed incredibly important.

I ran across the roof to where she was hitting something.

When I got to within a few feet, the smoke cleared and I saw she was trying to break a chain that held down a huge advertising balloon that loomed above.

"You'll kill yourself," I said.

"You came back to New Seattle to find something that would make you feel human, right?"

"I don't know why I came back."

"I do; it's in your eyes. You're about to feel a jolt of adrenaline that should make even a corpse feel human. Hold the chain."

"You always live life like this?"

"With purpose, you mean? You forgotten what that's like?"

I looked at her. And through the dingy half-light and pouring rain, I saw she had the kind of inner confidence I had once felt. And I tried to recall when that sense of being me had slipped away.

"I didn't have you down for kidnapping and social care in one package," I said.

She fired five or six rounds from the gun, and the chain snapped in a shower of sparks. I was dragged ruthlessly across the roof as the glum bulk of the advertising balloon began to wander off in the evening breeze.

We're in The Last Chance Saloon now, I thought as my legs caught on one of the air-con units, *although it has probably been turned into something with individual table lamps, and renamed The Last Chance Bistro, if an architect has gotten hold of it.*

I felt her hands grab me. Then she began winding the free end of the chain firmly around my chest.

"If we get split up, I've a room at the Halcyon motel, okay? It'll be safe for the night."

"Who the hell are you?" I said.

"Nena," she said and then pushed me off the roof and I hung, swinging, chained below the massive balloon. The thing began to drift, and a moment later she jumped, catching me around the waist, and her added weight sent us spiraling down through the cloud of red smoke until we broke clear into the evening lights. She was staring straight at me, and for a moment I smelled her perfume. Then she looked down into the cold rush and her face blanched.

I followed her gaze and the blurring images coalesced into something with hazy edges that made the scene below look like a Raoul Dufy painting. Maybe this was how Raoul Dufy got the idea for his painting style. Maybe he jumped off a lot of tall buildings and then remembered the hazy, undefined edges of the scene so he could paint it later when he had got out of the hospital . . .

We smashed into a man with a sandwich board.

Then we were spun and dragged into the crowd of hawkers and sellers. Their goods were sent flying around us as we skidded across the sidewalk. I tried desperately to get untangled from the chain, but I was snagged somehow, and snapshot images of people flashed before me, their faces made Technicolor by the adrenaline coursing through my veins.

Finally I was knocked free, brutally smashing apart a stall of fresh-cut flowers. The balloon dragged Nena on.

I fought my way to my feet, and suddenly saw it ascending again. She was still attached.

"The end of the world is so nigh there's hardly any time to do anything!" cried the man with the sandwich board, knocking me out of the way so he could stagger back to his box. "It's much more nigh than it was last Tuesday, and it was pretty nigh then. The end of the world is nigh! Who wants a sticker?"

I looked up again to see Nena float up to roof level.

Cops who must have spilled into the area fired through the dispersing red smoke. I heard the sickening crack and the crowd froze as one. Or maybe I just stopped hearing them. Nena dropped, looking inhumane and entirely wrong and landed half on the sidewalk, a little way away. I fought my way over to her.

"Nena," I called. "Nena!"

"That your girlfriend, is it?" said someone, laughing. I pushed him out of the way and knelt down by her. "Nena," I said, and turned her over.

It was a mannequin.

I stared at the inane smiling face. For a moment I froze, and then realized she must have grabbed it from one of the stalls and made a switch.

I scrambled back into the crowd as the cops began to inveigle their way through, but there was no sign of her. A fleet of drongles had been slowed to a halt as the confused crowd spilled onto the road.

I clattered into one and the door sprang open, revealing a group of nuns.

They stared out.

I shouted the name of the Halcyon motel into the horn and threw myself in.

The drongle moved off and nearly ran down a couple of cops who had run into the street. And then we gathered speed and were soon swamped by the traffic. Behind us, the partially collapsed balloon landed on the sidewalk again, causing chaos. I took a long breath and made eye contact with one of the nuns.

"What makes you so sure there is a God?" she said.

"What do you mean?" I replied.

"I mean, why on earth do you think there could be a God?"

"Sister Rachel is not well," said another nun. "It came on overnight."

"I'm sorry," I said.

"She has a fever. You see how pale the poor girl is?"

"I mean, how could there be a God?" continued Sister Rachel. "Why would he allow smug names for different shades of paint? And why would any God not want us to swear? And would he really have invented knees? Or allowed the French to be so off-hand and do that shrugging thing with their shoulders? And why would he think women having mustaches was quite such a clever thing? And why would he decide that the natterjack toad should have sex—"

"That's enough, Sister Rachel," said another nun.

"Yes, Sister," the nun said and composed herself.

I nodded, not quite being able to take all this in.

"I'm sorry," I said again.

"She'll be fine again soon, I'm sure."

I took this as my cue to sink back in the seat and close my eyes. I could have died back there at least twice.

I tried to breathe away a thousand thoughts telling me I had been stupid.

Really dumb-assed stupid. But eventually my mind settled.

And I had a fleeting memory of the vivid images that had run through my mind during the head hack.

And I remembered how I had been walking the city streets but they had been empty of people. I opened my eyes, and the image stayed in my mind with a vibrancy that was unnerving.

chapter THIRTEEN

The drongle drew up outside a convent with dreary gray walls, and the nuns got out in a flurry of umbrellas, which popped open above them like flowering roses.

Rain had erupted again.

A serious summer rain, with fat drops that splattered the drongle roof as the sky convulsed with lightning.

"There simply can't be a God. I mean, what kind of a God would allow golf? It makes no sense," said Sister Rachel before she was hustled away.

A huge unwieldy receipt came chattering from the drongle and the last nun took it, folding it carefully into a massive paper wafer, before getting out. If the nuns all started questioning God they'd have to rename the place Convent of St. Agnes, the Slightly Confused. It wasn't so far-fetched: I'm sure somewhere I had read of a saint called St. Howard, the Slightly Racist.

I shut the curved goose-wing door. My arms ached and I realized my clothes had been torn.

The drongle moved off dodging through the traffic. And then I felt a chill as I stared ahead.

Police checkpoint.

The drongle slowed to a crawl.

If I was pulled in now, they'd put me in a cell and lose the key, and it wouldn't just be down the back of the sofa.

We rumbled into line and stopped amid a group of cops. A man in a drenched suit was gesturing forlornly, his hair flat on his head as he talked to some cops who had turned up their collars to keep out the slanting rain. I could see their tired sneers run across their sodden faces. Then the man lashed out and the cops flattened him, pressing his face against the wet sidewalk slabs. The drongle edged forward so I passed within a few feet of his face, and I stared into his terrified eyes.

And then I was through the checkpoint and rumbling into the traffic again. Another five minutes and it crawled up a hill before it finally crunched to a stop across from the Halcyon motel.

"This is the Halcyon motel," said the drongle. "Please leave the vehicle now. Your lucky color today is yellow. Your lucky ombudsman is one who works for the Financial Services Regulator."

I heard the voice, but I was loath to rush from this snug, dry oasis, so I just sat there for a moment, trying to recollect what it actually meant to be alive.

I had been in this part of town many times before as a cop.

But that had been another life.

And for a moment I saw the image of Abigail run through my mind again. Nena had been right: I was paralyzed by the past. I was a stopped clock. I could appear sane and even content, but it was all an illusion. Even the hands of a stopped clock show the right time twice a day.

I looked out. The neon lights of the Halcyon motel's sign tried to shine gamely, to cheer the place up, but it didn't make a scrap of difference. The place hadn't had any sheen to it in years. In fact, it wouldn't have surprised me if they had built this place with the grime already included.

I remembered how this neighborhood had always specialized in seedy motels. The sort that smelled of old wiring, memories of lost youth, and badly printed Technicolor photographs of some faraway place that seemed all the farther and unobtainable for being associated with these droves of damp-carpeted buildings that had no ambition to ever be anything else.

I still couldn't bring myself to move, then I let the feeling slide and heaved myself out. The hotel sat among an unambitious set of small high-rise buildings that clung to the side of a hill.

I dodged halfway across the street, weaving through the traffic as it plumed up spray, hunching my shoulders pointlessly against the rain as though that might somehow keep me drier, until I found myself stranded on the central divider with drongles wheeling past on either side.

And as they whipped at my clothes, I tasted a strangeness in the moment.

And I recalled the dark presence that had invaded my mind during the head hack, and wondered if I had stared into the presence of death.

chapter

FOURTEEN

At Porlock, Inc., the whole situation was unraveling.

Mendes felt as though he had a cold coming on as he stood staring out at the lines of consoles that sat in the smoldering green neon light. It slid softly over the sleek walls and bathed the operatives in a ghostly ambient glow that was bordering on really-too-dark-to-see-properly-but-the-architect-was-fiercely-defensive-about-having-it levels.

The system had not responded at all.

The mainframe was now repeating the same question over and over: "Does anyone know any clever techniques for remembering a lot of numbers?"

He went back into his office and picked up the phone. Damage limitation. He should call the Pentagon. It would be an admission of defeat, and there was a chance he would be shunted into a backwater of D.C., but they might be able to help.

He hesitated and pulled a face, as though he had smelled something bad. Then he put the phone down.

FIFTEEN

I ran across the street, dodging the skidding drongles that looped spray up over the sidewalk in huge lazy arches, and headed toward the motel.

Above a New Seattle Health and Safety screen flashed: "Vacations can be stressful. Only go on vacation if you have the strength. Otherwise, stay at home where ALL YOUR NICE THINGS ARE."

A Health and Safety logo of a small squirrel wearing some ear protectors followed me with its gaze as I scurried across the sidewalk and into the lobby.

The main door clacked shut behind me, and I paused to let my eyes adjust.

To call the lobby dingy would have been a disservice to the word. It was drowned in gloom, then coated with a strong layer of murkiness. The air was thick with a musty-damp, recently-cooked-food smell that irreversibly impregnated my clothes on contact.

A large, dark-skinned man with a white-patterned shirt straining at the buttons was on duty behind the desk. He was lost in the shadows, so I only got a sense of his huge frame.

"I'm visiting a friend. Her name is Nena," I said. "I need the key." He didn't make any move.

I was about to repeat it when I caught the intense white of his eyes gleaming through the darkness, staring at me. The blood began to pump around my temples more forcefully.

"I see you have the red collar," he said.

I took a long breath and reached up and touched the thing. I didn't need more hassle and I sensed this wasn't his idea of small talk.

"Yeah," I said. "I have the red collar."

He nodded. "That'll be twenty for the key and an extra twenty for the collar."

Forty was pretty much all I had, but this guy was nothing but trouble. In fact, "trouble" could easily have been his middle name—along with "terrifying psychotic maniac." And I was in no shape to fool with anyone. I took out my wallet.

"Forty," I said putting it on the desk and noticing he had a gun under there. "If anyone asks for me, you don't know anything. They'll be another forty in the morning if it's all quiet tonight."

He came forward into the light and I saw his shirt was clean and well ironed. He slowly took down the key and placed it on the desk. I reached for it without breaking his gaze.

Another person in the darkness of the corner I hadn't even seen began laughing like a machine gun. The guy with the eyes just kept staring. But he added a nod and then said: "That's everything. Unless you want me to plug your details into the registry?" He waved a lead from the hotel feed reader.

"You have a quiet evening," I said, and got the hell out of there.

The police would trawl the motels and dark places with

their dull and overzealous brand of efficiency tonight, but some things never change. There will always be people scraping by on bribes at the seedy ends of society. Baksheesh has been mankind's closest companion since the dawn of time. Perhaps that's why God created the universe—someone had simply given him a bribe. And then maybe he did it on the cheap.

That would certainly explain a great deal.

Particularly about the shape of some fish.

I headed down the veranda to the room, and thoughts trailed after me as I worked the key into the door. Would he still call the cops? It seemed unlikely. There were probably more scams going on around here than in D.C. He wouldn't want them poking around.

I got the door open, flicked on the light, and saw four fridges and a tumble dryer in the room. "What the hell is this?"

"Hello," said the nearest fridge, opening its door so its light came on. "Would you like some Primula?"

"Primula?" I said.

"Yeah, it's processed cheese that you squeeze straight from the tube. It might make you feel better." It opened its door farther. The shelves were all barren but for one tube of Primula that was so empty you'd need to hit it with a mallet to get anything more from it.

"It looks pretty empty," I said. "What is all this?"

"It's a welcoming gesture. Nena said we could stay a couple of nights, just until she worked out the details," said another fridge. "And then we're all going to Mexico. Ah . . . Tequila!"

"Great," I said feeling my clothes drip onto the carpet. "That's just great. She's just full of surprises."

"She's gone to Bolivia," said a blue fridge with a deeper voice.

"Bolivia?"

"Yup, that's where she is. It's a big place where they have yak."

"How do you know?"

"Are you a cop?"

"No."

"Don't trust him!" said another fridge.

"Hey, I'm not a cop, okay?"

"He's not a cop. Where's his mustache?" said the one with the Primula.

"Okay, the truth is that we don't know where she is. Do you?"

"No," I said.

"Oh," said the tumble dryer.

"She told us to tell the cops she'd gone to Bolivia if they came calling, and we were working on a song. But we couldn't come up with anything that rhymed with Bolivia," said one with Frost Fox written across its door.

"That's a great idea," I said.

"You think so? Want me to dry your clothes? I feel a spin coming on," said the tumble dryer, nuzzling into me.

"Oh, yeah, you should. It'll make him so happy," said another fridge.

"Yeah, you can dry my clothes while I take a shower. She may be awhile. But stay quiet, all of you. If the management find out you're in here, they'll get angry. And if the guy in the lobby gets angry, we're all in trouble."

"Sure. We'll be quiet. And I'll have that Primula waiting for you when you come out."

"Okay."

I peeled off my sodden clothes. I had ripped gashes through a lot of the material and the gel had stripped the color from my shirt. I wasn't going to be making it to any flashy parties in those again. I put them in the tumble dryer, which squealed happily, and went into the grimy bathroom.

My head was throbbing, probably as some aftereffect of the head hack, and now it had become harder to ignore. It felt like I had a nest of bees in there.

Everything that had happened in the past few hours shimmered in my head, refusing to coalesce into any kind of shape, so my thoughts did little more than shamble around at half pace and I did my best to ignore them.

The bathroom was pretty disgusting. Nobody had done more than run a mop around the place in living memory, and green mildew was hidden behind the sheen of grime. The cockroaches were in cockroach heaven.

I turned the shower on, but it clearly wasn't used to this turn of events and began hammering away like a malfunctioning engine. After a minute, water spluttered defensively from the head. It was entirely cold. I waited awhile.

It got colder.

I forced myself under it, and my chest contracted with the shock. Then the water turned scalding hot.

I hopped in and out of the tiny jet as I tried to wash my hair and clean out the cuts and grazes. That's when I caught a glimpse of myself in the steamed-up mirror across from the cubicle.

My hair was blond.

My hair was completely, fucking blond.

I stumbled out of the shower and stared. The realization came at me in a confused ball.

The head hack gel. It had bleached it. The woman had said something about that and I began to recall that was why we had never used the stuff at Memory Print.

I looked at my appearance and it seemed as if in the space of a few hours I had begun turning into somebody else.

Maybe this was how Kafka's first draft of *Metamorphosis* had been. Perhaps the protagonist had just woken up with a different hair color and the idea of him turning into an insect only came later. The story possibly wouldn't have had the same impact on European literature, but it might have been more of a hit with hairdressers.

I dried myself off, managed to cut off the red collar using a broken tile, and went out into the main room.

The fridges immediately started singing.

"Where's she gone?
Here's a bit of trivia,
It's got the highest lake,
That's right! It's Bolivia!"

"Sh! Quiet!" I said.

They went silent. Most of them closed their doors nervously. My head throbbed. "Okay, listen. I'm in trouble, right? I need to keep a low profile and having four fridges and a spin dryer in my room singing loudly about Bolivia is not a low profile."

"Sorry. We thought it might cheer you up," said the Frost Fox.

"I don't need cheering up. I need to stay alive and away from the police."

"Oh." The fridges shuffled.

"So let's all just chill out, okay?"

They all began humming with intense vigor.

"No, I meant relax," I said. "Just relax, okay? How are my clothes doing?"

The tumble dryer padded over and opened its door happily. They were pretty much dry, so I slipped them back on.

"Thanks," I said. "Good job." Then I flicked off the light and lay down on the bed. Ideally I needed food, but that would have to wait. If Nena made it back, we could find a place to eat later on. I could really do with some coffee and whatever else they served in this part of town at night. And, ideally, pastries. Pastries always made everything better.

In any hijack situation, it was well known the negotiators always sent in pastries; it just took the edge off the terrorists' anger. You can't bring yourself to start shooting people when you've just eaten a nice Danish. They're too sticky and flaky.

I reeled in my thoughts. The police didn't have anything to go on. They weren't going to find me tonight.

"Anything suspicious and I'll do an owl call," said a fridge by the window.

"Just stay quiet," I said and tried to get comfortable, but there was a lump in one pocket. I felt to see what it was and found the memories printed off at the head hack. Nena had stuffed them in there as we left the room. Now they had been fused together by being soaked and dried. A few peeled apart and I thumbed through them under the light that spilled in through a crack in the curtains.

Most were out of focus, but then I came to one that was as clear as a bell.

My heart jumped. I hadn't seen her face in eight years.

I looked at her smile and her hair. And I traced the shape of her face.

Abigail.

chapter

SIXTEEN

Bryce Canyon.

The crunch of snow as we stooped under the pine branches that smelled sweet with resin to find the bar. The ice-hot freeze of the snow that fell on my neck from one of the trees. All around was the glimmer of pinprick white lights, flickering with fierce magic, and the jagged silhouettes of the encircling mountains.

We drank enormous brandies in outlandishly bulbous glasses at one of the outside tables that came supplied with soft, thick blankets. And as the evening went on, we snuggled up together and talked about the places we'd been and things that meant something to us. Raoul Dufy paintings, the lilt of the writing by Tennessee Williams, the calm quiet of an empty dawn sky in Nebraska. And for a while, all my cynicism, irritation, and anger with the world melted away as we watched the stars and listened to the background chatter and laughter around us, rosy with celebration and hope.

In that moment, I would probably even have had a forgiving word for people who thought spray-on stencils were a worthwhile aspect of interior decoration.

It was as though she was someone I already knew, and yet could not place. A person I felt I had been through fire with, yet had not enjoyed the stretched-out, delicious days of learning about who she was.

She was familiar and a total stranger, all in one.

And then, as it got toward midnight and the carol singers were gathered a little way off, singing without any kind of caution around a huge fire, she snuggled closer and said she wanted to stretch this moment out so it would cover the rest of her life with its warm glow.

And it was actually perfect. It was all shadows and magic.

And I couldn't think of a better way of spending my life than with this girl. She was full of a wide-eyed, innocent passion about life, as though she felt the heartbeat of the very earth inside of herself.

And maybe in that moment I finally understood. Maybe, for a brief second, I finally got the point of it all.

It's here. It's all around. We just need to stop and look. Then we'll feel the wind on our arms. Then we'll hear the swifts wheeling overhead with their soft screeches. Then we'll feel the gentle warmth of the fire.

All we need to do is take a deep, overslow breath.

And actually look about.

She was right. In that moment, I was home.

chapter
SEVENTEEN

Porlock.

In his office, Mendes stared down at the New Seattle buildings, swathed in a stony, stiff-necked gloom far below. They seemed to hunch down and grip the earth as the lightning forked. The last time he had looked at the screens they said: "What is it with pressing those keys so quickly?"

A plume of red smoke coiled into the air near Puget Sound. He watched it snake up, forming an elegant curve, and it felt like a painful metaphor for his career. The early optimism about cleaning the virus from the system had gone, and now Kahill was defensive about the whole subject.

The air-conditioning was on full and the noise filled his head with a tired white moan. "I need air," he said.

He headed out of his office to the lobby. Eventually he found the fire escape stairs that led onto the roof.

The cool air was a relief and it froze the sweat across his forehead. He walked to the parapet as an advertising balloon bobbed above him, yanking against a thick chain that was secured to a massive, rusting fixing.

He suddenly detested the whole project. It was a sham.

Down there in the city, the engineers had planted sensors. They scanned the population for a specific length of brainwave that was associated only with someone on the verge of doing something stupid. It was generated from a part of the brain that people didn't use very much—and that was why when they did something really stupid, it felt like it was not really them in control.

Computers pinpointed exactly where the signal was coming from and sent someone to interrupt. After some experimentation, they'd found that eyeliner and a large swamp of wild hair had a massively distracting effect, but all the agents had their own style.

They'd be down there now, waiting—like him.

It was an elegantly simple solution to the whole DST problem, but he didn't feel comfortable interfering in the lives of people like this. He wanted to be through with Porlock.

He had been told the name was a reference to Coleridge, and he had been sent copies of *Kubla Khan* by the marketing department.

He now knew most of it by heart.

"So twice five miles of fertile ground, with walls and towers were girdled round," he said. He made out the main city gate through the gloom. There were stories of people hacking into the drones that had built it. They were supposed to have reprogrammed them to put in tunnels and rooms that weren't in the original plans.

"With walls and towers were girdled round," he said again, then walked slowly back across the roof.

chapter EIGHTEEN

I felt a jab in my throat.

I clawed my way back from sleep, back into the darkness of the motel room. It felt like a knife. I twisted around in a daze and banged my arm. Through the gloom I saw the outline of a fridge, poking at me with the corner of its door.

"Stop that," I said lying back down. "I do not want any Primula cheese from a tube, and I don't want to play with any fridge magnets, if that's what you wanted to ask."

"Listen," said the fridge. "There's someone trying to get in."

A shadow.

"Make yourself at home," said a woman's voice through the darkness. "Sorry it's not more upmarket. I thought it would be less obtrusive for the fridges."

"Nena?" I fumbled for the bedside light and finally flicked it on. It threw out a sad yellow pool of light, but it was enough to see her face, flushed with the night air.

"Blond hair suits you," she said. "Want a drink? I have whiskey."

"You scared me." I heaved myself up on the edge of the bed, feeling the dry edges of my lips. "And I didn't mean to sleep. How long have I been out?"

"It's 1 a.m. Here." She had poured some whiskey into a glass and handed it to me. "You okay?"

"Yeah," I said.

"Good. You met the fridges, then?"

"Yeah. And they've made me really at home with their close-harmony singing and offers of processed cheese."

"You've seen what's inside them?"

"This fellow has some Primula, but I don't think they have a lot of food."

She nodded as I knocked back the rest of the whiskey and felt it course through my body, settling with a burn in my stomach.

"Better?" she said.

"Yeah. What took you so long?"

She poured another glass. There was a warm, comfortable silence interrupted by the chinking of the bottle neck.

"I was followed. And then I got to wondering whether you would have the cops waiting here for me so you could bargain your way out."

"That would have been the sensible thing to do, now you mention it."

She shrugged and then got up, rummaging through the closet until she found a blanket.

"But you decided I wouldn't? Am I so easy to read?" I said.

"People who have lost their way in life are always easy to read. It goes with the territory."

"What do you mean?"

"It's in your eyes. You might as well have a note stuck to your forehead. Get some rest. I'll take this side of the bed." She threw down the blanket.

"So, tell me what you see."

"No. Get some rest. You can spend the night here. But tomorrow you need to forget about me, okay? You just walk away. Get out of town."

"Why not tell me? What's the big deal?"

"You might find it harder to sleep."

"I'll sleep."

"All right. You want to start living again, but you don't know where to find the switch. You're trying to deny this is your life because you think you deserve a better one. And that maybe if you keep pushing the reality of your life away, that other perfect life you dreamed about will magically appear. But this *is* your life, isn't it?"

"Is that what you see?"

"Yeah."

"Well, it's bullshit. And you really think I'm going to run from this city tomorrow?"

"That's exactly what you're going to do. Now, get some rest. You were vulnerable, and I took advantage. That's all there is."

"Weird!" said the Frost Fox by the window. "The lot is full of red mist."

"Mist?" Nena got to her feet, flicked off the light, and peered through the edge of the curtains. "That's red smoke."

I looked out and saw shadows throwing their bulk about, and pinpoint laser lights were cutting the darkness into slices.

"Security Detail," she said.

"Should I do my owl call to signal danger?" said the Ice Jumper.

"Quiet, little fellow," Nena chided. "They sure as hell didn't follow *me*."

"I suspect they're here by invitation of the man in the lobby."

"You checked in at the lobby?"

"Yeah. Bad move, eh? Sorry."

"Hoooot!" went the fridge.

"Sh!"

"We're going to have to move fast," she said. "And leave the fridges." She froze for a moment, as though she had only just understood what her own words meant.

"Is that a problem? They do just hold food and hum a bit," I said, looking at her.

"Hey! Don't trivialize the important role we play in society," said the Frost Fox.

"Yeah! We fridges have a lot to offer. What about the Thermo King that became Washington State checkers champion four years in a row?"

"I heard about that," said the tumble dryer. "He wanted to take up chess, but couldn't get the hang of the horsey piece."

"Okay, I'm sorry. You guys take care," I said, as Nena grabbed me by the arm and pulled me toward the bathroom.

"Hell, we've been in worse corners than this," said the Cold Moose.

"I'll bet you have," I said. But I somehow doubted it. We both knew the Fridge Detail would be called, and they'd all be taken away to the Cold Compound and then the dumps in the desert. There were huge camps of refrigerators there. Some of them had gone completely feral. They were all going to hell. But Christ, they were only fridges.

The ceiling in the bathroom was made of cheap panels. Nena climbed onto the bath and knocked one out. Dust showered down. She put her foot on the sink and sprang up.

Then she turned and offered me her arm to help me through. I struggled up, flaying my legs hopelessly against the wall until I was lying belly down on a beam in the roof space.

It was unbelievably dark.

She replaced the panel, dousing the square of light so I could see nothing.

"Keep on the beam," she whispered and I heard her moving away. I tried to follow. We were still over the room when we heard the door being smashed in and a cacophony of muffled voices.

"Freeze!" the police were shouting.

Even from up here, I could hear the dramatic increase in humming from the fridges.

I smiled. I was actually getting to like those guys.

A pity they were all going to hell.

chapter

NINETEEN

I edged on awkwardly.

I could just about make out my surroundings now. We were in a small loft fitted into the pitch of a roof. Pipes ran about like they were looking for something. As I levered my way over a bunch of them, I caught one with my foot. The noise vibrated throughout the building and a shower of fine dust sifted over us.

I stifled a sneeze and scrabbled on, trying to keep up with Nena, feeling wooden splinters prick at my hands. Then I put my foot through the ceiling.

The tearing crunch made Nena turn and she grabbed me, but as I hung onto her I pulled her off balance. She slipped and broke through the ceiling. I froze, watching as she landed in a bundle on the floor. Thick red smoke began to drift up through the hole in the ceiling, and flashlight beams jabbed around me. I ducked back and fumbled on.

The loft kicked around a bend, and I saw a spot where the pipes all dived down in a mass. I crawled over and peered down.

It was some sort of duct.

Urgent shouts were marauding through the dead air now. Cocooned up here, it felt as though they were leaking through a tear in space and coming from another planet.

I hung my feet over the edge of the tiny duct and tried to find the one pipe out of the mass that wasn't scalding hot. I held onto it and eased my way down into the tight space. Eerie clonking noises vibrated from below, as though I was descending into the stomach of a dinosaur.

Then the pipe gave way with a shuddering growl and I slipped alarmingly. Water spurted out with an excited hiss. I might as well have put up a sign telling everyone where I was.

I forced myself downward quickly, but the space was so tight that I pulled another pipe free. More water gushed out.

Slanting gashes of flashlight cut across the duct above me now. The cops were in the loft space.

I forced myself down, then felt the duct open out at my feet, and dropped onto a concrete floor so hard my ankles felt like they'd broken.

It was a small basement. A huge boiler bloated with caking rust hunched in one corner. It was steaming hot and gurgling like a young child who had just told his first joke.

A small window poked up at ground level covered in layer after layer of cobwebs. Flashing lights flickered in from outside. On the other side of the room was a heavy metal door that stood ajar.

I heaved it open and found a set of worn wooden stairs that led up to a trapdoor. I ran up them and cautiously opened the trap an inch to peer out, expecting it to be flooded with cops.

It was quiet.

I went back down, jammed the metal door shut, then ran up the stairs and flapped back the hatch.

It took me a second to realize I was behind the desk in the lobby. I shut the hatch just as someone came in through the front door. I was caught, but hidden down behind the counter was a shotgun.

"Trouble?" The guy had a lilt to his voice.

"Yeah," I replied, "but it's under control." I fingered the gun.

"Good. I couldn't sleep with all that noise. I once nearly got a job with one of those security units. It was down in Los Angeles. The pay was so-so, but Sally wanted me to take it. She said the climate down there was good for her knees. The damp here makes them swell up, you see."

"Swell up?" I said. He had a looping mustache and a clothes sense suggesting he might have been brought up in the wild.

"Yeah, they balloon up, but she has pills and they work just fine. Little blue ones."

"The wonders of modern science."

"Seems like a long time ago. We had a dog then called Chico. Funny old feller he was. He could run like the wind, but he was always hungry. You ever eaten dog chocolate? It tastes okay, but you wonder what's in it. My wife used to buy it for him, but I had my share. You ever tried that stuff?"

"No," I said as the door scraped open again. This time, it was a cop. Even in the dingy half-light, I could see he had the sort of overtired eyes that meant he'd been around the block a few too many times. I took hold of the gun in two hands, but kept it out of sight. I hoped the thing was loaded. I repeated my answer as he approached, trying to enforce the impression that the man and I been chatting for some time.

"We lost the woman *and* the man. All we got were some goddamn fridges," said the cop.

"Fridges?" said the other man.

"Yeah, a load of fridges, and they won't stop singing about Bolivia. It's 1 a.m., for Christ's sake, and they're all singing about Bolivia. Sometimes I wonder about this job. You the one who saw the guy?"

"Yeah," I said.

"This him?" He pushed a picture of me over the desk that they had taken when I was in the head hack chair. I had black hair. And it was blurred.

"Yeah, that's him. That's the guy." I kept in the shadows.

"Yeah, well, we'll get him. We'll check every motel tonight. They've made this a top-priority sting now. And when that happens, we get free doughnuts. I guess that's why I stay with this job."

"Does your wife have knees that swell up?" the other man said to the cop.

"Swell up?" The cop looked at him.

"Yeah. Do your wife's knees swell up in the damp? Like balloons?"

"Are you making fun of me? Get out of here!" The cop lifted his hand and the other guy left hurriedly, letting the front door shut with a clack. "What is it with these people? So, this is yours. Thanks for the tip-off," said the cop, handing me an envelope. "If he comes back looking for his fridges, let us know."

"I'll keep an eye out," I said, putting the gun gently down on the shelf under the desk and taking the envelope. "With compliments of New Seattle P.D." it said. I slipped it into my inside pocket without opening it. The cop nodded and headed for the door. He took four paces then stopped, took his gun out, and spun around.

"Why do you have your hand on a gun under the desk? Why would you do that?" he said.

I stared, trying to summon up the kind of disinterest people felt for Canada.

"Habit," I said. "You get a lot of weird people in here."

There was noise above our heads.

"That right?" the cop said. "Habit? Maybe habit would make you do that, or maybe you're nervous. Maybe we should hear your mood."

But as he moved back toward me, the ceiling collapsed in a shower of broken plaster and another cop landed on the floor in a thumping, wet bundle.

"Ah!" cried the one that had fallen. "My back! And I've only just gotten it fixed. You saw that, didn't you?" he said to the one with tired eyes.

"Yeah, you fell through the fucking ceiling."

"My back! Don't stand there. Help me up!"

"Okay, okay." The event was swamping the first cop, but he kept his eyes on me, perhaps ensuring that I wasn't going for the shotgun.

"Get the Police OURU here, quickly," said the guy on the floor.

The cop with the baggy eyes seemed confused. "Who?"

"The Police Osteopath Urgent Response Unit. Get them down here. I need my spine looked at," said the other cop.

"Okay, sure." Well-worn eyes had put away his gun.

"And tell them it's an emergency."

"Okay." He got on the radio and called. "Don't you go anywhere," he said pointing at me as he helped the other man hobble through the door. "I want to check your mood. You understand? Or you'll be in trouble."

"Yes, sir. No problem. I'll be right here all night," I said as the door clacked shut.

Then I bolted through a back kitchen and got the hell out of there.

chapter
TWENTY

The night was clear and cold.

As I was sucked down the streets, my thoughts shambled, trying to coalesce into order. But they wouldn't do it. The situation was a mess.

So I walked, letting my feet take me where they wanted under a night sky filled with gleaming buildings, overinflated with a sense of prestige, past groups of drunken teenagers bursting with bravura, and on through the city that had once been my home. Occasionally I sank back into doorways to avoid the gaze of the police drongles. And all the time feeling the sidewalk under my feet, hoping the rhythm of my steps over the wet, gray slabs would tell me what the hell I should do next.

After an hour, I found myself standing outside Mending Things with Fire.

I stood stupidly, looking at the bar, telling myself that I hadn't come back to New Seattle to trawl over my past. But the place was unchanged, looking just as it had eight years ago, almost to the day when I had last been here.

It was as though time hadn't quite made it down this alley, and wave after wave of the years had only lapped at the end of the street.

Had it really been so long ago that Gabe, Marcy, Abigail, and myself had all stood here convulsed with laughter as we watched the Trivia Machine run off because it couldn't think of any more questions?

A couple of coffee tables slipped out of the shadows and began hassling me with insurance deals before I ushered them off into the night. I should have turned and walked away as well, but instead I headed into the bar—knowing I wasn't opening a Pandora's Box of the past, but probably a whole set of Pandora's Suitcases and matching luggage as well.

The familiar sweet smell of the place greeted me as I let the door flop shut behind me.

Inside it was confusing. It looked the same with its nooks and crannies, bookshelves, and wide beaten-up sofas, but the faces had changed.

And I was struck with the thought that this place didn't actually belong to me anymore. I had only been passing through.

I was slightly alarmed to see that a country singer had just begun playing up on a little stage—country music is just about all right as long as you don't give it your full attention. If you do, its credibility collapses like an elk shot between the antlers and you see it for what it is.

Utter maudlin nonsense.

This whip of a girl was cradling a guitar and had her head tilted over to one side so her long hair hung in a wide curtain. She was singing a song that seemed to have the refrain "That's why Susan became an ostler." I instructed myself not to listen to it too closely or I would get insanely irritated.

I headed through the wide sofas and battered tables that had been imported from improbably far-off places. The memories came at me thick and fast, but I did my best to dodge them.

Finally I stood dripping at the bar with a scorching headache and ordered fourteen mojitos.

The bar girl had small, pretty features and looked as if she was in that period of life where she believed she understood clearly what things were about. But my order made her hesitate and she seemed about to say something, but she finally changed her mind and just nodded.

Evidently, I looked like I needed them.

Standing here, I felt shoulder to shoulder with so many memories that I might have passed out with the strain of keeping them at bay, so I found a small table and sat down.

Then I took out the envelope the cop had given me and opened it. Inside were five hundred New Seattle dollars, in ten-dollar bills. I mentally raised a glass to the New Seattle P.D.

There were also two VIP tickets to the fireworks at the opening ceremony of the city wall the next night.

The girl singing country music brought her song to a close and smattering clumps of applause broke out around the bar. Someone shouted: "More songs about ostlers!"

"Hell, I only know one other," said the girl into the microphone. "But I'll play that later, if you like."

Eventually the bar girl ferried the mojitos over to my table. I drank one and finally allowed myself to let the memory of that last day wash over me, and I felt it catch at the back of my throat.

The gap Abigail had left hung in the air so palpably I could feel its shape, like a void still alive with its own emptiness.

The image of her came again so vividly I could touch it.

chapter
TWENTY-ONE

She had come home one day, carrying a brown paper bag full of shopping, placed it on the table, and said, "Have you seen the sky out there? It's like someone has taken the lid off the world." And then she collapsed and lay in a weird tangle—limbs folded over at strange, unsleeping angles, and the air around her stark with shock.

I had tried to bring her back—frantically—but she was already gone. She was falling through that deep blue sky even as I tried to blow life back into her cooling lips.

We had been married less than a year. That was all.

I could still feel that empty house. And how we had the funeral, and the endless aching tears. How I had tried to carry on with my life, but there was a heavy stupor of death covering everything, squashing away all sense of joy.

How I had left that place and gotten out on the road where there was room to breathe.

I had worked in endless dead-end jobs until I couldn't stand it anymore and moved on. Always moving on, when the pain got too much to bear.

I had wallowed in self-pity because I was furious at the world for having taken her from me. But more than that, I was furious that I had been unable to protect her. It was childish and stupid, but I was angry.

And then, after much too long, I began to realize that sometimes bad things happen. They just do.

But by then I had become a refugee in my own life, unsure how to go forward.

I had become a stopped clock.

chapter TWENTY-TWO

Mendes coughed.

He listened while the girl from admin explained.

"Sometimes it stops moving and then insists it's in Kazakhstan, three thousand miles from any grass," she said, raising her voice to such a high octave that it was approaching a frequency only dogs could hear. "And that, frankly, it isn't happy about it. But if we turn it off and then back on again, it carries on fine."

"Thank you, Sara," he said. "And if this was a lawnmower and not one of the most powerful computers on the western seaboard, we would have the solution right there. Now, I'd like you to go out and get me some medication."

"Herbs?"

"No, not herbs. Some drugs. Pills. I have a fever coming, and I need to stop it."

She put her hand on his arm. "It'll all be all right. But if it's not, you just have to laugh, don't you?" She laughed like a seal that was being machine-gunned.

"Please, be as quick as you can."

"I'll get them now." She left the office and he sat down. Security here didn't seem tight enough to him. The whole project was supposed to be only known to a few people in the Pentagon.

But there had been rumors in the press. Some journalist or other who'd gotten wind of it had already been complaining loudly that the government should not be allowed to meddle with free will. If people wanted to do something stupid, as long as it wasn't against the law then it was their right.

He'd gone on about how, throughout history, Americans had always been allowed to do stupid things. Even presidents had been free to be stupid if they wished. In fact, they had been pretty much left alone to be as stupid as they wanted to be, and it was partly that which had made the country great. So this government had no right to start stopping people from being stupid. Having the right to be stupid was all but in the constitution.

But he'd been told the economy just couldn't handle that sort of idealistic attitude.

There was a knock on the door.

"What?" Mendes said.

It was Kahill.

chapter TWENTY-THREE

I downed another mojito, feeling the bittersweet kick at the back of my throat and the familiar warm after-burn. But the memories wouldn't leave me alone.

So I drank most of the night, until it was nothing but a blur.

And when I had run the bar dry of lime and rum and glasses, for all I knew, I stumbled outside.

I sure as hell wasn't going to run from this city a second time. In the morning I'd track down Nena and see if she knew where I could find that goddamn switch to start my life again. But right now I was going to find her fridges.

I had been to the Cold Compound once as a cop, following up a case that no doubt had a sad ending, and I headed off down the alley with purpose. But the mojitos had blurred my mind so that the layout of the streets made no sense. They veered around corners that shouldn't have been there, and new buildings sauntered up to greet me, annihilating the New Seattle I had known. I passed a Health and Safety sign that declared: "Don't fall over. It can hurt." The thing was lit up in a gaudy green that spilled onto the surrounding buildings and across the sidewalk. I walked on, feeling the alcohol fuel my steps with a superficial, shivering energy, but my mind was missing one moment in three.

I kept on through the driving rain, becoming more desperate to find somewhere I recognized, and after a while I stumbled out down by the wharfs. The warehouse clock showed 4 a.m. Above it, the huge bulk of an advertising balloon bobbed in the night sky with its light ablaze.

I walked down and watched the rain fall across the water in a spluttering sheet as the drops tumbled from the windless sky and shattered the calm of Salmon Bay.

Most of the moored boats were abandoned to the darkness, but on one, some women were unloading a catch, the harsh lamps throwing pools of fierce, unearthly light around the cold, squat vessel. Rust streamed from the rivets of the panels on the hull, and I could see where the metal of the massive cogs and jib arms had been rubbed raw. It was a savage kind of machinery, speaking of crushed fingers and sailors swept away screaming in the cold, roaring darkness. A shiver ran through me.

Farther along the wharf, blue flashing lights washed past and I knew the police drongles would be trawling the cheap motels and dark corners of the city for me.

Another cop drongle came into view and I dodged down an alley and into the first bar I came to. The place was full of fishermen, some still in wet-weather gear, boisterous and excited about fish.

A group near me shed their yellow coats, which were crudely printed with the name of their boat, the *Mighty Fish*

Finder, and then shouldered up to the bar like it was all their birthdays at once.

These people knew how to live, and it felt like a little oasis of reality in the midst of all this Health and Safety crap. Maybe it was because they had all stared into the face of death more times than an average man could shake a stick at.

I watched them plow into their drinks with fervor. Their weather-beaten eyes seemed to be burning bright with stories, and it occurred to me that perhaps each of the lines that formed rivulets on their face could be traced back to one specific time when their souls had been bared to the real possibility of death.

Their expressions were ablaze with an unbounded sense of life. And in that moment, I loved them for it. In this messed-up city, there were still people who were actually living with a sense of spirit and were not just passing through, filling in time until their lives were over.

Another police drongle scurried past outside.

Sooner or later, they would check this place out. I approached the nearest fisherman and offered him fifty New Seattle dollars for his yellow coat, saying I'd had enough of being drenched for one day. He laughed and handed it to me, telling me I was insane. I partly agreed with him. The pungent smell of fish from it was overpowering.

I pushed my way out through the doors again and onto the street, putting on the coat and pulling up the hood, which muffled the sound of the city.

I looked like a walking yellow beacon, but sometimes it's better to stand out when you're trying to hide.

I headed on past the wharf, feeling snug in the coat and still insulated from the harsh cold and rain by the cozy effects of the mojitos. Another police drongle rumbled by, its lights casting long shadows that stretched like witch's fingers.

But the rain had begun to relent, and the wharf was mostly silent now but for the slap-slapping of the water on the harbor walls and the wind tapping the shrouds against the masts, sending out a long, unanswered cry.

chapter
TWENTY-FOUR

Dawn was still holding off.

The only clue that I had found the right place was a small sign near the door: New Seattle Secure Holding Area for Fridges, Coffee Tables, and Other Feral Electrical Goods.

I walked around looking for a side entrance, circling the rusted, barbed-wire walls. There was one in a side alley. "Four trees have been planted in Australia to offset the poor design aesthetic of this building," said a small sign. The lock was old and it gave with a grouchy murmur on my third attempt to force it. Inside was gloomy and damp, and somewhere I heard a police radio. A pool of yellow light shone at the end of the corridor. The radio crackled with static and I stopped to listen, but all I heard was my own heartbeat through a thick gauze of alcohol and adrenaline.

I edged in farther, trying to soften my steps over the hard floor. Each second stretched out in my mind until it was the size of Kansas.

I came to the corner, steadied myself, and peeked

around. A figure was sitting with his feet up at a desk, his cap tilted forward, and a red gun lying lazily in his hands.

The police radio crackled into life. "Drongle 34, you are cleared to deal with the suspect, but please ensure you have appropriate footwear."

The guy was asleep.

I moved closer until I could hear the rasp of his breath as his chest slowly rose and fell, filling out a faded uniform that once, as a younger man, he had probably worn with pride.

Now it was his ticket to a retirement pension.

A huge bunch of keys were lying next to him.

"Drongle 34, if you are at all nervous about which kind of footwear to use, call for a risk assessment," said the radio. "There's a fifteen-minute wait on Health and Safety at the moment in your area."

The cop shifted, then settled. When he was still again, I picked up the keys. They jangled softly and, as I moved away, the radio picked up a rogue frequency and a voice with a heavy accent began talking excitedly before fading away.

The Cold Compound was visible through a window to my left and I slipped outside. Most of the cages were empty, although in one a coffee table crashed up to the bars as I passed.

"You want to buy a hedge fund?" it chirped.

"Maybe later," I said and moved on. For a moment, the next cage appeared empty as well, but then I saw the fridges from the motel room huddled sadly in the far corner, trying to escape the rain.

"Hey!" I whispered, as I tried to find the right key. "We're getting out of here, okay?"

"Hey," said one, waddling over. "It's you! Did you come

back for some processed cheese? It's such a great snack straight from the tube."

"No, thanks. Get ready to move."

"Oh, boy, can we keep some beer cold for you?"

"Sure," I said, still fiddling with the lock.

"One cold beer coming right up!"

"Sh!" I said. "Less noise."

"Just so we're clear, I definitely don't have any pizza," said the Cold Moose. "Only a carrot so bendy you could tie a knot in it."

"That's no problem. This way." I got the door to the cage open.

"There is some pesto sauce, so you could have that with it. I hear they serve that at some top restaurants now."

"Let's move."

"Shall I make my owl noise again if there's danger?" said the Ice Jumper, opening its door.

"No," I said. "No owl noises. Just be quiet."

"Sure. We're good at being quiet," said the Frost Fox, and waddled out. "And we're very good at quiet singing."

"Right now, not even humming. This way." I fumbled with the key to the main gate.

"Okay, but we've been working on some harmonies. It's pretty special."

"Save it," I said, getting it open.

"Do you have a plan?" said the Frost Fox.

"I never make plans," I said, and saw that the small motel-size fridge was still trying to hide in the corner. "This way, little fellow," I called. "Come on."

chapter TWENTY-FIVE

Frankly, walking down the street in a yellow coat with four refrigerators and a spin dryer for company is not the easiest way to keep a low profile. They shuffled along as quickly as they could manage, hugging the edge of the sidewalk, their little feet waddling from side to side, but they were really designed for just getting about the kitchen. Their banter grew more breathless as the cold dawn light chased over the city.

Finally their chatter stopped altogether. The longer we were out in the open, the more chance there was of someone seeing us and deciding to call in a Fridge Detail. But at least it wasn't raining now, and the dawn sun meandered through the stack of buildings, its white rays diffused by the sweet-smelling clouds of drifting smoke that rose from the remains of small nighttime fires from the poor back streets. Someone had been burning cherry wood, and the odor hung in the air unmistakably. We passed a run-down anchovy emporium, which had a lot of anchovy-related offers in the window, and also some negative press about gherkins. There had always been some hostility between the two food groups.

Next to it was a musical mood stand that had been vandalized and was now playing a Motown track happily to itself. And next to that was a head hack stand that also looked broken. The street booths were pretty basic, and only gave grainy pictures from the last few hours. I watched the rest of the fridges patter past when I realized one of them was missing. I told the others to keep going and went back. Eventually I saw it hunkered in a doorway

It was the Frost Fox.

"I'm not as fit as the old days," it said. "Back then, I could get to the liquor store, fill up with beer, and get back without even getting tired."

"You need to keep moving." I said. "We mustn't get split up."

It began to waddle down the sidewalk.

"In those days, I was friends with this washing machine. We once talked about escaping up to Canada," it said, puffing slowly along. "So one day when everyone was out, we ran around the kitchen to get fit. Made a real mess of the breakfast bar and they had to call a carpenter."

I cajoled it along until we finally caught up with the others. I could see they were all old models, apart from the Tiny Eiger, and they were struggling more and more over the uneven slabs. Eventually, we made it six blocks, and I began to seriously wonder what the hell I was doing.

This had seemed a decent enough idea through the haze of mojitos back in Mending Things with Fire. But now, as the world struggled to cough itself back into life in the heartless dawn, the whole thing felt strange and desperate.

chapter TWENTY-SIX

I hadn't seen Gabe for eight years. I hadn't written. I hadn't called. Now I was ringing the buzzer of his second-floor apartment at 5 a.m. with a lot of fridges in tow.

I felt pretty bad about it.

But some friends—the ones that really matter—are friends for life, whether you spend time with them or not. And Gabe and Marcy were firmly in that category. I was astonishingly lucky to have met them.

Eventually a light came on and spilled from under the door.

"Give me a chance, here," I heard Gabe's voice mumble as he unbolted and swung it open, his eyes full of sleep.

"Gabe," I said. "It's me. It's Huck."

"Huck? Huck! Goddamn it!" He put his arms around my shoulders and hugged me. "Look at you! Huck!"

"It's good to see you, Gabe. Better than good. I would have been here years ago, but . . . my life had other ideas."

"You're here now," he said.

"I'm sorry to do this to you, but I've come with company," I said, looking into that familiar, worn, open face. "Quite a bit."

"No problem. Who?"

"Five refrigerators."

"Hey!" called a voice from down in the lobby.

"Oh, yeah, one is actually a tumble dryer."

Gabe looked at me quizzically. "It's complicated," I said. "And a bit bizarre. And slightly dangerous."

"I would have expected nothing less from you. And I'm glad you came here. Bring them in," he said. He had saved my ass more times than I probably knew when we had been out on the streets together as cops, and now he was doing it again without a second thought.

Just like old times. The man was pure gold.

We helped them through into his tiny apartment and closed the door.

"Marcy okay?" I said.

"Yeah, she's terrific. She'll be back in two days. They send her all over the place with her job now."

"Good. I'm glad to hear that."

"She'd love to see you. She talks about you all the time. Huck, I'm guessing there's a reason you're turning up at 5 a.m. with four refrigerators and a spin dryer. Or is this some kind of fashion statement that everyone is making in L.A. these days?"

"Yeah, there's a story."

"Good. I'll put on some coffee. Okay?"

"That's more than okay. The way I feel, it's pretty much essential."

He walked to the kitchen and flicked the switch. He still had a limp. He had taken a slug to the leg one time when we had been out on the East Side, and that was how he had been retired, four months before I had left.

"You should be mad as hell with me," I said.

"Huck, I've spent eight years wondering where the hell you were," he called from the kitchen, then poked his head around the door. "I'm not going to waste time being mad. How was Mending Things with Fire?" he added.

"Gabe?" I walked over and leaned on the kitchen door frame.

"You turned up at 5 a.m. with a load of fridges. I know you must have spent the night drinking someplace. And where else would you go?"

"It hasn't changed. They still make half-decent mojitos."

"You still drink mojitos, huh?"

"Yeah. There are some things that aren't meant to change," I said, and the words hung in the air for longer than they might have, and the image of Abigail came at me again so vividly I could touch it. Gabe broke the moment, sensing there was something wrong.

"You also smell of fish," he said, looking at me. "You never used to smell of fish. The fridges, the blond hair, and the smell of fish, those are new things about you. Everything else is the Huck I've been missing."

"It's the coat that smells of fish. Not my best purchase ever." I took it off and jammed it in the garbage.

He was older and yet the same. There were more lines on his face, and his heavy frame gave greater hints as to what he would look like in twenty years.

But it was the same Gabe.

The years had done nothing to tarnish his gentleness.

He made coffee with a little half-and-half and we sat down among the fridges. Even at the worst of times, coffee resets my mind to an easy calm and clears away the hassle for a while. And now it simply added to the sense that the world was a sane place, after all. The apartment had hardly changed, still with the same books, the same chairs, and the same picture of the two of us on our police graduation day.

"You ever find out who left us in that building?" I said.

"No. And even if I knew, what good would it do?"

"I guess."

"Now, what the hell happened to you?"

As we drank coffee, I told him what had happened in the last twelve hours, from entering the city in a dongle, to meeting Nena and the aborted head hack, to my escape from the motel, and finally how I had sprung the fridges and dryer. He nodded and raised his eyebrows a couple of times, but there was nothing that could surprise Gabe. His feet were planted too firmly on the ground.

The fridges sat humming quietly with their doors all slightly open, but with hardly enough energy to put on their lights. They were recharging themselves.

"You've been busy then," he said, finally. "And slightly insane."

"Any clothes you need drying?" said the tumble dryer. "I feel a spin coming on."

"Later, little fellow," I said.

"Oh. Well, how about if I just warm up some clothes that are already dry? Sometimes it's fun to get an acrylic sweater and heat it up until the static is strong enough to stick it to the wall."

"Just take it easy. I have some things to talk about with my friend Gabe."

"Are we still going to Mexico?" said the Ice Jumper.

"Tequila!" sang the Frost Fox. And they all took this as the cue to start singing.

"La! La! La! La-la! La-la! La-la-la! La! La-la! La-la! La! Tequila!"

"Just keep it down, all right?"

"Okay, okay, I do have a pizza," said the Cold Moose,

opening its door. "Here, see? And a carrot so bendy you could tie a knot in it. You have it. It's yours."

"That's okay, we're not after your pizza. You hang onto it," I said.

"Gee. Great!" it said, and then sneezed. "Sorry. Got a bit of a tickle. Had it ever since a peppered steak went bad on the top shelf."

"I know some information," said the Frost Fox as it waddled forward.

"Do you?" I said. "And what would that be?"

"I know the date of the Klondike gold rush."

"Okay. Any of you know where I can find Nena other than the Halcyon?"

They all shuffled in silence.

"Someone did once tell me how to tell the difference between a weasel and a stoat, though," said the Frost Fox.

"Yeah, well, I'll let you know if that ever becomes an issue we need to resolve. Now I suggest you all get some more rest, in case we have to move again."

"Sure. But I'm feeling a lot more energetic now. I feel like I could keep a yogurt edible for a year."

"Just take a rest," I said, but there was no stopping it.

"Where's she gone—here's a bit of trivia," it sang. "It's got the highest lake. That's right—it's Bolivia!"

The other fridges all joined in with their harmonies.

"We refined it in the Cold Compound, put in some extra harmonies. What do you think?"

"It's excellent," I said. "But rest now, all right?"

And thankfully, the fridges and the spin dryer finally settled down on their feet, closed their doors, and hummed gently. Gabe poured me more coffee.

"Why did you help this girl? You could have run," he said as he handed it to me.

"She knows me. She can see through me."

"That's an illusion, Huck. The best criminals have always been able to do that. It helps them stay alive."

"She's different, and she's not the sort of criminal we used to deal with. She could tell my past was running like a loop in my head just from my eyes."

"And is it?"

"Yeah. All the time." I drank more coffee.

"I'm sorry. But I still say forget her. She's only going to lead you into more trouble. At the moment it's fixable. All you'll get is probably a fine."

"I want to find her, Gabe. I know it's irrational and stupid, but if anyone knows how to fix my life, it's her."

"All right. Why not sleep on it? Things may seem different in the morning. It's close to six now and we both could probably sleep for a week. You get this couch. I'll get you some blankets."

"Gabe . . ." I said.

"You're always welcome here, Huck, you know that."

"Yeah."

"Get some rest."

And I thought, *the older we get, the more we need the friends we made when we were young.*

I made myself comfortable, but even though I was exhausted, my mind was running too fast to sleep. So I lay awake listening to the hum of the fridges, and the rumble and sigh of the city, wondering how I was going to find Nena.

And I realized the city had changed. I remembered it being alive to the touch, ebbing and flowing by day and dreaming by night. But I didn't sense it dreaming anymore.

It was keeping one eye open, wary.

chapter

TWENTY-SEVEN

A flitting shamble of ragged dreams and brackish images hung in a no-man's-land in between my consciousness and the dark.

Then a clear image.

A wooden door. It opened and I walked down some steps. The air was cool. Two flights and another door and then I stepped out onto the street.

It was empty. There were no people, and no drongles. The sky was a wild mix of colors—blue and green clouds.

Now I could hear a voice. Someone was with me. And then he was running away. The noise of his steps seemed to waft and glide among the buildings.

I tried to run too, but my legs ached, and . . .

Darkness.

Just the sound of the breeze.

For a moment, I felt the sudden, unexpected peace of this place.

And then I was swept up into my own consciousness by the sound of wild hammering on the door.

I forced my eyes open.

"Health and Safety," cried a voice. "Open up."

My head was thick with the residue of too many mojitos and hardly any sleep—and that wasn't just from the previous night but from pretty much the whole of the last decade.

During the evenings that were filled with mojitos, I had always felt an element of ambiguity about my state of health, as though I might have cheated nature, but the cold morning light brutally extinguished that hope every time.

"Health and Safety," called the voice again as Gabe came through, buttoning a shirt. "Routine check for hazards. Open up." I tried to shake the sleep from my head.

"What is this?"

"It's okay. Just be polite."

Gabe hustled the fridges back out of sight into the bedroom. As they shuffled through, the Frost Fox tried to tell me the date of the Klondike gold rush again, but after some coaxing Gabe managed to get him to be quiet. Then he shut them in and opened the door.

"Just a routine call. Health and Safety," said the man, stepping in. "How are you today? Feeling healthy? Feeling safe?" He was wearing a yellow hard hat and a yellow reflective vest.

"Feeling safe?" echoed a taller man, hovering at his shoulder and rubbing his hands.

"This leaflet explains the latest guidelines on opening doors safely," said the shorter, fatter one, looking at me.

"Feeling safe?" echoed the tall, thin one.

"Ignore the bit on osprey housing on the reverse. That's a printing error," said the shorter guy. He offered me the piece of paper.

"Printing errorrrrrrrr!" said the other one.

"Thanks," I said, trying to seize the moment, but I couldn't help feeling I'd left sizeable parts of it behind. Some of it as far away as Wisconsin.

"People miss the most obvious dangers, and that's why we go house to house." He smiled to reveal a set of badly brushed teeth. "You got any tigers in here?"

"Tigers?" I said. "No."

"Good. We don't like tigers. Very dangerous things." He nodded.

"No, no tigers," said the tall man. "No fucking tigers. We hate fucking tigers with their big teeth. Feeling safe, are we?"

"What about this? Have you stubbed your toe on this at all?" The fat man kicked a table leg near him gently with his boot.

"No."

"What, not even in the dark? Not even once in the dark?" The tall man laughed in a high-pitched squeal. "Not ever stubbed his toe on this?" They both laughed, and then the short guy suddenly grabbed my lapels and pulled me close.

"Do you think we're stupid? Do you think we don't know our job?"

"No," I said, catching sight of his dark pupils. "I'm sure you do."

"Feeling safe, are we?" whined the man over my shoulder.

"Any fool can see that you must have stubbed your toe on this in the dark at some time, you get me?"

"Yeah, I get you. You're making it very clear."

"Good! Now give him a toe-stubbing leaflet."

"Toe-stubbing leaflet! Toe-stubbing leaflet," crowed the other man, presenting me with a piece of paper.

"That wasn't so difficult, was it?" said the first one. "We're having a big crackdown on sharp edges at the moment."

"Feeling safe, are we?" The tall man rubbed his hands.

"Maybe you've seen our exhibition?"

"No, can't say I have," I said.

"Oh, well, we've got a really nice collection of sharp and smooth corners. Not too many sharp ones, but not too many smooth ones, either. Right. Well, our roster has us due upstairs, so I need you to sign here to say you have accepted the aforementioned leaflets." He handed it to me. "And fingerprint and kiss it for me as well. There and there. These are your copies. And that one's a copy to confirm you have your copy. And that copy is a spare of the confirmation copy, but it's in larger print."

"Thanks."

"Thank you. And here's a leaflet on the safe housing of industrial machinery. Stay safe. We all owe it to Mother New Seattle."

"Feeling safe, are we?" said the tall, thin man and then they were gone, their footsteps clomping away up the stairs.

I looked at Gabe and opened my mouth to say something, but the sentence that tried to form in my head had the word *fuck* in it so many times it didn't mean anything. So I just closed it again.

Gabe said simply, "I'll get some strong coffee."

chapter

TWENTY-NINE

The only lead we had was the Halcyon motel.

So I made a decision to go back and pump the staff for information. I didn't relish the thought of facing down the guy I had met there the previous night, but I didn't see any other option.

Gabe was adamant about coming along and I didn't like it. I'd tried to argue with him, but I knew my voice lacked conviction.

"I was a cop for seven years and I still know how to smash my way into a motel and scare the hell out of the people. They taught us that on day one."

"Huck, you're my friend. That's why I'm coming with you, okay?" he said. This time with such finality that I agreed.

But this was my senseless chase after a girl, not his.

All the same, a part of me was relieved. I had not lived life near the edge for years and his help might see me through. In fact, I had been so far from the edge, I had probably been closer to the middle where even signs for the edge were few and far between.

I settled down and had enough coffee to wipe away most of the effects of the mojitos while we talked about Marcy, and Mending Things with Fire, and the scrapes we had gotten into when we were young. And it reminded me there had been plenty of good times, too, and that came as a surprise.

Eventually I took a shower.

And after, I shaved my blond hair down to a stubble to avoid the attention of the cops. But it felt cold. And strange. Gabe loaned me a suit, and when I put it on and looked in the bathroom mirror it was hard to recognize myself.

I picked out the thick wad of head hack photos from my old clothes and walked back to the living room, feeling detached from myself.

"Nice suit," said Gabe. "Now you look the part."

"Yeah, thanks. I feel like a diplomat. I still have my head hack photos. Shall we have a look? Maybe there's a picture of Nena in there."

"Sure."

Many of the pictures were still welded together, but after some careful work we pried them all apart. The majority were ruined. Others were out of focus and hazy, but a few had survived. Some were from my stop in Portland on the way up, but there were also a couple of Nena in the drongle with me, and one of her taking out the doctor in the head hack room while I had been hooked up to the machine. It must have gone into my mind and then been pulled straight out again and printed. "That's her," I said, placing the photo on the table. "Nena."

"Brown eyes."

"Like Abigail? Is that what you were about to say?"

"No. You still want to find her?"

"She can see what's going on behind my eyes, and right now that seems important."

"Then I'll help you find her."

There were also a few pictures from the long-term hack. Most of them of Abigail and New Seattle at that time. They seemed foreign and almost meaningless, but I slipped them all into my inside pocket. They were a link back to a time when my life had meant something.

"You want me to alter your feed profile?" said Gabe.

"Yeah," I said. "Let's change everything about me. Why not?"

He opened a drawer and pulled out an old Handheld Feed Reader. Then he plugged in to the feed on my neck, but after ten minutes he shook his head.

"This thing is too old. You'll have to stick with who you are and take your chances," he said, pulling out the plug and sending a shiver through my spine.

And somehow, that seemed appropriate.

chapter

THIRTY

*S*ergeant Maddox was alone.

He stood at the gates of the park, feeling the wind whip his hair.

It was cold. He leaned against the fence rail and stared up at the giant steel and glass buildings.

He felt his heart jump. The man in black was suddenly there next to him.

"We had the fridge," said Maddox, "but it was taken from the Cold Compound. I didn't find out about it until it was too late. Now I have the FDs searching, but I have to be careful."

The wind cut through his shirt and he shivered.

"I don't know who would have taken it, unless it was the couple from the Halcyon," he added.

"Find that fridge. We must put an end to this."

"Sure. I'll—"

But the man had gone.

chapter
THIRTY-ONE

We tried to hail a drongle.

Gabe had given me a gun. It sat in my left inside pocket, and it felt like some kind of clumsy metaphor for a heavy heart.

The harsh morning light made the search for this woman seem almost childishly stupid.

More drongles. Most were full, and others were feral. Disposing of the wild ones wasn't easy, and City Maintenance preferred to leave them bumbling around on their own in the traffic until they broke down or exploded. The burned-out carcasses were not uncommon.

After ten minutes, one ground to a halt in a scuff of wheels and scattering sparks from the electrics. I shouted the address into the horn at least three times and eventually the light flickered on.

Inside, the screens plagued us with Health and Safety announcements as we nosed our way through the early morning traffic. They were mostly related to the dangers inherent in falling over, and there was another plea by the mayor to call the slightly-on-edge help line if you felt scared, but he still rounded it off by imploring us not to die for no reason.

"Is this what I came back for?" I shouted above the whine of the engine. "To listen to this mayor and his inane philosophy?"

"Take it easy, Huck. It's just the way things are."

I shook my head and tried to tune it all into the background, but that slogan was gnawing away at me.

Outside the smart and bizarrely dressed people on the early morning commute were struggling down the packed sidewalk. The city was squeezing these pedestrians in so tightly that, at some point, physics dictated they had to collectively implode. And if that happened, I wondered whether it would rain designer couture for ten days solid.

"There's a warehouse this way where we can store the fridges. They'll be safer there than in my apartment."

"Yeah?" I said. "Okay."

"We'll have to wait until after dark. It'll be quiet by about 2 a.m."

"It never used to be this busy."

"Yeah, the city wall is meant to cut congestion on the central sidewalks by 50 percent, but there are stories that the drones building it have been hacked into and that the whole wall is riddled with tunnels and rooms that aren't in the official plans."

"And you don't think that's a myth?" I said.

"I don't think so," said Gabe. "Health and Safety wields a lot of power, but it's not well organized."

"It's a shambles," I said as we eased our way through the hopeless muddle of traffic. Outside hawkers, brokers, and beggars mixed in a panorama of chaos under the flat, dark sky. The bedlam made me uneasy.

"You nervous about this?" said Gabe.

"Busting in on the Halcyon? Yeah, it's been awhile."

"But you never forget."

"No, you don't," I said. "Even if you want to."

Now we slowed to a stuttering crawl. And then stopped. None of the drongles showed any sign of moving.

Outside, a highly manicured woman with a small dog perched within a hat on her head walked past. She was with a man who had an identical dog in a hat on his head. I wanted to get out and give them a hard time about it for so many reasons I could have produced a small pamphlet on the subject.

Possibly a novella.

A group of nuns, clad neatly in wimples, were carrying clear plastic riot shields to protect the mother superior, and were causing a big commotion as they crossed the highway.

"Hail Mary, mother of grace!" said one, shoulder-charging a businessman out the way with her shield on the word *grace*. The shield glanced off the man and clattered across the drongle hood.

That kind of thing hadn't happened in Saratoga. There was something unhinged about this city. Maybe being right on the border of the country had finally gotten to the people here, and suddenly they felt like they were eternally on the edge of something, teetering on the cusp, ready to fall into the abyss. Maybe that's why they made such a big thing about pointing out their existence, just to reassure themselves they were all still here.

And perhaps that was why they were so concerned about health and safety, because they secretly knew they were doomed but they didn't know why, or how to deal with it.

The drongle stumbled along for another ten minutes. Then it hobbled up onto the curb, partially blocking the sidewalk. "This is the Halcyon motel," it said. "Please leave the drongle now. Your lucky color is green. Your lucky mausoleum is one with a nice plinth. Your receipt is being printed on re—" But the voice cut off as it spurted out a long sheaf of blank paper.

We were still three or four blocks north. Maybe more. "It's at least four more blocks," I said and banged on one of the panels.

"This is the Halcyon motel," repeated the tinny voice. "Please leave the vehicle now. Your lucky number today is seven. Your lucky famous engineer with strange first names is Isambard Kingdom Brunel."

"Four. More. Blocks," I repeated.

"Your receipt is being printed on material that may contain traces of nuts." And the thing spurted out more and more paper. "This is the Halcyon motel. If you are allergic to nuts, please wear the protective gloves," it squeaked, as the paper spewing out began to rise above our feet and a pair of gloves dropped through a slot.

"New Seattle Health and Safety" sang a jingle. "New Seattle Health and Safety. Stay safe. Watch out! Stay safe! Watch out! Stay safe! Watch out for that—"

There was a long, excruciating sound effect of a crash, and then the voice went dead. Someone on the sidewalk banged against the domed roof and the drongle rocked.

"Looks like we're getting out here," said Gabe, gathering the paper.

"Yeah," I said, and I made a mental note that if I ever met anyone from City Maintenance, I would give him such a massively long lecture about the state of these things that he would need warm clothing and food to see him through the conversation.

"Who maintains these drongles?" I said, yanking back the goose-wing door. "Someone brought up by bears?"

Gabe crumpled the armfuls of paper from the receipt into a bundle and eased himself out into the street. A gaggle of street kids dressed in dark denim clothes flocked up to him.

"Take your receipt away for a dime," they cried, converging on us. Gabe bundled the receipt into the nearest kid's open arms, pressed a coin into his open palm, and watched as he ran off with the others trailing after him, amid cries and shouts.

"The warehouse is a block this way."

"Okay," I said. The crowd around us was alive with hawkers selling strange bits of meat on a stick and glazed fruits of colors so vibrant they were almost blinding. A particularly truculent beggar attached himself to me and wanted fifty dollars to tell my fortune by punching me in the face.

"The face knows all," he said. "How a man's face reacts to the primeval force of being punched is revealing to those who can read pain."

"Maybe, but no thanks," I said.

"But think about it," he said, skipping after me. "It's an ancient technique. It was used by the British royalty. Have you never been confused as to why Henry IV had a wonky nose?"

"Actually, no," I said, virtually tripping over the guy as I forced my way past him.

We turned off down an alley and through some derelict lots and passed a tenement block abandoned to graffiti. Ahead was the warehouse.

The double doors were firmly shut, but Gabe took me to the side entrance and forced it open. We stepped into a tiny office cramped by years of papers and unopened mail. There were boxes of old smoke canisters hastily piled in one corner. And on the wall hung an out-of-date calendar from a company calling itself the Mighty Wump-Wump Engine Company. A shamble of wrenches and oiled-smeared paper was strewn across the desk.

There was a door to the back.

It led to a vast hangar, full of old cop drongles.

"Cop drongles?" I said. "Is this safe?"

They were jammed in and propped up against the walls in any way they could be squeezed in. Most looked ancient and wrecked, with their bodies full of gaping holes, disgorging wires. Dried blue liquid dribbled everywhere across the floor. A few had painted red stripes, but most of the others had the old police colors.

"It's abandoned. I used to do security here sometimes after I left the force, but they don't bother with it anymore. You think we can get the fridges here tonight?"

"Sure," I said. "Why not? They'd like it here."

We made our way back out through the office and onto the street.

I tried to hail another drongle but they were all full, or just unhelpfully grouchy, so we walked a block back to Main Street.

"Dan Berber," said a small man suddenly walking alongside me, leaning into my line of vision.

"No thanks, Dan. Whatever it is."

"I look like a regular pedestrian to you, right? But I'm not. Here's my card. Health and Safety. Undercover. And my badge. And I have some photos of me graduating from walking classes. You want to see them? No? No problem-o. My mother has one on her wall. She shows everyone." He had a tiny mustache that seemed uncertain of itself. "But I just want to give you a few safety tips on walking this morning, if you don't mind, sir."

"I do mind," I said. We were shoved sideways across the sidewalk.

"Okay, but you did some below-par walking back there.

●

Your steps were disjointed, you were a menace to other side-walk users, and that's why I'm on hand to intervene. I can get your walking up to the standard required for New Seattle in only a few lessons, just like that." He clicked his fingers with only partial success. "A few tips, a bit of practice. Maybe you should come to one of my weekend retreats. You'd end up with better walking skills than most of the people here."

"Honestly, I know how to walk. I'm doing it now."

"No, you just think you are. Everyone *thinks* they can walk, but they can't. You should be thankful to have someone like me on hand. You don't get this kind of service in Chicago. They have a safety squirrel as a mascot, too, but boy, are they a bunch of losers."

"Look, thanks, but no. I need to catch my friend."

"You're in a hurry, so let me give you just a taster. Keep your ankles in line and concentrate on posture. Chin is for-ward and up," he said, grasping my head. I came to a halt.

"I know how to walk," I said. "I've been doing it since I was two. Now go away!"

"Hey! I spent a year qualifying as an H and S walking advisor, and I passed with special merit in two of the six classes. I think I know more about walking than you, all right? I also did a class on skipping, if you were interested in branch-ing out."

"No, I don't want to do any skipping."

"You might have just slept with the girl of your dreams. Then you'd want to skip."

"I don't want to skip. And I don't need any advice on walking, okay? I can walk fine. It's easy."

"Okay. Your choice. But let me give you this. This is a leaflet specifically aimed at people with your problem."

"I have to go."

"Take the leaflet. It's on basic walking." His mustache seemed to vibrate, then he grabbed my arm as I tried to move off and stared into my eyes.

"Take the leaflet, sir. That way we'll all be safer. For Mother New Seattle. You do love Mother New Seattle, don't you?"

I took it.

He nodded, saluted, and slipped off sideways into the crowd at a huge speed, swerving neatly around someone carrying a chicken.

I threaded my way through the crowd as fast as I could to catch up to Gabe. But I couldn't see him. How could a man with a limp walk so fast?

After fifteen minutes of being pummeled and heckled by enough street hawkers for a lifetime, I took a left and noticed that the streets were run-down.

Another block and I saw the motel ahead.

In the harsh light of day, the place looked even more apologetic, the walls grimy with neglect, the lot strewn with wind-scattered rubbish. A fern tree someone had planted in a fit of enthusiasm now billowed out of control, and even the birds eyed it with suspicion.

This whole chase seemed more and more childish the longer it went on.

Why the hell was I going after this woman anyway? What did I expect from her? Answers to why my life had gone astray?

Because it was obvious all I was going to find here was trouble.

chapter
THIRTY-TWO

I made another ten yards before I was yanked into a doorway. It was Gabe.

"Cops might be staking it out," he said. "The tall building across from the motel, second window along. You see?"

I peeked out from the doorway and down the street. At first I saw nothing. Then I just made out the glint of something in the early morning sun shining from a second-floor window. It might be nothing, but it might be someone with binoculars. There was no point risking it.

"Yeah," I said. "I see it."

We retraced our steps and then took a right.

We passed the carcass of an advertising balloon that lay in a pool of its own broken structure. "Things Ain't What They Used to Be!" it said in gold letters on the side, but for what reason I had no idea. Another turn and we approached the motel from a back alley. It stank of rotting garbage.

People say that, in cities, you are never more than six yards from a rat. Right now, I sensed that figure was down to a few inches.

I took out the gun, and it sat uncomfortably in my hand. I had done this hundreds of times as a cop, but now the whole process felt foreign, and the memories seemed secondhand. It had been another me who had known how to do this—one who had given me a taste for perfectly made mojitos and a dislike of metal sculptures displayed in woodlands, but who had now gone and turned out the light.

The back door hung open. Gabe edged in and I followed. It was a kitchen.

The smell in here was as bad as in the alley, except it was mixed with cooking.

Remnants of breakfast were strewn across a table that was covered with a plastic tablecloth decorated with red roses and jelly. The linoleum floor was streaked with ruts riven by the legs of too many chairs, over too many years.

"Hey!" said the fridge, opening its door. "Fancy a piece of cheese?"

"No, thanks," I said. "We're just passing through."

"What, my Edam not good enough for you, eh? Okay, how about some wonker? It's like water, but not as good."

"Sh," I said. "Maybe later, okay?"

I heard the front door of the motel clack shut as someone left, and Gabe looked back. I nodded, leveled my gun, eased past him, and stepped into the dingy lobby. It was lit with a small desk light that silhouetted a single figure.

"Nice and easy," I said. "Step away from the desk and leave the shotgun under the counter."

The guy turned. I could only partially see his face, because it was smudged by the shadows. He moved his shaking hands slightly out from his sides.

"I don't want no trouble," he said. "This isn't my place." There was a rough edge to his voice, as though his nerves were fraying the edges of his words.

I kept the gun on him.

"What's your name?" I said.

"Buster."

"Okay, Buster, we don't want any trouble, either," I said as Gabe sat the guy down in a chair and checked him for weapons. He was clean.

"But no one calls me that anymore," he added.

"Okay. Well, it doesn't matter. We just want to ask you a few questions," I said.

"Do you want to know what they all call me now? Intercontinental Death Star officer, second lieutenant," he said, and his voice suddenly had an excitable edge, as though the words were desperate to be out of his mouth. "You want to join my army?"

"No. We're after some information about a girl," I said.

"You should join my army. I could teach you stuff. You know what this sign means?" He tapped the top of his head with his hands, looking around excitedly at us.

"We don't know. We just have some questions."

" 'Everyone gather around me.' You make that sign in the firefight, and everyone gathers around you. I've trained my dog to recognize it. He's called Juniper, after the tree. I tried to train the cats as well, but they aren't interested. They pretend to watch while you show them, but they don't give a fucking damn. Self-centered bastards."

"Listen, okay? A girl was in room fourteen yesterday and the cops came for her. You remember?"

"Yeah, of course I do. I saw her. Know what this sign means?" He touched his elbow excitedly.

"Did you talk to her?"

"Sure, I talked to her. 'Enemy coming from around the corner.' Just touch your elbow like that. No ... or is it 'helicopter landing zone is secure'? That one depends when you do it.

It's like Mandarin; one sign can mean lots of things, depending how you use it. This one I know for sure." He shot his hands out quickly into the dark and I flinched.

"Hey! Sit still, okay? Forget the signs."

"All right. All right. 'My antitank weapon is jammed and I need a big mallet.' In case you were wondering. My dog brings me a ball when I do that. Dogs are good at picking up this stuff. I tried it with the hamster as well, but the attention span of a hamster is pretty low. Are you thinking about joining my army now?"

"No. What about the girl?"

"What about her?"

"Did you talk to her?"

"Yeah, I talked to her. She was tired."

"The girl in room fourteen? You're sure it was her?"

"Sure I'm sure."

I held the gun on the guy and for a moment his eyes came into the light, but they didn't match his voice. They had a depth to them, not a flighty insecurity that should have gone with this character. "She paid me forty dollars not to plug her feed into the register. I'll show you the money if you don't believe me."

The guy went for a drawer and I knocked him out. There was a sickening crack and he crumpled to the floor.

"Something is wrong with that guy," I said. "Just wrong."

Gabe walked over and looked in the half-opened drawer and took out a gun.

"Yeah. This'll be what it is. Very wrong."

"You think he was a cop?" I said. "This wasn't the guy I saw yesterday."

"Could be." Gabe went through the man's pockets. Nothing.

Then he plugged into the back of his neck with the motel Handheld Feed Reader and scrolled through his details.

"History is way too clean and neat. This looks forged. I think he's a cop." Gabe played his mood, and it came out as a short piece of heavy metal. He let the man's head fall back to the floor. "Which means we don't have much time."

chapter
THIRTY-THREE

I pulled back the trapdoor.

Then I led Gabe down the steps into the cellar. Damp musty air. Sunlight dropped through a small window in the ceiling and then swam through a gauze of cobwebs before falling quietly on the floor. The giant boiler sat sweating. I looked up through the duct that I had squeezed down the night before and it seemed impossibly small.

"I'll check out her room. You keep an eye on our friend in the lobby." There was no way Gabe would make it with his bad leg, and it was better someone stayed with the guy, anyway.

"Sure. Have fun up there," he said, giving me a lift as dust showered down. The boiler shuddered and then began yammering away with an overexcited chatter.

I scrabbled at the pipes, hauling myself up until I was jammed against the dirt-caked sides of the duct. I steadied my breathing and then struggled up a few more inches, wedging my body into the tiny space. My shoulder hit one of the scalding pipes and I jerked it back. It was dark. What little light that had filtered up from the cellar was gone now. Cramped spaces always made me feel utterly alone. A pipe juddered in a squall of noise. I waited until the sound echoed away, then forced myself on until my head broke into the heavy, dead air of the roof space.

Somewhere, a shower was running. I hauled myself out and crawled along a beam, trying to work out which way Nena's room had been. A patch of light speared through the ceiling to my left and I guessed that was the spot she had fallen. I squirmed over and found the hole had been hurriedly patched up with tape. I squinted through a gap.

But there was nothing.

I listened for a moment, and then jumped feet-first off the beam. I broke through the flimsy ceiling with a tear of tape and cardboard and landed amid a shower of debris. Whoever was watching from across the street would have seen only a confusing blur.

I rolled back onto my front. The room was empty. Everything was smeared with red residue. It streaked the walls and the floor was covered in spent smoke canisters. I crawled to the window and peeked out.

The lot was quiet.

I made a quick search of the room. There was the usual clutter to support life on the road, clothes, a few books, and leaning up by the hangers was a plastic bag. I emptied it and found some brochures and bottles from a local herbal fair, along with some name badges with Nena's name. I stuffed one of the brochures in my pocket.

Then I crawled forward and checked the front window again. A moment before it happened I sensed it. Then something caught my eye to the left and the front door of the motel lobby opened. Gabe staggered out and the undercover cop followed with a gun in his back. A group of cops began running across the lot.

I bolted through the front door and out into the back alley. I took a right down and then another, coming out on a street that was bustling with drongles.

I dived into the crowd on the sidewalk and was sucked along for a block. I looked back but couldn't see anyone following. As we approached the corner, I heard a voice crying:

"These are the phone numbers of the beasts. Goat: eight, zero, zero, seven, eight, nine, eight, three, seven, one, one. Tortoise: eight, zero, zero, seven, nine, four, four, three, two, two. I have all the phone numbers of the beasts..." the woman began and then her voice was absorbed by the body of the crowd as I cut across the traffic and pushed my way through the throng on the opposite sidewalk, before cutting down another couple of streets. Then I stopped retching for breath and eased into a coffee shop.

I had a good view through the window and ordered coffee and a pastry. Across the street, a huge Health and Safety poster proclaimed: "When you're walking along the sidewalk, don't suddenly stop, turn around, and start going the other way. People will bump into you." Underneath it concluded: "A strong Health and Safety means a strong city."

A couple of workmen came in, one releasing a cloud of curly hair as he took off a woolen cap.

I berated myself for not trying to help Gabe. They would head hack him, and probably get a picture of me. Maybe they would link that to my escape last night from Head Hack Central. Then they would have Gabe for aiding and harboring a criminal.

I felt sick but I knew that now was not the moment to wallow in remorse.

I pulled out the herbal fair brochures I had collected from Nena's room. There was an address on the back page that was on the other side of town. If she had been working there, maybe I could get a lead. Maybe I could get some help.

I pulled out the wad of head hack pictures from my pocket as the waitress brought me my coffee and pastry.

"Can I get you some yam and goose waffles, or cakelike snacks with those?"

"No, thank you," I said.

"What about some wonker?" Her hair was swooshed back with a hair band that had the effect of making her face look constantly surprised.

"No, just the coffee and pastry is great. That'll do me."

"You're sure about the wonker? It's like water, but not as good. It's popular with the youngsters." The waitress hovered.

"No, thanks."

She shrugged, put her pencil away, pulled a smile that said "fuck off, then," more clearly than if she had shouted it, and left wiping her hands on her apron.

Why does the whole of New Seattle think I want to drink wonker? I thought.

A police drongle rumbled to a stop outside the window. I hunched over my coffee as two cops came in, brushing past my table. One knocked some of my head hack photos onto the floor.

"Beg your pardon, sir," said a cop reaching down to pick them up and hand them to me.

"Thanks," I said. The picture of Nena was right on the top. The cop held my gaze a moment longer than he needed to as he handed them back, but I knew that kind of behavior was second nature to the cops.

The other cop returned with a bag of doughnuts and they were soon on their way. I looked at the photo of Nena.

She was probably just a criminal who had stolen something or killed someone.

Across the street, three large birds perched motionless on the top of the Health and Safety sign.

"More ravens," I said to myself as I picked up the mug of coffee. "Why does the city have all these ravens?"

chapter THIRTY-FOUR

I walked.

There are only so many Health and Safety announcements a man can sit and listen to in a drongle before ten o'clock in the morning.

But if reincarnation turns out to have some basis in fact, I'm making it clear now that there's really no point in my coming back as a mountain goat. I simply wouldn't put in the miles to make a go of it. I'd be the goat sitting at the bottom of the mountain having a snooze and imploring the other goats to bring him back some nice bits of grass.

I passed a massive city health alert sign. Ticker tape letters ran busily across it warning of the illnesses sweeping the city that day. A flu virus was running amok with an epicenter on Capitol Hill, and there would be a bad hair day on Thursday in and around Yesler Terrace for people with light brown hair.

The bad hair forecasts had become prominent a few years before, when a well-known singer had refused to perform at a major concert because her hair forecast was bad for that day, and the concept had been adopted as part of the public services in many cities. But there was no evidence that they were accurate, and a good many scientists got angry about the very mention of them, which just made everyone snigger because they seemed to have bad hair all the time.

I made it a few more blocks along the sidewalk before I got some hassle from someone trying to sell me advertising space on his head, which he had shaved for the purpose. He had one advert for a pizza firm tattooed there already, but he soon lost interest.

Another twenty minutes and I caught sight of an advertising balloon with the words: "National Herbal and Healing Fair. Healing with Feeling."

People were heading up the steps en masse, and they jostled me toward the building until I was squeezed in through the doors.

A rich burning bouquet of herbs hit me like a wall.

The crowd fanned out and I found myself some space at the side to take it all in. Stalls stretched as far as the eye could see.

"Complimentary Healing Rock?" said a man, approaching me. He was struggling to walk because he had a large rock clasped to his chest.

"Actually, not today," I said, and headed down the first aisle. A minute later, I heard a commotion behind me. When I looked back, an elderly lady had collapsed on the floor.

"It's a healing rock," the man was saying as he bent over her. "Collapsing under its weight is good. It's part of the healing process."

I headed on. Nena could have been working at any one of these booths, but asking about randomly didn't seem ideal. If the cops had staked out the motel, they might be staking out this place, too. A girl approached me from a huge tentlike stand with long hennaed hair, smelling of a rich musty perfume that could have been described as the smell of a secondhand bookshop mixed with horse liniment.

"You really should try a diet with borage and woodruff. It would give you more energy and more connection with the world. You look like all your yin has gone into your left foot," she said. Her eyes were sunken around the edges, as though she was living in such a deep place inside her head that the darkness had seeped out.

"Yeah, perhaps it has, but borage and woodruff? That's not a regular pizza topping, is it?"

"Pizza topping?" She repeated the words but without any kind of meaning attached to them.

"Yeah. That's going to be a problem," I said. "I don't know how I would fit it into my diet. Unless you can add them to a mojito?"

She didn't say anything more but simply nodded, and her eyes glazed over. I sensed she was living in a place down so many twists and turns inside her own head, it would be hard to be sure you had ever truly reached her. And even if my words did finally find her, the time delay would be too great to make conversation a practicality.

I wove my way past the tent and saw it was filled with a swath of women who all looked exactly the same.

The aisles were overflowing with stall after stall selling infusions and herbs, which filled the air with an aroma that had cleared out my sinuses so effectively you could have driven a truck down them. Around me, people were buying this stuff like crazy. And it was not just middle-aged women trying to recapture a youth they'd never had in the first place, but the general population as well—as though these things were the nectar of life, and they would make them not just well, but better people.

Everywhere, liquids and potions and small heaps of seeds or twigs were being measured and packaged and sold, sometimes with small gestures of sincerity—a touch on the arm, a smile and a laugh—and at others with a perfunctory nod. This place was the front line between the cynically commercial and the sincere but mostly poor. Maybe it encapsulated the struggle for the city itself between those who valued the land for its spirit and soul, and those who wanted to bleed it dry.

After ten minutes of being offered a chance to cure myself of everything from an unwashed aura to housewives' knee and a fractured skull, I decided I'd have to start asking around whatever the risk. I took out Nena's photo as I browsed past another stall that was selling an infusion that was supposed to help vegetarians tempted by the smell of bacon sandwiches.

An older woman with a shopping bag on wheels browsing next to me thrust a leaflet at me. "I went on a spiritual weekend with these people about getting in touch with my inner self. And after a while I felt this calmness. But the people in the next yurt were doing shamanic journeying, so I couldn't sleep, and that's when I began to see their whole approach to health and safety was disgusting and I left. What's the use of reaching nirvana if the next thing you know you're tripping over a guy rope and breaking your wrist?"

"No use at all," I said and then, after she moved away, I asked the woman working behind the stall if she recognized the photo, but she shook her head.

I walked on down the aisle asking at the smaller stalls about Nena, sensing they were likely to be more independent, and less likely to be suspicious. But none of them seemed to have any idea who she was, and I was beginning to think this was going to be a dead end when I was pulled aside by a young girl.

"Put that away," she said pushing the head hack printout into my jacket.

"You know her, then?"

"What do you want? You shouldn't have come."

The girl was young with long dark hair and I saw she had a nametag saying "Chloe."

"I need to see her. You know where she is?"

"I can give her a message. That's it."

"Tell her it's Huck. Tell her I need to see her."

"That it?" The girl looked around, and I sensed I was losing her interest.

"No, tell her I have her fridges."

"Her fridges?"

"Yeah. She didn't want to lose them. I got them out of the Cold Compound. I have her four fridges and a spin dryer."

"Okay, I'll pass the message on. Go to this bar," said the girl, writing something on a card. "If she wants to see you, she'll come within the hour. If she doesn't, don't come back here, okay? Now go. Go. Wait! Take this. It's a free sample of healing balm. It might make you stand out a little less. Now go."

I took the small bag and headed off, dodging between stalls, toward an exit, feeling upbeat. Maybe she would help me spring Gabe from Head Hack Central.

At the end of the aisle a man in a suit abruptly stepped out and stopped me.

"Hold it," he said.

"What is it?"

"Can I interest you in some bombs?"

"Bombs?" I looked around. "Who are you?"

"Pulitzer's the name. What about a nice Howitzer shell?"

I realized his face was glistening with enthusiasm and his eyes shone like fairy lights.

"Are you shitting me?"

"Oh, no, I'm selling good-quality bombs."

"At an herbal fair?" I said, incredulity lacing my voice. "In fact, don't answer that. I don't need to know." I began to walk away.

"They're not just any bombs. Not just your normal ones that go bang," he said, chasing after me through the crowd. "These do go bang, obviously, or they wouldn't *be* bombs, but these ones leave the rich after-aroma of lavender so that anyone hit by shrapnel dies in a calm and relaxed environment."

"That's great, I guess."

"I can do you a job lot."

"No," I said, and I began walking quicker, but the man followed, bobbing at my shoulder.

"What about a land mine, then?"

"No. I really don't need any explosives. There are no large objects I need to break down to their constituent parts."

"But wait! Listen. After you tread on it and it goes off, it leaves the aroma of ginger and ginseng. How about that? If you've just had your leg blown off, you'd really appreciate a touch like that."

"Do I look like I need a land mine?"

"Okay, no problem. Sure. I understand. What about a trebuchet?" He had circled around and was standing in front of me.

"What?"

"A trebuchet. It's a huge wooden medieval contraption for hurling rocks. I haven't actually got one, but if I had, would you be interested?"

"No."

" 'Cause I think I know where one is. I've had my eye on it. It can probably hurl a lot of things—potted plants, furniture, even a small dog. I'm guessing it has a range of somewhere around half a mile. Yeah, I'll bet you could fling a dachshund half a mile. Not that I would condone you doing that, but, wow!"

"I don't have a dachshund and if I did, I wouldn't want to fling it across the city."

"Oh. No. Well, if you're sure? But think about it. Can I slip a card in your pocket just in case you change your mind? Think about the dachshund rolling through the air when you have a moment, its paws tucked in, and its ears whipped by the wind. It might change your mind." He pushed a card into my top pocket and his eyes glistened again with enthusiasm. "Stay safe for Mother New Seattle."

"Yeah," I said as he vanished back into the crowd. "I'll try." Then I wove my way on to the exit.

"An infusion for people who need a pick-me-up," called a girl wrapped in outlandish dress, carrying a tray of thimble-sized glasses filled with liquid near the exit. She smiled and pulled a weird angular shape with her body as I approached, and I sensed she was one of those girls who thought she was being alluring and coy when actually she was just being really fucking scary. "Would you like to try it?"

"Thanks, but I have my own personal recipe for that," I said, trying not to get freaked out by her expression, which was moving so fast that my eyes were struggling to keep up. "It's called a mojito."

PART TWO

chapter

THIRTY-FIVE

It's caught what?"

Mendes stared at Kahill. His collar was open and his tie had been loosened. There was a weary, unkempt edge to his words, where tiredness had slackened off his pronunciation.

"I know it seems crazy, but this is all we get from it at the moment." Kahill proffered a sheet.

"What does it say?" said Mendes.

"It's requesting an abacus to do some adding up. And before that it was asking us if we can remember how to do long division."

"But still. An irony virus?"

"The sensors are very sensitive. They are far more advanced than anything that has ever been used before."

Mendes threw his hands up in a gesture that he regretted almost immediately. It reminded him too clearly of a dance move he had had to make when he had been in a musical in first grade.

"My brief was: babysit this project for a month. If I ring them up and tell them that one of the most sophisticated computers on the western seaboard is asking us how to do long division, I'll be the laughingstock of the whole department. We have to keep this quiet, you understand? Destroy all documents relating to this. I have to get back to Washington with my career intact."

"I'll try, sir. Really. We have the top people in every single field of computer—"

"I know who we have. Get out there and sort it out."

Kahill nodded and headed out. "Oh, and if we need to destroy documents, we'll need maintenance. The paper shredder is broken," he said, stopping at the door. "It just scrunches up the sheets and throws them across the room."

"Scrunches them up?"

"Yes. It takes each sheet, scrunches it up, and throws it across the room."

"Kahill, it's not broken. Haven't you figured that out? On security setting one, it crumples the paper into a ball and throws it roughly at the trash. On setting two, they all go in the trash. It needs to be on setting four or five to shred documents. It's a document destroyer, not just a paper shredder."

"Ah, that explains it. I hadn't realized that was the problem. Clever. Very clever."

Kahill left.

Mendes took a long breath and sat down. If they couldn't work the document destroyer, how were they going to sort out the computer?

Was this just chance, or was someone targeting his operation? Was he the victim of some interdepartmental mud slinging by a face back in D.C. who held a grudge and wanted to end his career?

chapter

THIRTY-SIX

An abandoned drongle.

It was slewed up on the sidewalk in a backstreet, looking like some kids had disabled it and dragged it there.

"Today is your lucky day for buying osprey housing," it said as I caught one of the wheels. Blue lights flickered inside it, and then died again.

The alley was cold. I passed a stack of pallets and crates and took a look back. No one was following. Broken windows and cracked walls rose above me.

Then I heard a hiss. The drongle was now glowing blue. I watched as the blue grew in intensity, sending an ethereal glaze over the walls. Then it became brilliant white. I shielded my eyes.

The blast threw me back and into a pile of trash.

Pieces of drongle rained down, in masses of white sparks and a deluge of smoking, blackened metal. I waited until the noise of the blast and the aftershocks stopped. Then I raised my head.

The drongle remained slumped.

"Your lucky cutlery today is a spoon," said a voice among the flames. "No, wait! It's the little cake fork that only has two prongs and a flat bit." Another smaller explosion blew the dredges of life from it.

A furball of wires flopped out, and a stream of gungy blue foam trickled slowly down the alley.

I finally got to my feet.

The explosion was due to bad maintenance.

A handful of the drongles in any given city were feral. They cruised around with no one in them, having forgotten what they were supposed to be doing, until they either broke down or blew up.

It occurred to me there were probably a handful of people doing much the same thing, and I wondered if, right now, I wasn't one of them.

I ignored the thought as I headed down the main street and took out the card the girl had given me. She had written the name of a place called the Chewy Flamingo on it. The address was only a couple of blocks away.

After a little searching, I found it. Outside was a sign that proclaimed: "We are open twenty-five hours every day and a bit." A blue neon sign struggled to compete with the sunshine as it pointed down a dark corridor.

I squinted into the gloom and walked in. I heard a drongle pull up outside and I could just make out the harmonized singing. "New Seattle Health and Safety. Stay safe—watch out—stay safe—watch out. Stay safe—watch out for that—" Then there was the gurgling cry of: "Ahhhhhhhhhhhhh!" And then a crash.

"New Seattle Health and Safety," said the voice, "asks you to stay safe and not die for no reason. What's the point? Right?"

For a moment I felt my anger rise. Why did they have to keep on with that slogan? I closed my eyes and saw the un-sleeping hang of Abigail's head. And felt the sensation of the cold touch of her dying lips.

I shook the feeling away and followed the blue thin neon lights until I came to three bouncers in overly sharp suits with blotchy red necks as thick as salad bowls.

"And where do you think you're going, sir?" said a bald bouncer, turning his head toward me by swiveling at the waist.

"For a drink."

He laughed, and he was joined by the bouncer on the left, who hopped from one foot to the other.

The remaining bouncer said: "Just let him in."

"With an attitude like that?" Sweat glistened on his pate, and he looked pale. "Not a cock-sucking chance."

"Let him in," said the one on the right. He had a scar on his cheek like a crawling lizard. "Look at him; he's a suit. Let him in. You can't keep doing this. You'll have a hernia."

"We have a job to do. There's no way he's coming in here behaving like that." The one on the left took this as a cue to laugh again and hop from one foot to the other. Then he stopped abruptly as the bald bouncer took a step closer to me. His eyes were so deeply set that I couldn't be sure they were actually there. He lowered his voice. "Correct me if I'm wrong, but I don't think I've heard you offer to punch me yet."

"No."

"Don't do this," said the one with the crawling-lizard scar.

"So, you're threatening not to punch me? Is that right?" said the bald one.

"Clearly."

"Right. Let's chuck him out," said the bald one.

"Wait!" I said, as I felt a hand grab at my suit. "What is the problem? I want a drink, that's all."

"The problem is, you need to punch me." The bald one smiled.

"He's in a strange mood," said Scar-Face. "He's got a fever."

"Management policy," said the bald-headed one.

"It's not management policy," said Scar-Face. "You're acting weird."

"Yeah, and who's in charge here?" The lead bouncer turned and took another step toward me. I could smell shaving cream on his face. "So, are you going to punch me or not? It's your call." He continued to stare at me, his shaven head glistening in the blue half-light. "Or do we have to do this the hard way?"

"I just want a coffee," I said.

"Management policy," he whispered.

"Right." I looked into his eyes, then thumped him in the stomach as hard as I could. My fist felt like it had hit a brick wall, and the bouncer doubled up, almost going down on his knees. "How was that?" I said.

"Thank you, sir," he coughed. "That's very kind of you. Please go through."

"It's unhappy hour at the moment. All drinks are twice the normal price," said the bouncer who had been hopping about, and I saw he had missing teeth as he held the door open with a massive smile. "Stay safe. We all owe it to Mother New Seattle."

"You see?" said Scar-Face, bending down to his buddy. "Now look at the mess you're in. What was the point?"

Maybe he thought that kind of door policy would attract a lot of students once word got out. I sensed he was right.

Inside, sharp pools of light fell through the darkness. I came to an atrium where huge flowing banners hung down, gently wafting on a breeze that must have been made by a wind machine. It ruffled the material and blew hazy, whisping threads of dry ice around the bar.

I craned my neck to read the words on one: "Rage, rage against the dying of the light."

Maybe it was a rant against the ambient lighting that made it hard to see anything at all, but all it brought to mind were the bad memories of Abigail—the ones of her dying.

I walked on through the gloom of the atrium. There was a scattered clientele, strewn in clumps. But their unwashed appearances were at odds with the faded, hanging quotes. It was as though the giant words had been exposed to so much lowlife that they had lost the power to impose any meaning.

I headed on past wide sofas and battered tables to the bar. A man in a thick green shirt, sitting on a stool, watched me approach. He made a guttural sound as I got near as if he was trying to plagiarize an owl.

I made a point of not making eye contact, because he seemed to be one of those people with a lively insecurity. Always wanting a fix of recognition. When it came, he would feel contented for a while. And when it didn't, he'd start to get edgy, and I didn't have the patience for him right now,

As I got closer, he shuffled his overlarge stomach back around and his head followed on a slight delay, as though it was fixed with lame elastic.

Memories of too many nights spent in seedy places that smelled of this same sticky mixture of alcohol and faded chatter came at me thick and fast, and I did my best to bat them away.

Finally I got the attention of the bar girl and ordered.

"Would you like some wonker with that?" she said,

unscrewing the coffee holders from the espresso machine and whacking the dead coffee sediment into a bin. "It's like water—"

"But not as good. I've heard. No thanks," I said.

I became aware that the overweight guy with the green shirt was staring my way. I had spent my fair share of time in lost conversations with people like him, and however sad his story, I didn't feel like getting dragged down into the remnants of his life right now. But I felt a certain sense of empathy, seeing him washed up in a bar, midmorning, wearing a checked wooly shirt.

His life and mine were too close for comfort.

"Can I ask you something?" I said as I waited.

"Sure."

"What am I doing here?"

"Buying a coffee you mean?"

"No, I mean, what am I doing in New Seattle?"

"Are you on vacation?"

"No. What do you see in my eyes?"

"Oh. You're a Scorpio?"

The bar girl served me my coffee, and I used the moment to nod to the guy and find a table tucked away in a corner and sit down.

The aroma of the coffee caught at the base of my throat.

A jazz band was playing somewhere. I couldn't see it, but in any given jazz trio, one person will always be wearing a trilby hat jauntily on the back of his head and I had no doubt this would be the case here. Why do they do that? Please someone stop them. It's annoying.

I took a sip of coffee, sat back, and stared at the words laid out stylishly on a banner stretched up to my left: "Is all that we see or seem, but a dream within a dream?" And, for a moment, I was mugged by the dream I'd had of New Seattle, but the substance of it hung at the edge of my consciousness. And although I tried to pull at its threads, all I got was a general feeling of walking through the buildings and the place being empty of people. I took out my head hack photos and shuffled through them until I found the one of Abigail and placed it on the table.

That's when Nena sat down next to me, her familiar brown eyes glistening in the half-light. "Is that the woman who left you?"

"Yeah."

"Don't you find the past is a dull place to live, Huck? The same things happen all the time there."

"How can you see through me like this?"

"I just can. Chloe said you have the fridges? Do you have the small one? The Tiny Eiger?"

"Yeah. I have them all."

"And they're safe?"

"The cops have just taken my friend Gabe and they'll head hack him. They may easily get a lead. They may send a Fridge Detail, so they need to be moved."

"Where are they?"

"They're in his apartment." I looked at her. She was wearing dark trousers, a plain sweater, and she had pinned her hair back. "I can help you with this," I added.

"You think?"

"Yeah."

She measured me for a long moment—I wondered what she thought she was seeing.

"What's the address?" she said.

I looked at her with her fierce brown eyes, and her long hair in straggling curls.

"I'm coming with you," I said.

"No."

"You need my protection."

She shook her head. There was a pause large enough to issue its own currency, and I suddenly realized the jazz trio had stopped playing midline, as though someone had given them a strong sedative—which in normal circumstances would have had my wholehearted support, but an unnatural quiet ran around the gloom.

My coffee cup, which was sitting happily on the table in front of me, suddenly exploded in a blather of china and liquid. A hissing canister of smoke landed on the carpet, spewing a rabid, choking cloud.

The smoke was a thick, dark red.

chapter

THIRTY-SEVEN

Canisters came out of the gloom, one after the other, landing with a gentle thud and filling the bar with acrid smoke that sat at the back of the throat.

It tasted of a sickly, delicious suffocation, and a part of me wanted to breathe it in until I entered a dreamy state of unconscious. I began coughing. Figures appeared, in featureless black helmets. I had about a quarter of a second to do something, but I spent it going "oh."

The next moment, I was crushed by a scrum of bodies. About five people pinned me down, then another figure bent over to take the gun from my pocket. He grabbed my shoulder and fiddled around, trying to find the feed in the back of my neck. The smoke had begun to coalesce on his suit, and one sad, red tear ran down the visor of his helmet.

The plug felt insanely cold as he rammed it in, and for a moment I became overly aware of the shape of my skull.

His muffled voice seeped through the helmet as he talked on his radio, but I couldn't make out actual words.

Sniping red beams of laser sights tangled in the smoke as more and more figures gathered around, looming over me. The one with the Handheld Feed Reader scrolled through my details, and I noticed he had a red plume of feathers wagging on top of his helmet. It must have been there as some mark of rank, but it accentuated his head movements so that he seemed like some highly excitable chicken.

I heard a snatch of Motown come from the Handheld Feed Reader, and I guessed he was playing my mood. It seemed upbeat. I would have expected my mood to be more akin to heavy metal.

Another member of the detail descended hand over hand through the smoke, down the banner. Perhaps he was unaware the frenzy was over. When he was halfway down, the rivets gave up in an excited frenzy and a rip galloped through the material, slicing the whole thing apart. He fell, crashing heavily into a ring of Security and reducing them to a clumsy pile of shields, guns, and bodies.

The group got back on their feet as more red rivulets of coalesced smoke dripped down, so that it looked like they were all trickling thin lines of blood, and for the first time I saw Nena pinned down a little way away. She had obviously made a run for the door.

Finally the guy with the plume unplugged his handheld from my neck and called over two others. They dragged me off by my feet through the crowd, and someone dropped his riot shield with a clatter.

He picked it up, then took off his helmet to reveal a face dripping with sweat.

"It's new! You've put a ding in it," I heard him cry as I was pulled toward the main doors, my head thumping across the floor. "Hey! You hear?"

Someone had alerted this unit—probably the same people who had been at the Halcyon. Maybe they had been on my tail all along.

The corridor was packed with enough high-tech paraphernalia and personnel to invade Switzerland. Tired eyes stared below, propped up helmets, their faces pouring with red-tainted sweat. They looked like a deflated and defeated army.

"Hold it! What's this?"

The two guys dragging me were stopped in their tracks by a man holding his helmet under his arm. It had a massive, sprouting, red and white plume.

"Removing the insurgent, sir." The man's glum expression mirrored his speech. It was as if he had a speed alarm in his head, and if any of his sentences rose above lugubrious, the thing would shut off his brain.

"Are you? Really? Good for you." The plume wagged madly on the helmet. "And who taught you to drag a suspect?"

"It's what we always do."

"Well, it's breaking every Health and Safety rule in the book."

"Oh. Really?"

"You're both putting an enormous strain on your vertebrae! When you drag a suspect by the heels you must keep a straight back—dorsal spine in. Otherwise, you'll stress your vertebrae here at T3. What did they teach you at college?"

"There was a lot about mustaches..."

"Almost too much," said the other cop.

"Forget mustaches!"

The two guys shuffled. "I don't think we'd be allowed to do that, sir."

"Don't let me see you dragging a suspect like that ever again."

"No, sir."

"Because if I do, you are both on an H and S report. And I'll have you doing the Alexander Technique until you're so bored you might as well be a slug."

"Sir."

The two guys picked up my heels again and lugged me to the street, my back scraping over the sidewalk slabs. A huge jam of police drongles were parked up at angles and the whole area had been cordoned off.

"So it hurts using the side-handled baton, but what about when you lift up your riot shield?" A medic was talking to a man in a chair near a tent.

"Yeah, it's agony."

"Show me where exactly." The guy got gingerly to his feet.

"I can lift it up to here. But it hurts if I try and go any higher. I can give someone a glancing blow, but I can't smash them unconscious. That's why, recently, I've been kicking them all in the groin. But I don't get anything like the same satisfaction. I don't get into bed at night and think: 'Yeah, well done, Maurice, a good job done today.' "

And then I was dumped on my back in the middle of the street.

Above, I could see huge birds circling. And across the road, a large Health and Safety sign declared, "Please do not fall over. You could hurt your knee!"

Then a face blotted out the sky and someone loomed over me, reached down to flick my jacket apart. He placed a heavy machine on my chest and forcefully squashed down a handle, collapsing the air from my lungs so I was left coughing. After a minute, when I got my breath back, I leaned forward. I could just see the word *arrested* printed straight onto my shirt in large red letters, along with the date and a lot of smaller writing.

Another figure with a Handheld Feed Reader bent over me and began talking. He smelled of garlic.

"You are hereby arrested by the New Seattle State Department for being some kind of major pain in the ass," he said. "You have all the usual goddamn rights—and this does not affect your ability to buy wholesale electrical goods on credit or to apply to be a foreign national of the following countries." He consulted a list. "Belgium, China, and the Cayman Islands." Then he called to someone: "Get some cuffs and a collar on this guy, then get someone to bag him and track him out ASAP. Book him and hook him!"

I was rolled over, and my hands were cuffed behind my back. Then my legs were stuffed into a red sack and I was hauled to my feet so the sack could be pulled up to my neck. Someone across the street shouted: "This response squad has a target in ten minutes. Ten minutes, people. So let's get this show moving like a cow with a hot ass!"

A cop began winding me up in yards of heavy chain.

"I've breathed in too much smoke," he said, coughing. "You want to know why they use that? It's because of the marketing department. They want us to build up a brand. And when people see little plumes of red smoke all over the city, it gives our brand a boost. But they don't understand that it gets everywhere. Gets under your nails. Look! You see? My nails have been red for six months now. And my eyebrows. You see my eyebrows?"

"Hey, where are the free doughnuts?" someone called. "Free doughnuts when we're on a top-priority sting!" But whoever was asking was just met by a chorus of jeers. I looked across and saw them dragging Nena out.

"And you know our helmets?" The guy was still wrapping the heavy chain around me. "Health and Safety has gotten hold of a film of a cat sneezing and they're playing it on a random time loop for us on the heads-up display. It's supposed to make us all relaxed. You know, so we're not stressed. And it's a funny film. I laugh every time I see it, but it's a pain in the ass to have a cat suddenly sneezing in your line of fire."

"What'll happen to us?" I said.

"Head hack and mind wipe, I guess."

"A mind wipe?"

"They'll destroy your memories from the last day as a precaution."

"But they can't. That's illegal."

"Illegal? The twenty-four-hour wipe was instituted three months ago."

He clipped a massive rusting hook to the end of the chain by my neck and left. I fought desperately to think of a way out of this but I got nowhere.

Then Nena was brought across.

"Stay safe for Mother New Seattle," said a cop, slapping Nena on the shoulder and leaving us both standing there in sacks, wound up in enough chain to anchor a battleship.

"Lean over and kiss me," I whispered, urgently.

"What?"

"I need a bobby pin from your hair. Kiss me."

She looked at me, then tilted her head to one side and leaned across. I felt the soft touch of her warm skin and the smell of her perfume. It was supposed to be a casual gesture, a cover. But the sensation ran through me like a spear, and for a moment I felt myself reconnected to feelings that I had not experienced in years. I almost forgot the reason for the kiss. And then I brushed her on the forehead with my cheek and finally pulled one of the bobby pins from her hair with my teeth.

When the cops saw what was happening they began shouting, but as they moved us apart, I deliberately fell, using the moment to work my hands to the top of the sack and spit the bobby pin into my fingers.

They dragged me to my feet. "You get it?" Nena said, looking shaken.

"Yeah."

"You took your time," she added, but I could see the confusion lingering in her eyes.

chapter THIRTY-EIGHT

When I was a cop, we had competitions to see who could get out of a set of cuffs the quickest using a bobby pin. It's not hard—just bend the end of the pin and insert it in the lock to release the ratchet.

It was harder if the cuffs were double locked, but these weren't. Back then, I could do it blindfolded in under thirty seconds. I opened out the bobby pin and bent one end between my fingers so that I had a little hook. Then I felt around, trying to find the keyhole on the left cuff.

All around, the detail was packing up and generally shouting at one another. The arc lights began retracting with a hydraulic shriek, as a cluster of the police drongles scuttled away in clouds of dust.

Another cop was dragging out the ripped remains of the banner from the bar. It was stained with red rivulets.

Finally, I felt the bent end of the pin drop into the keyhole, but either the thing was stiff or I had lost my touch, because the ratchet wouldn't budge.

"Hey! What are they still doing here?" Another cop with

a Handheld Feed Reader was pointing in my direction. "Will someone please track those two? We've another target in ten. So let's move, people. Move!"

Rain began to fall in a sheet as members of the Security Detail walked over, clapped hold of the huge steel hook that had been clipped onto the chain, and dragged me backward across the alley. Two other cops were doing the same with Nena. I felt a twist in my neck. Finally they hauled me to my feet again by a metal door. It had "New Seattle Police Department Prisoner Rapid Removal—Hookup 473" stamped across in huge yellow letters.

One of the cops plugged a feed from the door into the back of his neck, and after a moment it identified him. Lights blinked, and it opened.

They dragged Nena inside the tunnel first. I couldn't see what was happening, but a minute later it was my turn. They hauled me into the tunnel, grabbed me around the waist, lifted me up, and slotted the huge hook into a catch above my head. Then they left me swinging there next to Nena. I was dripping wet.

The taller of the two cops wiped his face. "Have a nice trip," he said.

"I hear the wine list is fucking excellent," I said.

They grunted, unsure how to take that, then shuffled out and eased the door closed.

It was utterly dark.

We swung gently, tightly chained inside a sack with just our heads free.

"Can you get out of the cuffs?" called Nena, and her voice echoed around the tube. My eyes began to adjust and I saw the bulk of her outline.

"I used to be able to do it," I said. Then I heard a creaking whirr of machinery, and she was abruptly swung forward.

Above my head, a track of clacking teeth, thick with oil, rang with an undulating tremor and clang.

"Listen!" she cried as she was hauled away along the track. "There's a conspiracy in the city and the police are involved up to their eyeballs."

"What?" I shouted above the rising din as she swung farther away.

"Get that small fridge somewhere safe if you get out of here. Promise me!"

"The fridge? What's so special about the fridge?"

"Doesn't matter. Just promise me. And don't look inside, okay?"

And then I lost sight of her as she was dragged into the darkness.

A screen flashed into life a little way ahead, casting a swath of flickering light over the metal walls, and I saw the tube we were in was huge.

"Hi, I'm Dan Cicero, mayor of New Seattle. You might have heard of me," said the thin voice, reverberating with a sad, damp echo in the shabby gloom. "People call me the Mayor of Safety. Thank you for being arrested today. We have a zero-tolerance policy on danger in this city and, by getting caught, you're helping us make this city a safer place. New Seattle Health and Safety is the finest in the world. And a strong Health and Safety Department means a strong city."

"New Seattle Health and Safety," sang a close-harmony group as I was yanked along the track toward the screen. "Stay safe! Watch out! Stay safe! Watch out for that—" Then there was the drawn-out sound of a long, tortuous crash.

The mayor's face returned.

"And remember, please don't die for no reason. I mean, what's the point? Right?"

His eyebrows froze as the screen crashed and the words

ran cold through my mind again. Why was this city torment-
ing me with this inane slogan?

"Sometimes people just do, all right?" I shouted at his
picture, and my words echoed around the tube. "Sometimes
they just do!"

Then it was my turn to be yanked along the track. The
damp darkness seemed to seep into my bones, as though this
was some abattoir of the soul. Rats were scampering about
on the floor below, confused by the noise and my swinging
bulk.

I fiddled the bobby pin into the keyhole and tried again to
flick the ratchet release, but it was so stiff. Ahead, a slant of
sunlight daggered through a grill above my head, and a much
louder roar began to drown out the noise from this tube.

I was pulled to a hesitant halt and my legs swung madly.
Above me, the machinery stuttered and scraped as though
it were having a mad fit. Then, with a splitting squeal, the
hook above me switched onto a new track and I was
yanked left. It felt like I had pulled all the muscles in my
neck. This was a bigger tube and I was moving much faster,
twisting and swinging like a freshly slaughtered carcass of
meat.

The noise of the track became deafening as I clacked
over another interchange, and the rattling yowl of machinery
felt like it would burst my eardrums.

Then the track stopped dead and I swung again.

Silence.

I worked desperately on the cuffs. Then I heard a voice
shouting far away. I strained my eyes, wondering if it was
Nena. But there was only the scamper of the rats below and
the squeak of the hook gently grating above my head. I hung
like that for maybe five minutes, and I got nowhere with the
ratchets on the cuffs.

Then the track kicked back into life and I almost dropped the pin. Music mixed with the roar, and ahead another screen shone, showing a man in a field of buttercups.

"You have been arrested by the New Seattle State Police," he was saying, "a force that is dedicated to your well-being. You should feel proud to have been arrested by one of the top-four state police departments on the Western Seaboard Area, as voted for by the readers of *Happiness, Money, and Golf* magazine." I saw him hold up a copy as I was ratcheted past.

The next moment, I heard footsteps. And a figure tripped in front of me, clattering against the metal sides in a sliding, spidery sprawl.

"Nena," I cried over the roar of machinery.

But whoever it was didn't look up. He pushed my legs out of the way and was gone.

The track gave another yanking halt and I swung in the darkness.

Silence again.

But then, far away, I could hear the drone of drongles. I made a frantic effort to release the ratchets on the cuffs and one finally gave a few clicks. I tried to pull my hand through, but the gap was small.

The track came to life again, and I dropped the bobby pin. Blazing light loomed ahead, and I saw a group of work-men in a side tube. They had a works drongle that was piled high with materials and tools. I tried desperately to force my hand through the cuff.

I could hear the crowd and the drongles on a street out-side now. I could even make out someone shouting in a hoarse voice.

"The end of the world is nigh! The end of the world is the most nigh I have ever seen it. And I thought it was pretty nigh last Tuesday. Who wants a nice sticker?"

chapter
THIRTY-NINE

Maddox ordered coffee.

Then he sat at a table staring at the city wall that rose up across the street from the Blue Lagoon café. The coffee machine behind the counter steamed.

"And then the lighting of the lamps," he said without knowing where he had picked up the line.

The man in black sat down opposite in one lithe movement. He was wearing sunglasses. He always wore sunglasses.

"We have the guy—the ex-cop and the woman," said Maddox. "Security Detail picked them up a few minutes ago, but there's no sign of the fridge."

"Find it," said the man in black, his words falling like a dead weight on the table between them. "Why did you pick one that was so nervous?"

"It was small. I'll put pressure on the head hack guys to find something," said Maddox.

His coffee arrived. When he turned the man in black was gone.

"See you later, Maddox. Thanks for your help," he said to the empty seat.

chapter
FORTY

A pool of gloomy yellow light spilled over the tunnel.

Grimy white tiles. My eyes struggled to focus as I passed a massive sign in spidery neon that declared: "This is New Seattle Head Hack Central. You will be booked and hacked for evidence."

The rise of classical music fought with the horrendous noise of the machinery.

"If you are a real estate agent, you must declare it when asked," said another sign. "And give up any property details."

And then another: "Take the edge from the disappointment of prison with some haberdashery! Haberdashery is more than just a friend. It's a big, lovely, supersoft companion for life!"

A huge counter flapped over to 146 with a crack like a gunshot, and I was dragged toward a set of double doors. I tried to raise my legs to break the impending collision, but I couldn't do it, so I smashed them apart with my head.

My vision blurred into darkness.

And then I saw the streets of New Seattle empty of people. And I was running through them but there was no one there.

Then harsh, white light. I squinted. The track lurched, and I fell back to the present. I was hanging from the ceiling of a small office corridor. The doors were still flick-flacking shut behind me.

White light spilled from the light-tubes. A couple of cops in rolled-up shirtsleeves nonchalantly edged past my swinging feet, carrying files below. I could smell the antiperspirant from one. The track swung me down the corridor as a woman with a coffeepot backed out of a door and we collided, causing her to drop the pot with a clatter.

"It's happened again!" she cried, straightening up. "I said this would happen again didn't I?" she shouted to the corridor in general. "I said I wanted an office away from this thing." Her voice floated after me as I was dragged on. "I demand an office somewhere else!"

Then the track kinked left and I was shunted hesitantly through a hole roughly smashed in the wall, and across a storage room. Files were stacked in tall, swaggering piles. The teeth gabbled away above my head, and the rich dark smell of burnt oil from the machinery filled my lungs. I swung sideways, catching my knee on a shelf before it yanked me up through a hole in the ceiling. The joists and pipes were still sticking out, and the broken edges of plasterboard shed little falls of dust as they vibrated. The room above was much bigger. The track wound around in a big loop.

And then, up in one corner, a board clattered through a trail of letters to spell: "Room 349, level two."

A buzzer sounded and a red light flashed by a spur. The hook above my head unclipped from the main track and I sailed down the rails through a long sweeping series of bends, twirling and slipping through a faceless, filthy tunnel.

chapter
FORTY-ONE

A jolting halt.

I was breathing hard. After a moment, I felt myself lowered down through a hole in the floor until I rested awkwardly on a sofa in a brightly lit room. The journey had loosened the heavy chain, so the links hung in lazy loops.

"Mr. Lindbergh? Make yourself comfortable." The man behind a desk didn't look up. "If you're unsettled by your journey, there's poetry you can read to yourself on your right. That will help to calm you down. It's the rhythm of the words." He continued writing furiously.

"I don't need to read any poetry right now," I said, briefly looking at the words and then back at the man. He wasn't tall, but he was powerfully built if overweight, and his suit didn't quite fit his frame and slightly lagged behind his movements.

"Just read the poetry, and I'll be with you as soon as I can," he said, "and if you finish up with that, then stare at the picture of the puppy. I'm sure that will chase away any unease." He kept writing and shuffling papers.

"Are you going to slice away my memory?"

"When you finish with the poetry, look at the picture of the puppy and pretend you are stroking it. His name is Charles III. I'm nearly done here," he said in a distracted monotone. Finally he looked up and widened his mouth in what I guessed he passed off as a smile.

"So, Lindbergh, H. How did you like the puppy?"

"Are you going to wipe my memory?" I said.

"Not just at the moment. Did you look at the puppy? The secret is to pretend it's on your lap and you're stroking it. 'Nice puppy, nice puppy.' Like that. Within a few weeks, we will have pictures of puppies and kittens on the walls all the way down the PRR system, and the smell of fresh grass clippings pumped through as well. I'd also like to promote the sack as a protective womb. Did you think of it as a womb on your journey?"

"Can't say I did. Are you from marketing?"

"Yes." He wrote some notes and I wondered what this man thought life was really about. I wondered if he'd ever taken a moment to stand back and ask himself what the hell he was doing. "If one of the officers had called it a womb, or it had the word *womb* on it in big letters, do you think that would have helped trigger that as a concept?" Since he was strangely economical with how far he was prepared to open his mouth, his words had a clipped edge to them.

"No," I said. "It's a sack."

"I know it's a sack, but you have to use your imagination. You have to give something to get something back. The same with the picture of the puppy." He put his pen down, got up slowly and precisely, and came around to sit on the front of his desk, his suit fumbling into some outlandish creases as it fought to keep up with all this movement. There was a pause as he folded his arms.

"This is cutting-edge stuff we're doing here. One day,

prisoners will be long-term head hacked automatically at the start of their journey along the track, and then images from their mind can be shown to them on big screens as they travel along, accompanied by stirring music. A bit like their life flashing before their eyes so that when they reach here to be interviewed, they'll tell us everything."

"I can't wait," I said.

"Yes." He stared at me, but the smile froze as the door sprang open.

"Just stretching my legs," said a fridge.

"You? Get back to the kitchen," said the marketing man.

"Okay. Sorry, I know I said I wouldn't come in again, but do you want some anchovies while I'm here? Or some cake?" It opened its door and the light came on with a flourish.

"No, get out," cried the marketing man as his suit creased up like a piece of unfolding origami. "What is it with that fridge?" he said, closing the office door behind it. "It's always coming in. We marketed them too well, that's what it is, and now they think the world owes them something."

"Maybe it does."

"What? Do you know some of them think they should have pension plans? The only people making money out of it are the lawyers." His breathing was becoming asthmatic, and he took out an inhaler. "The food bill at our main office over the summer was astronomical, because the fridge was secretly ordering deliveries of hummus. Every time you wanted milk, you'd find the thing was stuffed full of hummus. I mean, what is hummus, anyway? We had it taken away in the end, and got a regular nonspeaking fridge. That was a big relief. Now I don't get snide comments if I eat dairy products."

There was a knock at the door.

"Yes?"

A woman in a matching pencil skirt and top opened the

door. "It's Louise, Mr. Malbranque. Can I have a word? It's about the red-smoke meeting."

"Sure. What is it?"

"Confidential," said the woman, mouthing the word, but with hardly any sound behind it.

"Of course. Please look at the picture of the puppy," he instructed me. "I won't be a moment and then we'll carry on." He got up and walked from the office.

He left the door ajar, and I could hear him talking to the woman in a low voice outside in the corridor.

chapter

FORTY-TWO

How are you getting on with the puppy? Mr. Lindbergh?" The man's voice trailed off as he returned to
the room and saw the empty sack hanging from the
hook. He took another pace in.

I was wedged in above the door and looked down, imploring him to close it, but he hesitated, and I could hold
myself in this position only for so long, so I jumped. For a
moment, I felt his bulky frame resist my weight, but then he
collapsed onto his stomach with a strangled cry. I grabbed a
picture from his desk and cracked him over the head, and he
stopped moving.

I got up and shut the door.

I knelt down and searched through his pockets, taking
his wallet and red gun. Then I sat down in his chair and
worked at the cuff that was still on my right hand with the end
of a coat hanger, and after a minute got it to release.

I stood up, pulled his hands behind his back, and got the
cuffs on him. Then I dragged him into the sack, wound him in
the yards of chain, and hung him on the hook.

On the desk was a panel of buttons. I ran my hand over them like a kid selecting a chocolate, trying to read the tiny writing above each. Finally I found one that looked like it said "Prisoner Removal" and I pressed it.

"Thank you for pressing this button," said the console. I waited; nothing happened. I pressed it again. "Thank you once again for pressing this button," said the voice. "It really is appreciated. Nice one!"

Still nothing happened.

I tried the one next to it.

"Thanks for pressing this button, too. Fabulous!"

I tried another and some classical music boomed out. I frantically pressed all the other buttons, and finally I heard the whir of machinery as the chain took in the slack links and began to lift him from the room. Then it accelerated and he was yanked through a hole in the ceiling. "Stop this! Hey!" he cried groggily as he disappeared in perfect time to *Thus Spake Zarathustra,* and then the trapdoor in the ceiling flapped shut. "I'm in marketing. Get me out of this! Hey!"

His voice faded and then there was silence.

My hand was bruised and grazed where I had scraped it through the handcuff, but it didn't feel broken. I cut off the red collar, buttoned my jacket to cover the red printing, and slipped out of the office into the corridor, carrying a red pen and a file that had been lying around. And for a moment, I felt again that mix of tired optimism that I had carried with me over the years when I had been a cop, and I had tried hard to hold onto a belief that I was making a difference.

No one hassled me; I guess I knew how to look the part, and most people were too self-absorbed anyway. I passed a whole line of framed certificates hanging on a wall.

"Runner-up in the category Best Small-Arms Fire at a Female Suspect," said one. "Most Imaginative Use of a Riot Shield During a Riot—Interstate Police Awards, Second Place," said another, but I didn't catch the rest.

From an office on my left, I heard a cop singing: "This cookie is my friend! The diet is my enemy." As I passed I saw him start to drink his coffee.

I walked on, trying to recall where the stairwell should be, and came across a long line of prisoners hanging in sacks on a piece of stationary track. A cop was sitting nearby reading a newspaper. "Was it you I told about the time I sang at the New York Opera?" said one of the other prisoners. His wispy gray hair slanted across his face in a wave.

"Yeah, that was me. You told me," said the cop, without looking up. "But that isn't going to win you any favors. Opera doesn't cut any ice with the New Seattle Police Department. Now, Parma ham, I like that. You get me some Parma ham, then maybe I can help you out a bit." He switched pages.

I looked at the faces of the prisoners each in turn as I passed, and then a little way ahead I saw Nena and felt cold.

The prisoner who had been talking to the cop began singing softly. It was opera. The first note sounded flimsy and comic as it jarred against the heavy atmosphere as cops passed up and down the corridor.

Nena stared straight ahead. When I came level with her, she shook her head with the slightest of movement.

"Fridge," she said almost inaudibly.

I stood looking into her brown eyes. For a moment I had the intense desire to reach up and sweep the hair away from her face.

"Fridge," she said again, and I forced myself to walk on. The pure ringing tone of the opera grew louder, and I felt drawn into the rise and fall of the notes as it filled the corridor. Then I heard a crack and the singing stopped dead.

I looked back and saw the cop holding his truncheon, standing by the man who now hung in a limp pile in his sack.

"Parma ham, I told you," said the cop. "You other guys heard me warn him, didn't you?" He prodded the next guy hanging from the track.

"I heard you. I heard you," said the guy.

"Yeah? Good. What about you others? Parma ham?"

"Yeah! Parma ham. Yeah. You said Parma ham."

"Parma ham, right. Now I'm getting through to you guys at last," he said, and went back to his paper.

The violence sent my heart pounding and I turned back. My thoughts raced at one and three-quarter pace. I was going to do my damnedest to protect this woman.

"Hey," I said to the cop, "maybe I can help you out with some Parma ham."

"Yeah?" He looked up. I took out the envelope the cops had given me in the Halcyon and quietly gave him all the money inside.

"Enough for Parma ham?" I said.

"Yeah, that'll buy Parma ham. What kind of Parma ham were you after?"

"What kind?" I said, thinking the Parma ham metaphor had now definitely outrun its usefulness.

"Yeah."

"I'll be honest with you. You see that woman there? She's a neighbor and we've had an affair. They'll be pictures in her mind that would make my wife apoplectic if she gets hold of them. You know how these things have a habit of coming out?"

"Ah, I get you."

"So maybe she doesn't have to be head hacked. What do you think? It's just an idea. And maybe keep all this off her record."

"Yeah?"

"Yeah. Enjoy your Parma ham," I said and walked away.

Cops were wandering about or slouching in offices with their stomachs peeking over the edges of the desks. At any kind of slouching competition, cops would be right up there.

I passed more offices with ill-fitting doors and a room labeled Authorized Personnel Only, on which someone had scrawled Unauthorized Personnel, Tuesdays Nine to Nine-thirty.

The noise of the track was louder now, and the thin partition walls vibrated.

I headed down a stairwell, feeling my heart thump in looping beats, and I took a long breath, smelling that same familiar, underlying odor of disinfectant.

On the wall at one of the landings was a bulletin board, overflowing with cards. I stopped as a group of cops came past. "For sale: riot shield. Shoulder charge model, shaped by Ralf Semmens. Some scratches. And one ding from a brick, but nice repair. Must be seen. $300," said one.

I unpinned it.

It took me another five minutes to get to the exit.

"What kind of mood is that?" said of the security goons, as a piece of hip-hop at double speed filled the air. "It's weird."

"Yeah," said the cop who was plugged into the reader. "I drank a lot of caffeine this morning. I'll be running around all day and I won't sleep tonight. It does that to me."

I reached the checkpoint and the cop started to plug into my feed, but I thrust the card so close to his face that he had to jerk back.

"You know the guy selling this?" I said.

The cop took the card.

"No. Is he D section?"

"This is all I have."

He shook his head. I nodded.

"Okay. Thanks anyway." I took the card and walked swiftly out into the lobby.

People were milling about for reasons that escaped me. There were maybe fifty lines all labeled with boards saying things like Fines for Downtown or Fines for the Wharf.

In front of me, a drunkard wearing a cheap suit, which shone with plastic, was flattening out a filthy piece of paper he had just removed from his pocket. His limbs twitched awkwardly, as though his body were nothing more than a sack filled with otters. I stepped around him, inhaling a lungful of alcohol.

A couple of bums were waiting in line at a lane marked Tramps Who Just Want to Shout at the Police. They were dressed in layers of beleaguered clothing and carrying bulging bags.

I found myself trying to wedge my way past a man who had brought a metal filing cabinet with him on a cart and now was delving into various drawers.

The atmosphere trawled up a bad taste in the mouth as though this lobby was a magnet for madness, sucking in people who were slightly off balance. Maybe it could even send the blood the wrong way around the body. There was a palpable, down-at-the-heels heaviness here, as if the fear on the streets was being drawn in, and then getting absorbed into the fabric of the building itself.

Many of these people had seriously lost their way in life. They had unkempt hair and sad wandering eyes that were constantly searching for someone who would lead them to a better place. It had not been like that when I had worked here. There had not been this depth of hopelessness.

I barged my way toward the doors, but a furry, eight-foot squirrel confronted me.

Its whiskers trembled. Then it cocked its head.

"Rusty Ragtail the Safety Squirrel welcomes you to New Seattle, the city of safety," said a stunningly beautiful woman wearing a spangly leotard, who seemed to be chaperoning the fluffy creature. "New Seattle Health and Safety is having a big drive on sharp-corner awareness this week, so we have an exhibition here." She pointed to the other side of the lobby. "Please take a moment to browse. One of the sharp corners was brought in from Moscow. Rusty Ragtail likes that one, don't you?"

The squirrel nodded.

"Isn't he cute?" she said.

"Yes," I said.

"He's not scum is he?"

"Scum?" I said. "No."

"The Chicago Safety Squirrel is scum, isn't he?"

"Is he?"

"Yeah. How could they have sunk so low as to copy our idea of a safety squirrel?" The squirrel opened its mouth and put its hand in. "It makes him sick," she said. "Come on, Rusty Ragtail."

And they padded happily away.

I wove my way toward the exit and found myself near the exhibition. More women in spangly leotards were giving away brochures and, at the back, a close-harmony group began singing. "Stay safe! Watch out! Stay safe! Watch out! Stay safe! Watch out for that—"

They stopped singing and one of them let out a long piercing scream.

"New Seattle Health and Safety. Please, don't die for no reason."

Those words mocked me the more I heard them.

I tried to tell myself it was just a slogan as I accepted a brochure from a girl who was pressing it toward me with a smile that surgery had crafted into a permanent fixture across her face. But they resonated too deeply for me just to dismiss them.

And all this Health and Safety crap was mothballing everyone from reality, numbing their sense of what it was to be alive, stopping them from facing up to their own flimsy existence on this planet.

Just as I had mothballed myself away from my own life.

And I knew that that led nowhere. I wondered if only those who have truly come to terms with their own mortality can feel compassion. Perhaps that's how it worked. And it struck me that that was what Nena and Abigail had in common.

Compassion.

I battered my way through the crowd and outside to the steps. The remains of a smashed stone bird had been swept into a pile and I realized it was the one I had knocked off the roof the night before. The head looked like a raven.

I hurried down to the sidewalk where a man was busking with a massive gong. He had some music on a stand and struck the gong once theatrically as I approached. Someone near me gave him a few coins.

"Thanks," he said, pointing to the sheet music. "You came in at the good bit. There were four hundred and eighty bars of rest before that."

FORTY-FOUR

I headed along the sidewalk. "The end of the world is nigh!" said the man, perched on his battered box on the corner of the block. He now had a bandage wound around his head and I didn't get too close in case he recognized me. "With some mildly nigh periods later. Then the end of the world will become really nigh tonight, especially in the Denny Park area, before easing off and not being nigh at all in the morning."

I hailed a drongle. It was in a bad way, with a gash running clean through the roof, and dribbling blue fluid in a long line from one of the wheels.

I shouted Gabe's address into the large horn on the side and climbed in, aware that two other people were already there. It was a young couple that had been out shopping. The girl was snuggled into the shoulder of the boy. They were smart and clean. And happy.

To them life was simple. And I hoped it would stay that way.

The drongle slithered around a corner barely under control, but at least the screens weren't working.

"Nice shirt," said the girl, and I realized my jacket was undone but the red printing had run into a blur. "But red? Won't the cops be pissed if they see you with that? That's restricted."

"Yeah, you're right," I said, doing up the jacket.

"I really respect you for it. There should be more people like you," said the girl. "I'm a student doing my master's in 'Overly Long Moments of Coughing in Postwar European Literature,' but I don't know any students who would dare have a red shirt. But I am so behind you. You show 'em."

"Yeah, you must have been lying under the Tree of Courage," said the boy, who had shoulder-length hair. "I'm studying coughing in nineteenth-century literature, as well, but my classes have more of a slant toward flu and colds in general."

"Sounds useful," I said.

"Yeah, it's an amazing subject, actually. It has a real relevance. Get this. When you analyze Dostoyevsky, you find that without coughing his work is really nothing. The fact that his characters do a lot of coughing is what lifts it out of the ordinary, and makes it speak."

"Is that so?" I said, as the wedding-cake columns of Head Hack Central slipped from view.

They talked a little more about coughing in literature, going on about Circe and James Joyce, but I didn't know what they were talking about, and I was relieved when they eventually got out, no doubt off to drink cappuccinos and stare into each other's eyes and talk about the size of the essay crisis that was gradually enveloping them.

Someone had once worked out a formula for calculating the actual size of an essay crisis. It had something to do with the time until the deadline, the length of the essay, and a variable factor related to how much access there was to children's programs.

"Your lucky medieval instrument today is the crumhorn," said the drongle, coming to a jerky halt. "Your receipt is being printed on material that may contain nuts." Then I heard the extended sound of printing, but only a tiny receipt about an inch square appeared in the slot.

Then nothing.

I picked up the tiny piece of paper and heaved back the drongle door to be met by a rush of kids.

"Take your receipt for a dime," they cried. I showed them the tiny thing.

"What's that?" said one kid, and they turned away. I was still a mile from Gabe's apartment but I decided to walk.

chapter

FORTY-FIVE

The marketing man struggled inside the sack as he thrust down a final length of track to the head hack area.

"I'm Sky Malbranque! I am in marketing. Stop this!" he cried as he saw the nurse.

She smiled, but it was so laden with insincerity that it made unusually high demands on the muscles in her cheeks and the layer of makeup that she had plastered across her face.

She swung him toward the chair, maneuvering the chain.

"Please! He escaped and put me in the sack," said Malbranque, trying to wriggle to face the nurse.

The chain clanked madly in the track.

"That's very sweet," she said, "but the system is the most sophisticated on the Western Seaboard. Did you know they are going to have pictures of a puppy all the way down the tubes? We know you have to be Huckleberry Lindbergh."

"But I'm not! Lindbergh escaped and put me in his place. I am Sky Malbranque from marketing. Ring my department. Ring them now!"

The nurse slacked off the wire with a control and Malbranque sank awkwardly into the chair.

"Fire the head torsion please, Nurse." The doctor didn't look up as he spoke. He was engrossed in studying a chart.

Two flat hydraulic plates squeezed in on Malbranque's cheeks and it became impossible to make out any of his actual words. Only a squashed, fluctuating squeak and drawl.

"I'll just pop these on you," the nurse said, sliding some protective clear glasses over his eyes. "And I'll pop a bib on just to protect the nice sack," she said, fitting a small, pristine white bib awkwardly over the filthy sack and links of oily chain.

"I want to step up and use 3-C with alfalfa this time please, Nurse." The doctor gave her a hurried look and you got the sense he felt this was an overly generous use of his time.

"Yes, Doctor. I'll just pop the picture of the puppy there," she said. Then she put on a pair of latex gloves over the ones she already had on, dolloped a handful of goo onto the man's hair, and slopped it around.

The doctor moved so he was within Malbranque's line of vision.

"Mr. Lindbergh, you escaped a head hack yesterday, presumably because you have a memory you wish to hide. We will be checking your short-term memory, but if we don't find anything there, I also have instructions to probe back a bit further, so you may lose some of your past. I will do my best not to ferret around anywhere too deep. You have my word under the oath I have sworn to the Medical Council Bear. And, I am also part of the Lodge of Maculfry, which has a strict code of morals," he said, returning to look through the notes. "So, can you please sign here and here for me? And kiss the page here. Kiss. Thank you." He shoved the form in front of the man's face. "Kiss there again. Good. Look at the picture of the puppy to help yourself stay calm. Prepare the vault for the images please, Nurse. Sanction the input. Memory is on. We are locked. And stand by, please. Head hack in five, four..."

Malbranque erupted into a frenzy of muffled shrieks, but neither the doctor nor the nurse took any notice. "Pretend you are stroking the puppy. Three, two, one..."

chapter FORTY-SIX

At Porlock, the computer was displaying this message: "What's with all the numbers in brackets?"

And as soon as they deleted any infected files, more sprang up.

Mendes watched the world below through his window. A handful of rays burst from behind a cloud. A summer storm was moving in pregnant with soft, heavy rain. The world was moving on. The world was always moving on whether you were a part of it or not.

He was tired now, and he felt his career slipping through his fingers. If he was unable to babysit this project, then he would be farmed out to some desk job in a department on the edges of D.C., where they dealt with nothing more interesting than food allergies.

His arms ached and he mopped his forehead.

He had a fever.

chapter
FORTY-SEVEN

I tried the handle to Gabe's apartment, but the door was locked. I called to the fridges but I didn't get any reply. Finally I heard the tumble dryer asking me if I wanted my clothes dried, and it tried to open the door, but after five minutes I sensed it wasn't going to happen.

I kicked at the door and the lock burst in a splinter of wood.

"Hi," said the tumble dryer, waddling up to me. "Those clothes look wet."

"Hey," said the Ice Jumper. "You're back. Would you like some Primula?"

"No, thanks. We have to get ready to leave." I closed the door as best I could.

"Great," said the Ice Jumper. "Are we going food shopping?"

"No," I said. "How's the Tiny Eiger?"

"Quiet. He's always quiet."

"You know what he's got inside?"

"It's not taramasalata, is it? I love that stuff," said the Frost Fox.

"Hey, come here," I said to the Tiny Eiger as it loitered near the bedroom. "How are you?" It hummed a lot more for a moment, then tried to hide unsuccessfully behind a lamp shade.

"Come on, little fellow, open your door," I said, crouching down in front of it. "I need to have a look." It was a much smaller fridge than the others. Probably it came originally from a motel room.

"Maybe something went bad inside of him and he's hallucinating," said the Frost Fox. "I had that once. A mango went bad in my salad drawer. I felt really woozy for days. Kept warning everyone about a polar bear in the hallway."

The Tiny Eiger hummed a little harder.

"Come on," I said. "I'm here to help you."

It hummed harder still, opened its door a tiny amount, and then, after another few minutes of coaxing, swung the door wide. Inside were racks and racks of test tubes. I stared and then pulled one out.

"City of New Seattle Fear Virus," I read. "Where did you come from, little fellow?"

But the Tiny Eiger wouldn't say anything more. I put the rack of test tubes carefully back, and noticed a wooden box on the bottom shelf. I pulled it out.

"He was already in Nena's room when we arrived," said the Ice Jumper. "Are those test tubes inside?"

"Yeah," I said.

The box was heavy. On the outside it said Sergeant Liebervitz. I opened the lid and nearly dropped it immediately. It was the head of a man packed in some chemical with a lead poking out from the feed on the neck.

"Gee, what's in there?" said the Ice Jumper, waddling over.

"Nothing," I said, closing the box quickly and forcing the revulsion in my stomach to settle. I put it back in the fridge. Then I sat on the floor by the Tiny Eiger.

"Where did you come from? It's important."

"Nena," said the Tiny Eiger. Then it closed its door and shuffled behind a potted plant.

FORTY-EIGHT

I poured myself a whiskey and sat down. I needed to get out of here fast with the fridges, but it was no good just wandering the streets. The obvious place to take them was the drongle warehouse, just as Gabe had planned, but it wouldn't be dark for hours.

What the hell had Nena done? Had she killed that cop? Was that why she didn't want to be head hacked? And what of the test tubes? Had she stolen them? Or bought them in some black-market deal?

"Don't look in the fridge," she had said.

Perhaps Gabe had been right all along.

Perhaps she was just a criminal who had been playing on my weakness. After all, that was all she ever claimed, but I didn't want to believe that. I wanted to believe that she was the one who knew how to fix my life.

I had more whiskey.

There had been stories of people trying to control the population with fear strategies before.

There had been a clumsy attempt while I had been a cop

by a marketing consultancy firm working for police finance. As a marketing strategy, they thought up a criminal gang called Warriors from Nowhere You Would Actually Know. Their whole plan was to secretly create an atmosphere of fear in the city. That way, they argued, the people would be happy to see more money poured into the police budget to combat the threat. And the more money the police had, the more they could enhance their image through marketing without having to spend it all on actually fighting crime, because there was no crime. The plan was that simple.

So they had set out to spook the city by giving the impression that this gang—Warriors from Nowhere You Would Actually Know—was rife, even though it didn't exist.

But it all went spectacularly wrong.

The name of the gang was an error, for one thing. One of the marketing people came up with the idea of calling them "Warriors" and put in brackets, "from nowhere you would actually know," meaning that at another time they would think up some make-believe place.

But some marketing graduate with a degree in graffiti husbandry at Tampa Bay University had taken that to be the actual name. And before the error could be rectified, a graffiti spray team from New York had been flown in. They hit the city wearing a flurry of baseball caps and, with a dash of exuberant lettering, the name was out.

It wouldn't have mattered, but something else happened after that. Something way more sinister.

Kids on the street, seeing the graffiti, became intrigued and agitated, and they wanted to join the gang. And in the months that followed, amid the rumors, whisperings, and posturing, Warriors from Nowhere You Would Actually Know somehow slipped into existence.

And then it grew.

For a little while, Warriors from Nowhere You Would Actually Know became a powerful underworld player on the Western Seaboard. And initially, the New Seattle Police didn't have the resources to keep tabs on them.

They fired the marketing company, and I remembered how the new one was always scathing about what the old marketing company had done. They spent a lot of time going around and saying, "Who did your marketing for you last time? Cowboys they were."

So maybe it was police marketing. Maybe they had created a whole new generation of fear strategies.

Marketing companies wielded a lot of power.

Even the army had image consultants assigned to each unit who went into battle. They had major input in what the best way of attacking an enemy should be, so they put across the most aggressive image.

I had to get the fridges out of here, and I realized I was trying to form a plan.

And I'd deliberately not made any plans in years.

I made a real effort to get more information from the Tiny Eiger, but it just kept calling for Nena, and my thoughts returned to the head in the box. I coaxed the little fridge to open his door again and examined it further.

Presumably the feed on the neck still worked and that was why someone had gone to so much trouble to preserve the guy's head. The chemical in there reeked.

I searched through Gabe's bookshelves and pulled out a map of the city. I opened it up, flattened it on the table, and marked the drongle warehouse. Then I traced the tubes from the Prisoner Rapid Removal system. There was an entrance five minutes from Gabe's apartment and it was possible to get from there to an alley close to the drongle warehouse through the system. I marked the route in red on the map.

But it would only work if the feed on this dead cop's head would give me access.

I buttoned my jacket, picked up the box with the head, and left the fridges, telling them not to wander out of the apartment.

I took a left down the first alley in the slanting rain.

The huge tube ran down the side and I could hear a grinding howl of machinery. After a couple of minutes I found a door marked "New Seattle Police Department. Hookup 159." The fuck-off yellow letters had been newly painted. I opened the box and plugged in the feed from the head.

There was a pause.

I glanced around but the alley seemed deserted. Still nothing. I was about to give up when finally the door opened with a slow sigh. It was dark inside but there was easily enough room for the fridges. I closed it again and ran back to the apartment.

"Hey," said the Frost Fox. "Did you pick up any milk? Or fromage frais? I've never had any, but they tell me it's pretty special."

"No," I said. "We have to move now. We're going on a little trip." I searched around for a flashlight, but I couldn't find one. "We have to be really quick. If anyone calls the Fridge Detail, then it's over."

"Sure, we'll be quick," said the Ice Jumper. "What about singing?"

"No singing. Everyone ready?"

"Sure," said the spin dryer.

I led them out of the apartment, and jammed the front door shut as best I could. We had to go about twenty yards down the main street before we turned into the alley.

A kid passed us, then shouted: "Let's see your eggs then!" at the fridges. But when I turned to look at him, he ran off laughing.

A man with a dog had picked up a newspaper from a bin and held it like a sodden halo above his head as protection against the rain. The dog came over to sniff out what was going on, but the man didn't bat an eyelid at the fridges.

We turned into the alley.

Some faded graffiti on the wall declared Let's Party! The streets became choked with sodden wood smoke, and the buildings grew more and more dilapidated as I headed into the slum. I stared into a room as we passed, and saw it was lit by a swinging pool of faint yellow light thrown out from a bare bulb that was strung precariously on wires. Someone was banging on something far away. A piece of tin or metal.

Voices jumbled out of one window on my left in a weird soft language I couldn't place. "Ishi," someone seemed to be repeating. "Ishi."

Another woman's voice was shouting in rehearsed anger from a balcony up above. It rose and fell over ground I sensed she had trodden before. We walked on. Eyes watched us from dark rooms.

The fridges padded along as best they could, but the road was uneven, and the place was strewn with garbage, which jammed in their feet, so we had to stop a couple of times and free them.

I stopped. "Hide! Fridge Detail." About fifty yards ahead, I saw a group of figures in dark orange shirts saunter out from the alley in a shamble of shouting, and begin searching half-heartedly through the crates in the rain.

The fridges all hunkered down, using the alley doorways and garbage for cover. After another two minutes the detail left, headed the other way, and we continued down the alley, splashing through the puddles until we reached the door. I took out the lead from the feed on the neck of the severed head and plugged in.

A woman approached. Her face was drawn into a tight, pained expression that revealed her top teeth and made it look as if her cheeks had been taped up in folds toward her eyes. I sensed it was her form of protection, a shield to keep the world away. She walked by without even exchanging a glance.

Finally, the lights blinked sadly in the rain, and the door opened with a moan.

I eased the fridges inside, and then shut the entrance. They began shuffling along with their doors open, throwing just about enough light around to see as the track clattered noisily high above our heads.

After a while a woman came swinging gently toward us, her gray hair cropped short. Her wide eyes were full of fear as she was pulled past us, pleading.

After another five minutes, a man appeared hanging from the track in the distance and began shouting wildly. "And on the fifth day God created sin and blaspheming!" he cried, his eyes staring out of the gloom. "And man fell from grace into a great cesspool of sin. A huge steaming ocean of sin! A great big vat of stinking sin!" The track dragged him over us. "Sinners and thieves!" he shouted down. "Sinners, thieves, and electrical suppliers! All damned! All damned to hell."

We edged past his swinging legs, down into the increasing darkness as his voice faded. Faint red lights fixed high on the side blossomed into small pools.

Another person hung limply from the track in the darkness, her face picked out by a sharp slither of light so that it resembled a fifteenth-century painting. She looked unconscious.

A smaller tube ran off to the side, and I realized I had forgotten the map. I tried to visualize the route and took a left, hearing the clattering discordant cry of the track, punctuated now and again by shouts of the people hung in the sacks. Above a fraying cable spat white sparks.

I took another smaller spur to the left again, and I felt the metal floor rise as the tube staggered through the buildings and we were met by the groan of traffic noise.

Chinks of daylight speared through tiny holes in the rusted sides. The track over us was dead now and all I could hear were our stumbling footsteps and the heavy gasping of my own breath that seemed to fill all the spaces in my head.

I led the fridges on in the gloomy light. The noise of the wind tapping a wire on the outside of the tube let out a mournful cry. A door banged far away, and the thump echoed in waves. We came to a discarded cap lying pristine and un-touched on the floor like a calling card from the dead. And all the time, the musty, damp smell of filth—stale and heavy—lay on everything.

Here the track was utterly dead, and sheaves of wires hung down in tentacles.

A pool of red light. And we came to a doorway with a grimy sprawl of hydraulic arms. It was stamped "number 322."

"This one," I said as the noise of someone running through the tube far away echoed around us. I plugged in the lead from the head and the door opened.

"Hurry." I helped the fridges out into the harsh bright light.

The alley was deserted.

"It's one block and then you'll be safe," I said hustling the fridges through the mud.

chapter

FIFTY

Huckleberry Lindbergh?"

There was a *phwump* and hiss of hydraulics as the nurse released the torsion boards from his cheeks. They were all that was holding him upright in the chair and he slumped forward in the sack. But the chain connecting him to the track in the roof stopped him from collapsing completely.

"I can't make sense of it," said the doctor. "He seemed to have picked up memories of working in an office. Perhaps they are phantom images. I've heard it can happen. Anyway, I've wiped away a large chunk of memories to make certain he wasn't hiding anything underneath. But I can't find anything that would make him want to skip a hack. Strange. But there's probably a reason. I'll check my notes later tonight."

The doctor wasn't normally perplexed, and this was a mystery that he felt was a worthy adversary to his intelligence.

"Well, I'll put a copy of his pictures with him." The nurse trotted off.

Malbranque stirred. He looked sluggish, like a boxer who'd gone way too many rounds in too many fights.

"There, that wasn't too bad, was it? All done, Mr. Lindbergh," said the nurse clacking back into the room. "I'm going to staple a copy of your pictures here, to the front of your nice sack. You can have a look at them later. There are some nice pictures of a puppy for you."

"Where am I?" he said groggily. "And has anyone seen my Spanish homework?"

"We're just going to send you down to the cells now. We're all done here. Well done."

"Am I going to meet the wizard at Christmas? He promised me an owl," said Malbranque, and then his head fell forward again.

The nurse pressed a button and the sack was hoisted up and swung up to the track in the ceiling. He became conscious again just long enough to say: "He promised me a very happy owl."

The doctor flipped through the records while he was thinking, but more out of habit.

"Maybe he had his memories altered in some grimy back-street operation." He paused. "I've heard rumors of such things."

"Shall I get the next one in?" said the nurse.

"Yes. Actually, recommend this one for Fridge Detail. He won't know anything too much. And we don't want to make an issue of losing his mind."

"Fridge Detail recommended," said the nurse, selecting a huge sticker and placing it on his forehead. She pressed a button.

"I really do like the way there is so much variation in this job. Each day is different isn't it?" she said as Malbranque was lugged out.

chapter

FIFTY-ONE

I walked cautiously through the side door to the back of the store where the old cop drongles were stacked.

The rain dripped in through the ceiling, landing with an intermittent patter on a drongle roof nearby. "Hello?" I called, but my voice just echoed back, sounding strangely monotone as it shuffled around among the mechanical debris, old drongles, dust, oil, and cookie wrappers. "Just the rain and nothing more," I said. "Now I need you guys to stay here and hide if anyone comes, all right?"

"Sure," said the Frost Fox.

"What about a little singing?" added the Ice Jumper.

"Just not too loud," I said as I knelt down by the Tiny Eiger. "Open your door again little fellow," I said. And when he did, I slipped the box with the head back inside.

Then I left them and headed to the Halcyon motel.

It was only a few blocks. If Nena had killed that cop and my bribe had had no effect, they would find out from the head hack and lock her up for good. But if she was only wanted for some minor misdemeanor, they might just wipe her mind of the last day and she'd end up back at the motel.

I didn't fancy tangling with the guys in the lobby, so when I got there I headed across the parking lot and straight to the door of her room. It was locked.

I looked around, then kicked it in. The flimsy lock gave with barely a murmur.

The room hadn't been touched. The hole in the roof where I had jumped through was still there and the debris lay scattered across the carpet as though the moment had been frozen in time. I took out one of the head hack pictures I had of her in the drongle and wrote a note explaining that if they had wiped her memory, she would need to talk to me, and I left Gabe's address.

If she had killed that cop, and they found out, she wouldn't be back, anyway.

I placed the picture on the table by the bed hoping it would attract her attention without being too obvious to any-one else snooping.

I was about to leave the room when I felt a crack on the back of my head.

"Where's my money?" said a voice.

I staggered as my vision bled away at the edges and then finally fell. I felt a hand roll me over. Above loomed the shadow of a huge dark guy. He took another swing that caught me on my jaw.

"I haven't got any money," I said feebly, but it wasn't the best reply.

"You took the money. Where is it?"

"I haven't got any money," I found myself saying again, and he began roughly checking my pockets. He found the gun and the wallet I had taken from the police marketing guy.

"So you haven't got my money, eh?" he said riffling through the wallet and pulling out a wad of notes.

"Take it," I said, struggling to focus.

Then he whacked me again and I heard the sound of the crack of my jaw but felt nothing.

chapter

FIFTY-TWO

*S*huddering.

Much more than seemed ideal.

I opened my eyes to be met with the soft blue light that bathed the inside of a drongle dome and a smatter of rain on the shell. Outside, the leering swagger of buildings swept by as a wheel hit a pothole and the jolt spiraled through my lower back, jarring the air from my lungs.

I clawed my way up and sat on the torn seat, and I found my jaw ached like I had been hit by an angry wrecking ball. The blurred shaken forms of other drongles stumbled by.

I ran my hands over my head, feeling its dead weight as the bruises throbbed. I had been out cold, rumbling around, for God knows how long.

At least I was still alive.

I held my head more firmly in my hands as the drongle hit a pothole and threw me back onto the floor. A grouchy sneer came from somewhere deep behind one of the panels.

I had to get out.

I tried to force open the door as we slowed up without

any success. Then I pulled the emergency handle, but it came off in my hand. I braced my back on one side of the drongle and kicked the shell.

After a couple of attempts, the dome cracked. Then it shattered and my foot went through a small hole. I pulled it in, stuck my head out, and tried to squeeze through when we stopped in traffic. But the hole was tight and we picked up speed before I could get out and I was caught, half in and half out. Then we squealed through a junction, and the momentum threw me tumbling to the sidewalk in a ball of limbs.

I got to my feet. People were staring and I hobbled away before there was time for any of them to call the cops. Something in my inside pocket had dug into my ribs. I felt around and found out it was the bottle of healing balm I had been given by the girl as a free sample.

"Ideal for bruises," it said on the label.

"They were dead right about that," I said.

A coffee table lurking in the shadows was disturbed as I stopped and began coughing. They'd had a plague of them in New Seattle. Although most were culled, a few still evaded the catchers, living in the sewers and dark corners and normally coming out only at night. They all had pretty much the same personality, which had been bred in a computer program by feeding in data from thirteen thousand salesmen and seeing what they all had in common.

Top of the list had been the belief that golf was a sensible pastime, but I think they suppressed that from most of the models.

This one scooted up alongside and started to make small talk, one of its wheels squeaking wildly. They had been built to sell insurance and equities, but no doubt the companies that had made them had gone bust years before.

"Quiet out tonight, eh?" it said.

"It's ten thirty in the morning," I said.

"Sure. I knew that. What, you thought I didn't know that?"

"What are you selling, then?"

"I'm not selling. Do I look like the kind of coffee table that would sell financial products?"

"It would be easy to think so."

"No. Hedge funds, corporate bonds, stock-tracking medium-risk packages, I ain't selling those. I ain't selling equity bonds, even if they do look like a solid, long-term bet."

"I have to go," I said.

"All I will say is they give you 4.5 percent on a lump sum over a minimum of three months and you get a free gift of your choice. That's all I'm saying—unless you ask about the management strategy, or the start-up costs."

"Listen, little fellow. I'm not buying, so you might as well go away now."

"Sure. Sure," said the coffee table, squeaking along and nudging at my ankles. "But listen, if you signed up for a plan where you paid a fixed sum every month, you could choose a free gift. Maybe you'd like the carriage clock, or are you someone who would prefer a baby badger?"

"A baby badger?"

"Yeah, they make nice pets. It's a talking point to have a badger set at the bottom of your garden."

"No. And I haven't got a garden anyway."

"Okay, so maybe you've got a window box."

"Actually, no. Go on back to your hiding place."

"A badger might like living in a window box. He'd get a nice view."

"I'm not buying."

"Okay, but if you've got a lump sum, you should invest it. I'm offering you a unique opportunity here."

"Thanks, but no." We had nearly reached the junction with a much busier street and the coffee table was clearly nervous about being seen.

"All right," it cried, and began hauling itself back into the alley. When it was halfway back, it cried, "I have friends, you know. I know a coffee table who once held a mug for the president!"

chapter
FIFTY-THREE

The main operations room was doused in soft green light and Mendes struggled to adjust his eyes.

An object came flying toward him. It struck the wall and landed on the floor near the trash. "Hey, I need to destroy that," said a man over by the document destroyer, without turning, "but I can't work this thing."

"That's the wrong setting," called Mendes. "It needs to be on five. Can't anyone work that out?"

"Oh, sorry, sir," said the man turning around. "I hadn't realized."

"It's done it again," said Kahill rapping the screens. "Look what we have now! 'Can someone tell me what the fuck algebra is?'"

"So how do we cure the virus?" said Mendes, leaning against his console.

"I don't know. You delete files and then they all come back. We've never come across anything like this before." He swiveled his chair too far and had to backtrack.

A single sheet of paper rose in a small fireball from the document destroyer in the corner.

"Hell!" cried the operative. He pawed at the thing hopelessly as it drifted toward the floor. "Fire!"

"That setting is too high!" cried Mendes. "You just need it on five. Five shreds the documents! Can't you understand that?"

"Ahh, I see, sorry, sir," said the man stamping out the fire. "I had it on eight. Hadn't realized this machine had such a range."

chapter FIFTY-FOUR

H ealth and Safety guys were everywhere, wandering around in hard hats and yellow reflective bibs. They were fixing up a huge new Health and Safety sign across the street: "Do not buy clothes on holiday. Ever. It will dawn on you halfway through the first evening you wear them back home that you look odd. A strong Health and Safety Department means a strong city." The cheery logo of the squirrel wearing a large pair of ear protectors stared at me from the corner.

A drongle was flopped up on the sidewalk and struggling to close its door.

"Your lucky inhumanely produced pate for today is foie gras," it said as I passed by and into the block.

The door to Gabe's apartment was wide open. "Marcy?" I called as I edged in. The place was quiet. I poured myself a drink.

"You must be Huck," said a voice.

"Nena?" She stepped out of the kitchen. "How did you get here so fast? You want some whiskey?"

"You're a cop." Her voice was flat, shorn of any kind of recognition. It felt as if our friendship had been reset to zero.

"I was a cop. That was a long time ago. You saw the photo of us?"

She nodded. "So, you're not a cop now? You know what happened to me?"

"Yeah. Are you sure you don't want some whiskey?"

"All right." I poured her a glass and she finally sat down.

"Were you head hacked as well?" I said, handing it to her.

"I don't think so," she said. "They didn't give me any printouts."

"Good." The bribe had paid off.

I looked into her brown eyes, took a swig of whiskey, and recounted roughly what had happened.

"So that's it?" she said after a pause.

"That's it," I said, finishing my whiskey.

"No. You left things out."

"That's what happened, Nena."

"Yeah, that's *what* happened. But that's not *why* it happened."

"What do you mean?"

"You left out some things, didn't you? You want to know what I think? I think you lost your way in life. And then you met me and you thought I could help you find the switch that would start it again. And then...There's something else. There's something between us. I can feel it."

I stared at her as the door to the apartment swung open with a crack.

"Feeling safe, are we?" said a voice.

"Feeling safe?" echoed another voice.

Two Health and Safety guys swept in and loomed over us.

"We've been waiting. We found a problem with your kiss," said the fat guy.

"My kiss?" I said, momentarily disoriented. They were the same two I had seen that morning. But how did they know about my kiss with Nena?

"You'll have to come in. The DNA from your kiss on the form brought up a red flag."

"Red flag. Red flag. Feeling safe, are we?" The tall one rubbed his hands and leaned farther over me.

"There must be a mistake," I said, understanding. "I arrived in the city yesterday."

"Mistake? There's no mistake." They both laughed. "Mistake! The only mistake we ever made was with that tiger."

"Yeah, we hate tigers." And he held up a hand to show a finger missing.

"Right."

"So we'll check over your details and then send you in," said the fat one, waving a jack plug at me from a feed reader.

"Okay," I said, trying to think my way out of this.

"This isn't just a toe-stubbing hazard. This is a red flag. We need to get you down to Head Hack Central."

"There won't be a problem," I said to Nena, and she tilted her head to one side as if to contradict me.

"No? Let me give you a hand," said the fat guy, leaning in. I just caught the manic fire in his eyes and I tried to shuffle back as he jabbed me roughly in the shoulder with something sharp and a numb molten ache erupted in my arm.

"What the hell is that?" I said.

"A little Health and Safety cocktail."

"Health and Safety cocktail!" echoed the taller one and they both laughed.

My mind staggered under the weight of the drug and my thoughts collapsed into slurring colors as I slumped.

I heard the laughter from the two men run around my head. And then it stopped. Through the grainy drug-induced darkness, I saw Nena stand up and take them out so fast that they sprawled across the floor.

Then I felt her grab my collar and drag me out of the apartment as the drug swept away more of my consciousness.

"Don't pass out," she cried as we crashed out onto the street and I fell heavily, but felt nothing.

I could see her mouth shouting, but the words didn't make any noise. The drug was shutting down my senses, and the whole of the world was slipping to some other place. Behind me, Health and Safety people were everywhere.

Now we were moving.

The sensation had gone from my feet, so I threw my legs into as close a proximity to running as I could manage.

A raven screeched, watching me with its huge black eyes.

.

chapter FIFTY-FIVE

Nena forced me down the alley. I stumbled and came face-to-face with a kid, and I found it hard to tell whether he was real or imaginary. He was poring over the gutted remains of a coffee table.

"There are some great insurance deals out there," the coffee table said, its voice booming wildly around my head. "And a fixed-bond income might be just what you're looking for."

The child yanked at another wire and the thing went dead. Then I felt a hand pull at my collar and I was dragged on.

The alley got narrower. Washing hung from the higher stories, as if it had been put out months before and left as a signal.

Now the child was at my side, walking in fast step with me as though he was marching, and I felt the drug make me euphoric. Then I found we had stopped in a small square surrounded by high walls, all smothered in hundreds of peeling posters.

I heard shouts somewhere far away, as though they were coming from another life.

The world was spinning and I felt the energy sap from my legs as I stumbled backward against a wall and collapsed, scrabbling at the posters for support. But they tore from the wall and I fell. Up above, ravens screeched.

I lay on the ground.

When I opened my eyes, I saw Nena ripping at the walls. I stumbled over to her and saw she had found a handle. She pulled it, and the thick layer of bills ripped as the door opened. Then she hauled me through and clanked it shut.

Darkness.

chapter

FIFTY-SIX

Mendes awoke with a start, sitting in the chair at his desk, and found he was bathed in sweat. A bag was now sitting in front of him, and he recalled sending Sara out to get something for his fever.

"An irony virus?" he said out loud. "How could this god-damn computer have caught a virus that makes it start acting ironically?"

He'd wanted fuck-off strong drugs that would just kill his fever stone dead even if it destroyed the rest of his insides in the process and made him sleep for a week, but judging by the bag she'd gone to the health fair. He looked inside and found a bottle of elderflower, yarrow flower, peppermint tea, and an infusion of ginkgo and feverfew. He opened it and smelled the contents gingerly. The strength of the vapor took him by surprise and he pushed it away. He tipped out the remains of the bag, and a sheaf of papers and a rock clonked onto his desk. He picked it up, then set it down again.

He shuffled through the pamphlets and brochures, hoping for some straightforward pills, but there weren't any. Then he picked up a business card that had been tucked into one of the leaflets.

"Pulitzer," he said.

chapter FIFTY-SEVEN

I tried to focus my eyes, but the drug gave an aching, slurring tail to all my thoughts, so they overlapped without any apparent beginning or end.

Somewhere a picture screen was pumping away a game show. The audio echoed.

" 'Pish pash! Take the cash!' " said a smooth unseen voice. "Or is it, 'Pash pish, ask the fish'? Perhaps the fish has the money. What's your hunch? Is it 'pish pash'? Or 'pash pish'?"

I edged forward, feeling an overwhelming sense that we had fallen into a crack of normality.

"Pish pash!" cried some. "Pash pish!" said others.

Ahead I saw a faint pool of flickering light.

"What's your choice?" said the smooth voice.

"Pish pesh," said a woman.

"What?"

"Pish pesh!"

"There is no 'pish pesh.' It's either 'pish pash' or 'pash pish.' "

"But I thought there was a 'pish pesh.' "

The dim column of light fell from above. I shivered as the drug eased further into my blood. I didn't like this place. It had a touch of death about it.

"Ask the fish if he has the money or take the cash on offer. Those are the choices. What's it to be?"

The light seemed more hesitant the closer we got, as though the connection back to the real world had become flimsy.

"So there's definitely no 'pish pesh'?"

"No. It's 'pish pash, take the cash!' 'Pash pish, ask the fish.' Those are the choices. The lady in the pink top there thinks it's 'pish pash.' Are you going with her? Or what about this gentleman with the prosthetic arm who thinks it 'pash pish'?"

"Well, I don't think I can ask the fish."

"No?"

"No. Fish, what are they really? Trout for example? What are they?"

"They're fish."

"Yeah, but what does that mean?"

"It means they're fish!"

The audio faded away as though it had been sucked back into the real world and our steps echoed around the chamber in the hollow silence. After some indefinable length of time, we reached the base of the column of light. There was a ladder of rungs welded into the wall that led up into the flicking dim glow above.

"You have to climb it. Don't pass out! You understand?" Nena said.

I grasped the first rung and felt the cold slippery rust of the metal momentarily cut through the drugged haze.

I began to climb. Hand over hand. Now I could hear music. Jazz.

My mind wandered.

I tried to concentrate on the feel of my hands on the rough flaking iron rungs; on each little pitted nodule that poked from the wet slime that coated the metal, so that by force of will I could nullify the drug.

My breathing became staccato.

Then a massive metallic clank of a heavy door slammed below. The echo ran through the place and I felt the vibration shuddering through my cold hands.

Then silence.

"Keep going, Huck," called Nena, and I realized I had stopped. I looked up at the rungs vanishing above me into the gloom, and I lost focus. My arms ached. I was clinging to the soft underbelly of life. Scrabbling around in no-man's-land where nothing seemed to matter. I pushed myself on, trying to feel my hands on the rungs, but there was only the faintest of sensations. I tried to tell myself that this was all there was between me and falling into that abyss, but the word *abyss* had lost its meaning. It just hung in the dark, mocking me.

How had my life led me here? Climbing a rusting ladder in the cloying dark? The harsh, inhumane quality to this place seeped into every pore of my body. If I died here, my soul would be crushed.

I craved to be in a warm room in a house, with a fire that snapped and crackled with wood, and a kitchen filled with the smell of fresh washing. And a cat that sat with neat paws. And a girl curled up reading a book at my side. Why was I not living that life?

I tried to focus on the feel of my hands on the rungs as my thoughts sprawled and then I felt a waft of fresh air. I was near a vent and the noise of the game show clawed its way around me again.

"And then there's herring. What would you say they are?" said the woman.

"They're fish as well," said the host.

"You say they're 'fish,' but what does that really mean?"

The audio faded. My lips felt dry and cracked and my arms were so tired they screamed with pain. The metal rungs flaked paint in the darkness.

Then abruptly one rung gave and I swung out with a cry.

Time seemed to slow and then stop.

I hung.

My mind sidestepped away from me. I felt a dark presence rear up and I fought it. It leered in a shapeless roar. I flailed for another moment and then grasped for the next rung, clawing at the stale air.

Long staccato breaths.

I was shaking. I forced myself to climb again.

But my breathing was stretched.

More rungs.

Then, abruptly, I emerged through a wide hole in a floor and found myself in a tiny, grim room.

I stepped off the ladder and stood bent over breathing in lungfuls of air. That had been an awful climb.

I was shaking partly from fear and partly from exhaustion. A grubby picture screen in one corner was churning out flickering lines of static and that was the source of the light we had seen below.

The walls were made of rusty iron and the room was entirely empty. On the opposite side was a metal door.

I staggered over in the gloom and felt the surface of it with my fingers as it shed leaves of rust.

After a moment I found it was bolted from the inside and I hammered back the rusting arms with the palm of my hand until they gave in metal-flaking lurches. Then I pushed with my shoulder. The thing was heavy and grated, as though I had woken it from some deep children's storybook sleep.

Nena joined me and forced it farther until finally it swung in a shuddering whine letting in a shamble of shadows, light. It was just wide enough to squeeze onto the other side.

We were in a warehouse. It reverberated with a heavy, musty smell so full of the past it felt as though it might burst. Silence lay in piles.

And dust covered everything with a milky sheen. The roof was pitted with cobwebbed windows so that the sunlight fell from above in soft, sagging plumes. A dry stench made it feel as though the whole place was on the edge of the world's consciousness.

My vision began to fade. I tried desperately to stay alert. In front of me was a sign. It said: "Do not let your girlfriend cut your hair. Ever."

chapter

FIFTY-EIGHT

Nena pilfered a pile of metal signs, carving a groove through the dust and soft planks, and jammed them against the door.

"This way," she said, pushing me forward, and our footsteps hung in the silence, mocking us.

An old drongle had been slung up near the ceiling so that it hung like a dead bee in a web. The sunlight seemed to imbalance my senses and they swung in and out of my grasp, sometimes making everything loud and garish, and sometimes faint and lost.

I stumbled. "Don't trip over these annoying cables," said a sign stamped with the New Seattle Health and Safety logo. Then we came to a whole stack that declared: "Trying to dig out a tree stump will take days and make you look stupid." I felt my eyes close and Nena grabbed me.

In front of us was a grand piano. As my veins ran with the drug, she helped me forward and I slumped onto the piano stool. My vision swooped. A raven screeched, staring from the roof.

"Stay here. I'll be back," she said.

I leaned across the keys and a discordant chord rang out, swirling uncertainly around me. Then I began to hear a piece Abigail had loved to play. The notes swung around my mind, and I sank into the music, letting it hold me and take me where it chose.

And the memories coursed through my veins.

chapter

FIFTY-NINE

I was there.

I was holding Abigail's limp, soft body in my arms and crying. Crying stupid, big, childlike tears because I would not see her smile again. She still seemed so full of sleepy life. And I screamed to myself that she wasn't gone, that she would never be gone. That when I saw the surf break at dawn over at Higgins Beach, or when the butterflies were swooping around the bushes, she would be there. Because her passion for such things had burned so stupidly fiercely that it had become a part of me, too. And part of her passion would always burn like a hot coal inside of me. I cried at myself to believe that was really true.

It was all I had.

And I wanted something of her to remain so much. I wanted that essence that was her to be something I could always touch whenever I was lost or sad or confused. I wanted it to be with me in a form so pure it could swallow me up with its intensity.

I had opened my soul to her and she had understood.

And now I held her limp body, which still seemed so full of sleepy life.

And I realized that death was how the story ended.

But it's how all our stories end.

Larkin wrote somewhere that what will survive of us is love. He didn't mean it as simply as that because he was all wound up in irony and other poetic crap.

But he should have done.

Because love is the echo we leave behind from our lives. In that moment I felt that more clearly than I ever would have thought possible. It is the legacy we leave to those around us. And that was what Abigail had left me. It was a beautiful and sad gift and I felt humbled.

I closed my eyes and tried to feel thankful that I had had the chance to love her. That we had walked upon earth together. That I had felt the steady beat-beat of her heart as we had lain one summer's night wrapped in a blanket on the beach.

chapter

SIXTY

A clash of metal.

Tolling like a church bell ringing out for the passing of another soul.

I opened my eyes and stared like a mesmerized seven-year-old toward the door as it banged against the signs.

"Abigail?" I called, but it came out swallowed. "Abigail?"

And then a voice was shouting from down the warehouse.

"Huck! Come on!"

I turned and stared, feeling my consciousness segue between memory and reality.

I looked back at the door.

"Abigail?"

"Health and Safety," cried a voice. "Open up or I will shoot the hell out of this place." And a hand appeared through the gap, holding a red gun, and a round ricocheted down the warehouse. A second later, the piano creaked and then abruptly collapsed in an implosion of noise, notes, and dust. The cacophony folded out in waves, shaking the floor. The mounds of metal signs shivered and slid as I staggered away through the billowing dust cloud toward Nena.

"This is the Anchovy Emporium," said the drongle slung up in the roof. "Please alight from the drongle. Your lucky word in *Crime and Punishment* by Fyodor Dostoyevsky is the word *the* on page 264."

I tripped and regained my balance as more shots recoiled and snickered off the metal signs.

Stairs.

They swung down flight after flight, and my legs staggered over them in a hobbled rhythm trying to catch Nena. A large sign up along the way said: "Please do not die for no reason! What's the point? Right?"

There was no point.

The thought ran through me.

I came down the last flight, to find Nena waiting.

"There was no point," I said as she grabbed me, pushing me headfirst into a small hole, and then I was falling through darkness.

"There was no point!" I cried as I was scooped up and tossed around, through remnants of garbage.

My head caught the side, and I felt the shape of my skull as it bounced. The air echoed with the shrill empty thud, and I gasped as reality fell away. I hung suspended, weightless. The chill of the wind snapped at my jacket.

The blurred outline of buildings.

Then I dropped heavily into a mound of rotting refuse and my back arched with shock. I lay gasping, watching my breath pool in vapor clouds above me.

And then Nena was there, pulling me off the discarded crates and rotting garbage.

She pushed me to run, but my legs groaned with cold

pain. After a hundred yards, we took a left down another alley and then another turn.

And another.

Eventually she stopped, and I was breathing madly, hardly able to walk. I bent double pulling at the air. My mind swung about inside my head, blurring my vision and I staggered, catching at a drainpipe for support before sinking to the ground and closing my eyes. I counted in my head so I wouldn't pass out.

I forced my eyes open and saw the blue sky of the afternoon opened up over me in a floorless panorama. And there were more ravens circling overhead. So many ravens.

"I need pastries," I said almost inaudibly, as the thought rebounded about my head and gained momentum.

I had to get to my feet and find pastries. They were only a little thing. But right now they were important.

chapter
SIXTY-ONE

The man looked more out of place than ever. It wasn't just that he was too neat for the surroundings to cope with; there was some other dimension that seemed to set him apart.

"What's wrong with the café?" he said.

"I saw some spies meet in a park once in a film," said Maddox, "and they fed some ducks." His worn shoes were getting splattered with mud. They walked toward the remains of the gutless fountain that had once proudly spurted looping spools of water, but it was hard to imagine now.

"You get the fridge?" said the man in black.

"We head hacked Lindbergh. But they couldn't find any memories of the fridge. Seems someone had done a job on his memory. He ended up getting wiped."

The man in black took this in. "What a mess. He didn't deserve that." He walked on gingerly, taking in the surroundings with distaste.

The whole of Cal Anderson Park was little more than a scathing rant of windblown litter and overused syringes. Its main feature was a slab of grass, which hunkered down between a slurry of blocks that had been redeveloped so many times over the years that the buildings had forgotten which city they were supposed to be in.

And frankly, they really didn't care, because they were those cocky-little-fucker-type of buildings. But the park was their conscience. It carried with it all that was left of the soul of this neighborhood. The only vaguely tangible evidence that the past had once existed around here and was not simply a myth made up by historians for their own casual amusement.

Perhaps that's why the cop had wanted to meet here, because it was reassuringly human.

"In the film, they met in the park and fed the ducks," said Maddox. "It seemed more interesting than the café."

"There are no ducks."

"Well, there'll be something we can feed. I brought bread." The cop held up a plastic bag with a presliced loaf, squashed at the edges. It had been a crazy thing to do, but he thought somehow this would make the man in black more human. "Everything has to eat," Maddox said. They were walking on the sodden, uneven slabs of a side path. "There must be some birds around here we can feed. You want to throw some bread?"

"No, and I can't stay; you know that. What's the matter with you? Find the fridge and we'll make arrangements to collect it." They had reached the fountain, but the shallow lake that at one time would have held water lilies now shone with a thin sheen of gaudy licks of oil. The remains of a coffee table slumped over the parapet.

"Well, I'm throwing bread." He threw a few slices and they landed in the mud. "Maybe this is not a good time of day for them."

"There are no ducks."

"But what if this is their siesta period?" said the cop undeterred, chucking another slice into the sodden, ragged grass.

"Next time, we meet in the café," said the man in black.

They reached a small pavilion. It was scrawled with graffiti in long spidery writing. "The state of the economy is fucking awesome!" it said. Companies saw graffiti as cheap advertising. And the government still used it, too.

Maddox stopped.

"Hey, look! You see over there? What did I tell you?"

But the man in black had gone. "I knew there would be some birds. Over here!" he called waving his arms. But the large black bird flew off.

"Maybe I should have brought sandwiches," Maddox said. "Maybe ducks don't go for plain bread so much these days."

chapter
SIXTY-TWO

I needed pastries.

My mind was going walkabout, and dizziness swamped my thoughts.

Abruptly I remembered how I had once met a man dressed in a blue cardigan standing by a rail stop, and he had told me that if you ate noodles they absorbed words beginning with *k*. That the more noodles you ate the less you said words with a *k* in them. If you ate a lot of noodles it would cut down on your use of words with the letter *k* by about 50 percent. And the next time I'd visited a noodle bar I had eaten with reticence. The memory loomed in my mind like a bad song, so I couldn't shake it.

"Absorb words beginning with a *k*," I said as I stumbled down yet more streets with Nena. "They absorb words beginning with a *k*." My mind tried to lose the memory in a backwater as a heaviness returned to my body making my limbs unwieldy and foreign.

And then, tucked into a fork ahead, we came to a pastry shack, its tin roof waving haphazardly and its squat chimneys poking at the air. The whole thing steamed like a racehorse after a stiff canter.

Nena gave the man our order and he nodded. "No problem," he said, pouring our coffees into Styrofoam cups. I leaned on the counter, aware that he was wearing a white coat that hadn't actually been white for years, and he had the jowls of a man who knew how to stuff away pastries with the best of them. "You like a man with a toupee?"

"Sure," said Nena.

"You heard of a model called The Executive?"

"No."

"It's classy. I've researched them all, done all the stuff you need to do. You want to know where the best toupees are made? Vancouver."

"Never would have guessed it," said Nena.

"Yeah. And a toupee could really change things for me. Suddenly, I'd look like I was in the twenty-five-to-thirty category. But my wife says toupees are for sad people."

"Really?"

"Yeah. Do I look sad?" The guy was really fired up now.

"No. You look terrific," said Nena.

"Exactly. Sure I go through times when I feel down, but everyone has them. Everyone cries some afternoons, right? So anyway, I colored in the bald part of my head with a special felt pen and suddenly—bang—I was in the twenty-five-to-thirty category. They had all these words in the magazine you could choose to describe yourself. I chose *sleek*. Can you imagine that bit of my head the same color as the rest?" The man nodded at me and bowed his head. When I didn't reply he looked up. "Is he okay? He looks terrible."

"I'll be fine. I have a headache," I said. "The coffee will sort it out."

"Coming up. So, this could easily be the day I get The

Executive. Then my wife will stop looking at that guy from the bridge club. I should blow his fucking brains out. There you go. Twenty dollars. Nice talking to you."

Nena nodded and paid him.

My skull felt like it was constricting, and my legs were stiff and heavy. I straightened them as we sat down on some steps and the texture of the rough stone felt reassuring under my fingers.

I drank some coffee and felt it flow into me. Then I took a bite of a pastry. The taste made its way past my aching jaw and I felt my mind try and settle. It was a slim connection back to the real world, and it put a thin gauze of normality over things. I took another bite and tried to retrace my way back to who I was.

"You still alive, then?" said Nena.

"Yeah," I said and had some more coffee. "But I feel like I have one hell of a hangover so at least we have pastries. Did you know in any hijack they always send in pastries? It's supposed to be harder to kill anyone after you've eaten a pastry."

"I didn't know that," she said. The sun shifted from behind a cloud and the warmth made me begin to feel more alive.

I had some more coffee.

"Where did you learn to knock people unconscious?" I said.

"My older brother went to self-defense classes and used to practice on me when I was a kid. But then one day he got in a fight he couldn't handle, and he got himself killed."

"I'm sorry."

"Yeah. But it was a long time ago and I don't feel sad in quite the same way anymore. Sometimes bad things happen, don't they? Who was Abigail?"

"That was a long time ago, too."

"Yeah. But the memories still appear like reels of film, playing through your mind time after time."

"Yeah."

I sipped some more coffee and the taste ran through me, easing away the headache that had settled at the back of my head after making repeated trips around my skull. And suddenly I found myself telling her everything in a torrent of words and emotion. And as it came out I felt my chest release as if these memories had become some physical thing I had been holding deep inside.

Eventually I finished, and Nena was silent for a long time. "And you can't forget her, can you?"

I shook my head.

"So was I wrong about us?" she said and got up. "What does it matter anyway? People come and go. You know you wanted to find that switch to start your life moving again?"

"Yeah."

She threw the remains of her coffee across the alley.

"There is no switch, Huck. That's why you can't find it."

chapter
SIXTY-THREE

Fridge Detail 471 had been sent to comb the back-streets, looking for strays after a report of a sighting. There were five in the detail, all in orange Fridge Detail fatigues. And five didn't fit in a drongle. "He promised me an owl," Malbranque said, squashed in by the man next to him. His speech was light, shorn of the weight of meaning.

"Yeah, well, you can shut up about your fucking owl," said the man. He was sweating. It ran down his head and he mopped at it.

"But it was the wizard."

"I don't care if it was the fucking president of Azerbaijan. You're driving me crazy. And you're taking up too much space. You shouldn't be here. And I shouldn't be here, either. I once worked for an architect in a proper job. That's where I should be, not here with you."

"Oh." Malbranque stared wide-eyed, as though he had been told some great secret. "But I thought that the—"

"Don't you dare say wizard again."

"Okay, easy now," said a woman. "We're nearly there.

Keep your eyes open. There was a report of a spin dryer in this district an hour ago, and I want a proper sweep, with everyone working as a team. Is everyone clear about that? Huckleberry, are you listening?"

Sky Malbranque nodded.

"Good. We're on a bonus, here. This one could be high on the wanted list. So work as a unit. You all happy, people?"

They all nodded.

The drongle stopped.

chapter

SIXTY-FOUR

We passed a bunch of Health and Safety workers fixing up a new sign: "Do not eat Cheez Whiz just before you go to bed or you will have strange dreams."

"You see them?" said Nena. "When people get scared, they start trying to control everything. They become desperate for order. That's what that city wall is about. People are scared, and they're trying to rationalize their way out of it. Trying to make it all neat."

Eventually we found a lone drongle and clambered in.

"They say having people insecure is good for the economy," she said as we moved away. "The theory is people buy more stuff to feel better about themselves when they feel insecure. So there was a department in the government a few years ago, planting reports of fake burglaries in the press. And they even went as far as employing actors to perform petty crime in areas of the country where it was regarded as too safe. Maybe this fear virus is a more sophisticated strategy."

I nodded. "I had the same thought. You think it's the government doing this?"

"It could be. But whoever it is, I am going to find them and stop them."

"Why? Why go on with this when you can walk away?"

"Because I'm a part of it, and at some stage in my life I decided to stand up and be counted."

"What does that mean? That you'll start killing cops? Did you kill the cop whose head is in the fridge?"

"No."

"So what if it comes down to that? Then what?"

"I'll deal with it," she said. "You just show me where the fridges are and then you're out of it. Or do you still think I have the answers to fix your life?"

"I'm not leaving, Nena."

"No?"

"No."

She didn't reply. Just simply broke my gaze and stared outside.

Eventually the drongle stopped a block from the warehouse.

Nena climbed out and gave the massive receipt to a lone kid who spotted us from fifty yards away and came running up breathlessly with a smile.

He giggled, submerged under the pile of paper he struggled to grapple along with the dime I pressed into his hand.

Five minutes later we slipped into the warehouse office and walked through to the hangar.

"Hey," said the fridges, pedaling their way up to me. "It's you! Hey that's great. Guess what? Guess what! I've got something to tell you!"

"I already know the date of the Klondike gold rush," I said. "And I told you to hide if anyone came in."

"Oh, sorry. It's just that we've been playing murder in the dark. You should have joined in."

"Yeah, we missed you," said the Frost Fox, waddling across. "Hey! It's Nena!" it said and began singing. "Where's she gone? Here's a bit of trivia! It's got the highest lake! That's right, it's Bolivia!" They all joined in with the harmonies.

"I guess you met me yesterday, huh?"

"What say we have pizza to celebrate being back to-gether!" said the Ice Jumper. "I love families."

"Yeah, and let's have Primula. What could be better be-fore pizza? Processed cheese, straight from the tube!"

"Not a bad idea," said Nena. "The pizza, I mean."

I found a small kitchen in the warehouse, and a little while later, I opened the oven door to the smell of pizza. Pizza was definitely the way forward. In fact, it's always a strong fallback position in times of crisis. It's standard practice dur-ing the peace talks of warring nations to order pizza. Al-though, on one famous occasion, the only pizzas that turned up had pineapple as one of the toppings.

Those two countries were still fighting seven years later.

I had also heard of hospital recovery rooms that ordered a constant supply of fresh pizza because the smell was found to be the most effective way to draw people out from the anesthetic. They then gave the pizzas to the patients on the ward. Doubling up like that really pleased the management.

The two of us ate without saying a word, but it wasn't exactly a pause. There's no such thing as a proper pause when there's pizza about. If Harold Pinter had had all his characters always eating pizza no one would have even no-ticed the pauses.

And so, for a moment none of what had happened seemed to exist in any meaningful way. There was only pizza. And there was only the atmosphere that descends when you eat pizza.

The Chinese from ancient times used to call that kind of

peace chi energy, and trained long hours in martial arts to try and create it. They would have been astonished to learn that the same calm effect could have been gotten from eating a certain kind of cheese on toast out of a cardboard box.

"So," said Nena eventually as the Tiny Eiger hummed beside her. "You sure you can't think of anything else that can help us? A name of a street or a person, perhaps?"

The Tiny Eiger shuffled, then opened its door. "Sergeant Maddox."

"Sergeant Maddox? A cop?" I said.

"Sergeant Maddox," it repeated, then closed its door and nuzzled into her leg.

chapter SIXTY-FIVE

The rain smudged on the vaulted drongle roof, so Mendes could hardly see anything of the passing streets. And there was too much traffic. The drongle rambled gingerly along the wet roads until it snagged in a jam at the next junction. It was hardly moving now.

He closed his eyes as sweat ran down his cheeks.

"And all who heard should see them there,

And all should cry, Beware! Beware!

His flashing eyes, his floating hair!"

"So twice five miles of fertile ground with walls and towers were girdled around," he said, losing the thread of the poem. He fell silent, staring into the hazy passing chaos of people struggling through the regular day-to-day trauma of their lives, and he felt an inexplicable sweep of pathos.

Eventually, they reached the city wall and the drongle nosed its way grudgingly between the hawkers and beggars.

"Walls and towers were girdled around," he repeated softly as the drongle stopped sharply with a shudder. However much he wanted to, he could not turn away from this now. Something was forcing him on. He took out the card and checked the address, and then levered open the goose-wing door, which hissed gently, and stepped out into the hustle of the sidewalk. A gaggle of kids pressed up to him in the rain. "Take your receipt for a dime! Take your receipt for a dime!"

He bundled the receipt into their arms. Then he turned up the collar on his leather coat and slipped easily through the crowd until he came to the steps. He didn't feel himself. He had a fever.

He hesitated for the briefest of moments, as though by treading on the first stair he would be committing himself to a future he didn't want to disturb.

chapter
SIXTY-SIX

The red smoke was visible from ten blocks away as it curled into the air and started to form a mushroom cloud.

"Stop!" called the woman on the stairs, as she leaned on the wall, coughing. "Please!"

More canisters, tumbling in with stifling clouds, scooping aside the air.

She waved her hands at the stuff as a horde of bulky figures dressed in Security Detail uniforms broke down the door next to her and swarmed inside.

"Please!" she called again, and grabbed at the arm of the nearest person in black riot gear, who spun around clumsily and pointed his gun at her. "I have asthma."

The figure undid four straps and took off his helmet. He was dripping with sweat.

"Sorry, madam. I can't hear, and also we have a clip of a cat sneezing being randomly played. Very good, too, but it can get distracting. I'll show it to you if you like."

From the inside of his helmet came the tiny audible sneeze of a cat.

Across the way, another guy from the detail collided clumsily into the wall.

"Please, get me outside," she said.

"Oh. Could you hold on for the guys with the large picture of the puppy? That'll calm you down no end."

"No!"

"Well, okay," said the man, as she began coughing again.

He helped the woman down the steps and down to the hustle and bustle of cop drongles parked outside and handed her a drink of wonker. "Do you want a box of doughnuts as well? There's jam, apple, or goose pâté. Pretty disgusting, those last ones."

A figure still in full combat gear came striding over, wearing a helmet adorned with a massive plume.

"I know I should have waited for the detail to come in with the picture of the puppy, but she didn't feel she could wait," said the guy.

Maddox took off his helmet.

"The OURU. Where is the OURU?" His head was running with red-stained sweat. "My back is killing me."

"I got a strong smell of lavender earlier. I'll find out, sir!" He disappeared and after a few minutes a man with sunglasses strode over purposefully.

"Police Osteopath Urgent Response Unit. You have a lumbar problem, ma'am?" the OURU man said to the woman.

"Not her. Me," said Maddox. "It's me with the problem."

"We're onto it, sir." Soon more men with Osteopath Urgent Response Unit stamped neatly across their backs came running carrying a massage table. "Just relax, and we'll get treatment straight to your lumbar."

"You boys are quick. I appreciate that," Maddox said.

"In this business, you have to be quick. If you get to a patient fast, you can cut down long-term discomfort."

"Call for you, sir," said another cop.

"I've a lumbar problem."

"She said you'd want to speak to her. It's about a fridge."

"A fridge?"

"That's what she said."

"Give that to me." He took the phone. "Who is this?"

chapter
SIXTY-SEVEN

The corner of Seneca and Twelfth was among a jumble of backstreets. Hardly a drongle came by, and the tenement blocks had seen their fair share of tenants live out a slice of their lives among the increasingly crumbling walls. Some of the lucky ones had moved on to better things, but the majority had probably dissolved back into chaotic and vapid lives full of squalor.

Maddox waited, fidgeting on the corner.

"He's there," said Nena, squinting through a crack in the door from inside a tube of the Prisoner Rapid Removal system. "Take a look."

I moved closer, put my eye to the slit, and saw Maddox standing like a lost child in the rain. He'd turned up his collar and had his hands thrust into his pockets. I wondered what sort of a man he was and what kind of a life he went home to at night. Whether there were pictures on the walls, and ornaments on the shelves, or unwashed shirts strewn across the sofa. I stepped back from the slit as the sound of a woman's feet faded, echoing through the tube.

"Any backup?" I said.

"Can't see any." A drongle came juddering up the road. The noise vibrated through the metal, shaking the dingy sides. Then the engine faded away and the silence lengthened.

"Here comes the Frost Fox."

I could just see the fridge waddle up to him, and then stop.

Maddox looked around. There was a pause and then the fridge opened its door.

Inside, we had thrown enough red smoke canisters to create a cloud the size of Milwaukee, and a dense, red fog blew out.

I heard Maddox coughing as he stumbled back.

Nena tumbled out of the door, and I followed running blindly toward Maddox. The corner of the block was thick, with a balling cloud of red smoke now. When we got within a couple of feet, I saw his hunched gray outline and heard him coughing. Before he could straighten, Nena knocked him out cold and he went down like a dead rhino. We dragged him into the PRR tube and forced the door shut.

I was breathing hard and the noise echoed around in the darkness.

We each grabbed a foot and hauled him through the tube, our footsteps reverberating as Maddox's large over-weight body slid over the shiny metal. He had clearly been at the doughnuts. We came to a junction and took a left, and then a little farther on a right, until we had made a couple of blocks. The track above our head began to move with a gritty growl, and a dribble of watery oil ran along the floor.

We found the door.

I took out the box with the head from a bag on my back and in the darkness I scrabbled to find the point and then fi-nally plugged in. The door swung open with a cough of hy-draulics, letting in the light.

It was a street with a pool hall and a run-down mall.

We dragged Maddox down to a head hack booth, then twisting his body around we plugged him in. I held his head steady as Nena fed in the quarters.

In three minutes, we had a pile of photos. The quality from the street booths was pretty poor, but we were hoping this would be all we'd need.

I grabbed the images and we left Maddox there, collapsed on the street. He might be tagged, in which case the rest of the cops would be onto him in minutes. Either way, we didn't want him getting any kind of memory of us.

"Hey," said the spin dryer as we came into the cop drongle store. "Did it work out?"

"Are we heading down to Mexico now?" said the Ice Jumper.

"Yeah, it worked out really well. Any sign of the Frost Fox?"

"No, he's not back yet," said the spin dryer, but at that moment the fridge came bumbling through the door.

"Okay?" I said.

"I've never had smoke before. It was kind of tickly. Reminded me most of a Waldorf salad. Had that kind of nutty aroma," it said.

I laid out the pictures from the Maddox head hack on the floor. There were about thirty. Some hadn't printed well, but mostly the images were recognizable. There were a load of other cops, and a few of a block of apartments. We both kneeled down and pored over them.

Nena's hair brushed my face and the sensation sent a frisson through me.

"Look," I said eventually. "He's met this man twice in the last day. You see? Here, and here. That's him. Each time it was downtown. You see? Carl Anderson Park in this one, and that's the Blue Lagoon café on East Olive Street. That's the area where we should look."

"We find him, we find out who's behind this," said Nena.

"Yeah, and my guess is, we'll also find a lot of trouble."

chapter

SIXTY-EIGHT

Twilight, and clear.

The ravens circled overhead, and the sidewalks began to swell with the first signs of people heading toward the fireworks that were to celebrate the opening of the new city wall. I looked at them as they walked past, wrapped in coats and scarves, no doubt ready to shout and cheer. They were no different from the mobs that had turned up centuries before to watch a public execution, but it wasn't a person they were hanging tonight; it was the freedom of a city.

Finally, we hailed a drongle. As we sat down I saw it had a huge crack running through the dome.

I had heard stories of kids hijacking these things, messing about with them, and then putting them back on the highway so that they fell apart. There was even an urban myth about a hacked drongle that took two New York businessmen to Mexico when they only wanted to go a couple of blocks.

Or maybe it was a tale made up as part of some advertising campaign that now escaped me. The crack on this one grated alarmingly so that blue liquid seeped from one of the panels.

"What do you think has happened to Gabe?" I said.

"They'll head hack him and wipe his mind of the last day."

"But why isn't he out by now?"

"He'll be okay."

"I turn up after eight years with a load of fridges, wreck his apartment, and get him caught up at Head Hack Central. I haven't even tried to get him out."

"He'll be okay, Huck."

"What if they go back more than twenty-four hours in his hack?"

"You have no idea where he is, Huck. You could make things worse for him if you do something crazy. And he can't just run from the city. He lives here. He'll be okay."

I stared out feeling powerless.

We passed some graffiti mocking Quantity Surveyors. I remembered reading that they had become universally unpopular after it became public they had miscalculated how many practicing members they had.

Nearby, an outlet for the Quantum Physics Pizza Delivery Company was advertising for business, its facade a melee of neon squiggles. It was a chain that had done well. They operated by knowing either what your order was or where you lived, but as a matter of policy they made sure they never knew both at the same time. It was based on the Heisenberg uncertainty principle, and made no business sense at all, because either they delivered the right pizza to some wrong random address, or they turned up with a random pizza at the right address. But somehow, they'd made a success of the concept. I guess it was fashionable. And people thought it was amusing. And there was something about the

Heisenberg uncertainty principle that had caught the mood of the population.

Downtown New Seattle was alive with more people than it knew what to do with.

Nowhere else in the country had I seen people wearing such bizarre hats and frankly dangerous shoulder padding. There was such a wild display of fashion, an anthropologist would have struggled to classify these people as a single species.

For a short time, fashion had come under a governmental department, and had been controlled by a committee in Washington, but the whole thing had fallen apart a few years before, after D.C. had decreed that furry boots were to be trendy the following year. It resulted in sporadic riots, and the government had scrapped the scheme.

The drongle dumped us in an area that had been poured thick with concrete and then mobbed with weird steel and glass shapes that architects habitually passed off as buildings. We were two blocks from the Blue Lagoon café.

When we reached it we found a small place with peeling wallpaper and a steaming coffee machine that monopolized the atmosphere with a wild stream of noises until a waitress dropped a pile of plates and they smashed with a clatter. A wave of embarrassed silence spooled around the café.

We ordered a coffee and asked a few questions, showing the photo of the man in black around. But no one knew anything or they weren't saying.

I felt tired.

Afterward we wandered around Carl Anderson Park, but there was nothing to find. The place was a detritus of faded glory, and as the last rays of sunlight reached out through a gap in the buildings, I could feel the city steel itself to survive another night.

I sat down by the fountain.

"Even the rocks, which seem to be dumb and dead as the swelter in the sun along the silent shore," I said, reading an inscription on a plaque, "thrill with memories of stirring events connected with the lives of my people."

"These rocks don't look like they thrill anymore," said Nena.

"No, I don't think Chief Seattle had foreseen the onset of commercial office development at the expense of inner-city recreational areas. But you can't blame him for that."

She sat down next to me and I sensed the chase had come to a cold and unsatisfying end, but at least we were alive.

"They say you can wipe the memories, but not the feeling behind them."

"Is that right?"

She pulled out the head hack photos from Maddox and went through them.

"You want to go to a party tonight? I have two tickets."

"Are you asking me on a date?"

"I might be."

"Right. Well, I don't have anything to wear, but thanks for the offer."

I sat looking at the park, watching the shadows eat away at the paths and neglected flower beds. Eventually a raven landed and eyed us cautiously, perhaps hoping for the remnants of a snack.

"You know what the collective noun for ravens is?" I said.

"No."

"It's a conspiracy."

She shuffled another photo to the top of her pile. "A conspiracy of ravens?"

The raven took off untidily with a squawk and I watched it circle, then it landed far above, roosting with many more. "Yeah. There never used to be all these ravens," I added.

"No?" She put down the photos.

"No. You see them up there?"

"Yeah."

"I've seen too many ravens in this city, and now it's bothering me."

chapter
SIXTY-NINE

The building was the only old one I had seen in the district.

"We're chasing ravens?" said Nena, her head tilted to one side.

"There's something wrong about them."

"They're just birds, aren't they?"

"I don't think so. Not this time."

The lock clicked, and the door swung open tentatively. Crowds streamed past on the sidewalk at the bottom of the steps, oblivious.

Nena and I edged into a dark porch, and found ourselves confronted with a tall, cool lobby flanked with columns and arches that led off into dingy corridors. The faintest sounds rose up above us and filled the vast ceiling with a booming echo. I pushed the door and it recoiled in a massive sigh. And then shut.

It triggered a cool feeling at the back of my neck. Maybe the place was deserted. Maybe there was nothing to find. But a small tight knot in my stomach told me otherwise. My mind tried to pass off what I was feeling as a mixture of boredom and excitement, but it wasn't.

It was fear.

Silence folded over everything again.

The place seemed dislocated from reality.

We walked through to the lobby, scuffling over the marble floor. It was dingy as hell. Soft light fell through another huge opaque window, bathing the space in a gentle musty white shimmer. Particles of dust hung motionless in the air, as though time had slowed so much it would be months before they settled.

Somewhere way above, I heard the screech of a raven, and it reverberated down the wide stairwell.

"Hello?" I said, feeling the echo take my words and throw them about excitedly. Silence returned in heavy waves, cocooning us in a thick pall. Every movement seemed like an event.

We climbed the wide flights of stone steps and came to a small landing. A pile of papers was strewn on the floor, covered in spidery brown longhand.

Another flight, and then another—all bathed in the same diffuse dingy light that came from vast opaque glass windows high up in the walls. It was as though the place had been designed to keep out all signs of the outside world. There was a cool, tingling edge to the silence.

On the next landing an old man was asleep on a bench. He looked familiar, and I realized I had seen him in Head Hack Central. I stared for a moment as his chest rose and fell with each breath.

We reached the next floor. One of the doors was propped open, partly revealing a stretch of carpet that was little more than a nebula of heavily vacuumed stains.

Nena pushed through and I followed. A Raoul Dufy print

hung askew in its frame on the far wall. And at the windows we could see the silhouettes of the ravens, casting huge shadows across the room.

On the far side was another massive door.

I caught myself.

It was the one from my dream.

chapter SEVENTY

I forced it open.

It creaked, then grated tiredly over the floorboards in a surprised "what the hell?" kind of a way. A recoil of dust billowed around and we walked through. It clicked shut behind us with a soft thud. On the other side was a set of stairs exactly like the ones we had come up.

"I dreamed of this," I said.

"What?"

"This door and this staircase. Come on."

We walked down, hearing our steps echo off the treads. At the bottom was a door exactly like the one we had come in through. It led onto the street at the back of the building.

It was quiet.

We walked out at the back of the building, and then around to the main street. It was absolutely quiet. There were no drongles, no crowds.

Nothing.

There was absolutely no one anywhere. I touched the nearest building. It was solid. It was real.

Far away, a blue cloud slid in from the east as the sun set. I stared. The thing was really blue. And there were other colored clouds as well in the distance, some a vibrant red, others a brilliant green. And a few a shocking purple.

"Hello?" called Nena. But there was nothing. No birds, no people. "Where the hell are we?"

"I don't know," I said. "Maybe we're dead."

We walked, and I began to feel like we were in some gigantic game that someone had constructed, and that in a moment the picture would fade and be replaced by some kind of advert. Then I would wake up to find I was wearing a game helmet and the high scores would scroll across the bottom.

We were in New Seattle, but everyone had gone.

The sky shone and the eerie clacking of our feet echoed away into the silence. The intensity of the strangeness grew until it felt like the air was so thick it was almost solid.

And my body had stopped feeling like it was my own.

"A person," said Nena. And two blocks down we saw a figure. Nena took off and I tried to keep up with her, but my calves were too tight.

I stopped, breathing hard, and watched her chase off after the figure.

I felt like I was partly in shock. I walked to the corner of the block, and found Nena standing alone in the street.

"He went down there," she said.

We pushed open the door and went in.

It was empty.

Ahead was a counter. Above it was displayed a wide range of available pizzas.

"Anyone home?" shouted Nena.

"This is a strange place," I said. "They have a Fiorentina, but it comes without the egg."

"And that's all you find strange?"

A man appeared dressed in a black suit and wearing sunglasses behind the counter. "Who are you?" I said. "What is this place?" And part of me wanted to add, "and how come you have Fiorentina, but it comes without the egg?"

"Welcome to the Otherside," he said.

"What Otherside? Are we dead?"

"We have a table specially reserved for you upstairs."

"We didn't come for pizza," said Nena. "What has happened to us?"

"Please, your table is upstairs."

The man pointed, and after a long moment Nena nodded. We went up two flights of stairs, and my heart was beating wildly now.

Had we died? Had someone been waiting for us in that building and the memory of the moment of death had been taken from us? But would this be where we would end up after death? In a pizza place?

The room upstairs was busy, and that was comforting, even if everyone wore black suits. And they were all eating pizza.

Reflexively, I found myself looking for Abigail.

We were shown to a large table by the window that had been set for three.

"Any idea what is going on?" said Nena.

"Maybe we're dead. Or this is a dream. Perhaps we were taken out, and someone is inserting this in our memory."

"If we're dead, then we've been lied to by a whole range of theologians over thousands of years. I can't think of a single religion that mentioned pizza."

A man in black wearing sunglasses sat down with us.

"Why have you come?" he said. "Other than for the pizza?"

"We followed the ravens. Who are you? And what has happened to us?" said Nena.

"We are all guardians."

"Of what? Of pizza?"

"No. Of this city. Would you like to order?"

"But where are we? What has happened to us?"

"You're in New Seattle. It's the same city. We're just on the Otherside."

"What 'Otherside'?"

"You have heard of the Heisenberg uncertainty principle?"

"Atoms appear to change in character depending on whether you are looking at them or not. It's impossible to know the speed and position of their electrons at the same time," said Nena.

"Exactly. And that's because atoms exist on two sides of the same place at the same time. The same atom exists here as well as on your side of New Seattle. Everywhere has another side to it. It's just a case of finding it."

The man took off his sunglasses. His eyes were pricks of white light. "Do you know where the fridge with the virus test tubes is?"

"We have it."

The man put his sunglasses back on and nodded. "I suggest the Fiorentina. It's a house special."

"We didn't come here for pizza," said Nena.

"I see. But please, try some. You think it's just a kind of upscale cheese on toast, and yet eaten in the right way it induces a very particular sense of calm."

"We're still talking about pizza here?" said Nena.

The order came almost immediately and it was entirely wrong. I had asked for a quattro formàggi and I got a

Fiorentina. No one asked if we wanted garlic bread with that, which made the experience all the more strange.

"The waiters can never know the order and the table number at the same time. So the outcome of the orders is always uncertain. Enjoy."

So Nena and I ate pizza in a city that looked like New Seattle but was inhabited by only a few people with identical fashion sense.

"The mayor has created a secret laboratory, which is making a fear virus. He releases the virus into the city every few weeks, so that he can push through more Health and Safety directives, build a city wall, and do pretty much whatever he wishes."

"The mayor is behind this?"

"Yes."

"And the police?"

"He has them mostly in his pocket. But we have someone on our side."

"Maddox," said Nena.

"Yes. He contaminated the last batch of the virus, but the experiment didn't entirely work. It merely changed it from a fear virus to an irony virus. How's the pizza?"

"Good," I said, feeling the overarching strangeness of the situation return in a wave. It reminded me of a time when I had been small and had stood up on stage for the first time. I had never imagined that the world could feel so different. Or that I could be so aware of my own skin.

"An irony virus?" said Nena.

"Actually, that makes sense," I said.

"Yes. After that, Maddox stole the contents of the laboratory, so that when the place is destroyed, none of the fear virus will be released. But the fridge he had loaded up then escaped." The man in black shifted in his seat.

"The Tiny Eiger."

"Yes. And if all that virus was to be released at once, then the city would die. That much fear would cause a huge rip through from your side to this side. We wouldn't be able to repair it in time, and we would all die trying. And without the guardians, New Seattle would soon die, as well. The city would become prey to all kinds of bad people." The man had a calm assuredness about him, and a hypnotic quality to his voice than could eke out meaning from the most menial of words.

"So please, bring us the fridge as soon as possible so we can dispose of the virus. I would come with you, but I cannot survive on your side for more than a few minutes."

"And the ravens?" I said. "Why are there so many ravens?"

"They are attracted by the rips. The virus has already caused some small rips. And the gateway is in so much use as we try to undo the damage that they can sense its presence. I hope you enjoyed the pizza. Now you must go."

I wanted to mention the lack of an egg, but I held back. "The pizza was great," I said. "And we'll bring the fridge."

I felt a confusing sense of detachment from myself as we walked back through the deserted streets. It was as though my body had left my mind behind somewhere else, and I was only vaguely aware of it falling through some soft, unending abyss. The luminous sky glowed, melding from a darkening turquoise to a thin, pale green. A clutch of wisping clouds raced away to the horizon, dappled with fluorescent shafts that jabbed at the sea.

Nena didn't say anything. She was caught up in all that had happened and maybe we were both thinking the same thing.

That we wouldn't be able to get back.

So we walked tentatively through the empty streets. When we came to the building, it looked exactly as it had, but something made me touch the stone to see once again if it was real.

Then we found the door around the back. It opened. The stairs were still there. We climbed them and stood in front of the door at the top.

Weird thoughts ranged through my mind. Maybe we would find our two bodies lying on the floor on the other side, dead. Or maybe the door would be locked.

But it simply opened with barely a murmur and we stepped through.

The room seemed to shimmer as though we were infecting it with the strangeness we had seen.

The chairs and pictures took on a stark, wild energy. We made our way down the stairs, and I noticed the bench where the old man had been asleep.

It was empty.

chapter

SEVENTY-ONE

A storm of noise and confusion.

The sidewalk was packed. And now the presence of this crowd seemed wrong. They had invaded a city that for a while had been our own.

Nena pulled me toward the street. For a moment I got tangled with someone shouting: "The sins of man are but nothing compared to the sins of geese!" I came unexpectedly close to his face and his ruddy unshaven complexion. "Geese are the real sinners," he cried at me.

I pulled myself free and clawed my way across the sidewalk. Nena had somehow hailed a drongle and was shouting the address into the horn.

We both clambered in and sat down.

Wires hung from the panels in a long, dripping shroud, but finally we moved away as the screens struggled to life with a grouchy cough of static.

"Hi, I'm Dan Cicero, Mayor of Safety. You might have heard of me!" said the mayor, and then the picture froze, with his eyebrows at right angles to each other.

"Yeah, we've heard of you," said Nena.

"Did that really happen?"

"At the moment, I'm thinking that it did."

"Yeah, so am I." But there was also a part of me that had already washed its hands of the whole thing. It wanted to think about other, smaller and far more uncomplicated things instead. The drongle dodged on through the traffic as an H and S announcement about cushions began to play.

My mind skidded every time I tried to think about what we had seen. "They had a Fiorentina pizza without an egg," I said finally as I stared outside.

chapter

SEVENTY–TWO

Mendes was sweating as he folded the map again in the man's office, and droplets fell on the paper. It was a small place, tucked into a loft, and the roof ran at a jumble of angles. A ceiling fan hung above, unmoving. The corners were crammed with metal boxes.

"Are you all right?" said Pulitzer. "You seem edgy. Is it the explosives? There's no need. SEMTEX is as stable as anything."

"I have a fever," said Mendes. "It's nothing. And I have had plenty of training with explosives. I was in the reserves."

"Really? See any action?"

"No. Not really."

"Well, please tell your colleagues about my products. You have the lavender and ginseng SEMTEX, but I can do other scents. I hope to get a contract with an entire army, one day. Even it's only the Dutch. I hear they like reusable products, so I'm working on a reusable bomb. They should like that; it will help save the environment."

"How could that possibly work?" said Mendes, after a pause.

"We're working on it. You have a bomb, it explodes once and then, well, the next bit is the part we're working on. These scientists can do all kinds of impossible things. One of them can make an origami swan in about ten seconds. It's awesome! I can't believe you've cleaned me out of stock. That's absolutely all the SEMTEX I have here. The only other thing I could give you are some Howitzer shells."

"No." Mendes got up, but the ceiling was not tall enough, so he had to hunch slightly.

"Or a trebuchet. You want a trebuchet? You look like you could really use a trebuchet. I've sourced one, and it's cheap." Pulitzer's eyes fired up with energy.

"A trebuchet? I don't think so."

"Are you sure? Think about it. You look like you could use a medieval siege engine that hurls rocks or you could hurl other things if you felt like it; you know, odds and ends, ornaments. Must be a great way to get rid of all that unwanted clutter in your attic. Fling it into the distance. Job done. What do you say?"

"No. The SEMTEX is all I need. Now I have to go." Mendes stooped toward the door, carrying the huge bag, but the other man somehow got there ahead of him.

"Nice doing business with you," he said. "Stay safe for Mother New Seattle. And if you change your mind about that trebuchet, let me know." He slipped a card in the man's top pocket and patted it.

Mendes nodded and made his way down the stairs.

"It could definitely take a dachshund," Pulitzer called after him.

chapter

SEVENTY-THREE

I t was almost dark outside now and the warehouse was slipping into the gloom as the skylights above turned to a deep, impenetrable black. It was also cold.

The fridges had come waddling up to meet us as soon as we walked in the warehouse and I had chided them forcefully about the need to hide.

"What if we had been a Fridge Detail?" I said.

"We didn't think of that," said the Ice Jumper. "We were working on a new song. It's pretty exciting."

"Well, remember to stay hidden next time."

I took a walk through the abandoned cop drongles to try and clear my head as Nena found some candles and lit them in a little circle by the fridges.

The flicker of the light had a religious overtone to it. And somehow, that seemed appropriate. There was a pagan sense of awe about what we had seen—possibly not unlike how the explorers first felt when they saw an elephant, or how Galileo felt on discovering the moons of Jupiter.

The axis of the world had changed.

We sat down among the cop drongles.

"Maybe we were drugged," I said. "Or maybe they hacked our memories."

"You really believe that?"

"No. But I'm struggling to believe that there's another side to this city, one that's empty but for some people with a sharp fashion sense."

"They used to burn witches. They used to think Belgium was a good idea. Golf was once regarded as a sane pastime."

"I know. But perspective changes. The world moves on whether you are a part of it or not."

Fleetingly, I recalled the European law cordoning off large areas of Belgium with tape saying: "Much too dull. Do not pass."

Then something fell out among the drongles and the noise reverberated through the hangar, snapping the thought away.

"So we're going back?" I said, but I knew the answer. I had always known the answer. Of course we were going back. You don't make that kind of discovery then decide to forget about it and play cards instead.

"Yeah," she said.

We called the Tiny Eiger over and explained we were going on a little trip that was going to involve quite a lot of stairs. I took out the box with the head and put it in the Frost Fox.

"You can look after this," I said.

"What's in it?" said the fridge.

"It's a specialty of the area. You ever heard of a Fiorentina pizza without an egg?"

"Without an egg? Are you crazy?" said the fridge. "What kind of a place would serve you that? Hey! You guys, he's talking here to me about a Fiorentina pizza, but without the egg."

Nena went outside. When she had hailed a drongle, she came back in.

"Time to go," she said.

"You guys look after yourselves, do you hear?"

"No problem. Any chance of bringing us some yogurt?"

"I can't promise," I said, and led the Tiny Eiger outside to where the drongle was waiting. As we helped it inside, we heard the fridges all singing:

"Where's she gone?
Here's a bit of trivia,
It's got the highest bridge,
That's right! It's Bolivia!
So tell us exactly what he said
     about this Fiorentina pizza . . ."

Then I pulled the door shut with a grating crunch, and the drongle nosed off through the darkness, into God knows what future.

chapter

SEVENTY-FOUR

Rain.

We passed a police checkpoint and I felt my stomach churn. If they stopped us now, we'd be finished. The screens made a halfhearted attempt to flicker into life and then died.

Outside, more people were heading toward the fireworks. I tried to think about anything but where we were going.

"You nervous?" said Nena.

"A little," I said.

We pulled up near the building. I wrenched the drongle door open and we stepped out into the crowd. It was dark.

Instinctively, I looked around. A fiery red cloud of smoke hung in the distant sky, lit up by the wet city lights, and the full force of where we were going hit me once again.

chapter
SEVENTY-FIVE

Maybe this time, it would be death.

And for a moment, I remembered the dark rearing force that had swept through me in the head hack. I tried to steady my mind.

We climbed the stairs through the silence. There was barely any light. But the glare from the city found its way through the huge arched windows with enough strength to light the treads.

What was on the other side of that door was no more insane than the fact that slavery flourished. Or that people once thought Belgium was a good idea. It's just showing the world in a different perspective.

"It's just about perspective. And we are all free to choose any perspective we like," I said.

"Yeah, I guess we are," said Nena.

"You can even choose to ignore the truth," I said, looking at her.

"Yes, you can," she said, and she met my gaze.

And I had been choosing to see the world through a filter of the past.

We carried on climbing up the stairs, helping the fridge up the treads, which were each a bit of a leap for it.

But holding onto a healthy perspective, that's the really hard part, I thought. *Not forgetting it when you are swamped by events.*

"We're going to keep a mojito cold for him," said the Tiny Eiger unexpectedly.

"That's right," I said, patting the fridge. "You are. Good to hear your voice, little fellow. Come on." And I realized the revelation had swept away my fear.

We reached a landing and passed the bench where the old man had been asleep.

It was empty.

And for a moment, I recalled the gentleness of his face.

chapter

SEVENTY-SIX

Mendes slipped through the soaked crowds at the down-at-the-heels end of Rainier Avenue as the rain beat down methodically, rapping the tin roofs and spooning off badly made gutters in wild waterfalls.

The air was heavy, as though there would be thunder.

All about him, people hustled and shouted, scurrying under flimsy canopies, trying to stay under some kind of shelter. Someone up above was scraping a pan. The sullen metallic sound seemed as though it might be heralding the approach of a medieval body collector.

The drongles rambled lazily across the street and steam poured from the vent of a building that looked as if it long ago had given up the will to actually stand up, but somehow still managed to do so out of sheer habit.

Somewhere close by was an entrance to the tunnels in the city wall. He took out the map and unfolded it in the rain.

chapter

SEVENTY-SEVEN

The massive door opened with a recoil of dust, alerting the ravens, and their shadows dropped over the room as they flapped, screeching, at the windows.

We coaxed the fridge through, and the door shut behind us with a soft boom. The sound had a disconcerting finality about it.

We helped the fridge down the staircase, and it made a little leap on each tread until, eventually, we reached street level. Outside, it was just as before, except that now the wind was blowing furiously, and toward the horizon the dark sky was tinted with a deep purple.

Still no one.

The strangeness prickled.

We headed for the Quantum Physics Pizza Delivery Company through the empty, silent streets. Nena encouraged the Tiny Eiger now and again, and her words felt fragile in the emptiness.

The pizza company was alive with lights, exactly as before. We approached down the street, and I felt my life stretch out behind me, as though all the moments from my past were alive, and that each had had some kind of point to it that I had been unaware of at the time. But it had been to lead me here.

"Hello?" shouted Nena as we stepped inside.

But it was deserted, though the lights blazed and I smelled pizza.

"Service needs a little attention," she said.

"I guess we're not in any hurry."

I checked through the menu above the counter. They still had the Fiorentina but without the egg, and I looked systematically through the rest of the pizzas. Quattro formàggi, Napoletana, quattro stagióne, pizza Romana. All the ingredients on those were standard. They also didn't serve anything else, and I was reassured by that. Pizza places that also sell burgers are breaking some kind of unwritten but important law.

After a few minutes, a man dressed in a black suit and wearing sunglasses came through from the back to the counter.

"Ah, good, we've been holding your table upstairs. Please go up," he said.

"We didn't come for a pizza. We brought the fridge and the virus," said Nena.

"Please, go up to your table."

"We've had two pizzas today already. Who do we see about the fridge?"

"Please, you must go upstairs. I apologize that we are very busy today. I will take the fridge through to the kitchen. He'll be looked after there."

"You know about the virus?"

"Of course. Everything is taken care of."

Nena nodded and we made our way up the two flights of stairs. The room was packed. Tables had been jammed in at angles, all filled with people dressed in black, wearing sunglasses and eating pizza.

We were shown to a small table in the corner. It was more cramped than before. As soon as we sat down, a waiter came and took our order, and after a while a man dressed in black made his way across the room and joined us.

"I'm glad you came back for some more pizza. It's a great relief to have the test tubes. We will destroy the virus."

"Good. But we didn't come for the pizza."

"No?"

"No. What about the mayor?" said Nena.

"His operation will be destroyed. Maddox will see to that."

"How come Maddox is responsible for all of this?"

"He found the door as well. And we did a deal with him."

The waiter returned with our pizzas. The order was spectacularly wrong. I got a cup of hot milk, and Nena was presented with a bowl of radishes.

"Ah. They must be very busy. It makes the outcome of the order even more uncertain," said the man in black.

"Not even pizza?" I said, looking at the milk.

"No. Maddox will destroy the mayor's operation tonight, during the fireworks," said the man, adjusting his sunglasses.

"And the city wall?"

"We're working on it. That may take a little longer, but we'll try and nudge events in the right direction. Please, enjoy your food. You have done everything perfectly."

I tried the milk. It was smooth and comforting. I had not had hot milk since I was a child.

And I saw Nena was happily eating the radishes. I drank more of the milk and found I was going to have it all.

Fifteen seconds later I realized it had been drugged.

chapter

SEVENTY-EIGHT

A dream.

New Seattle, but the streets were deserted.

Except for a man dressed in a black suit wearing sunglasses, leading us somewhere. Someone else was there with me and I felt a huge sense of tenderness toward the person, but I didn't know who it was. Or why I felt like this.

Then a building. A set of stairs. And a huge wooden door and we stepped through. The interior was large and cool.

And outside in the street, New Seattle was throbbing with people.

chapter

SEVENTY-NINE

The mayor's eyebrows tilted viciously. "Still no sign of the last batch of the virus?"

"No. The fridge hasn't been found." The cop's jaw hung open out of laziness. There were ten of them around the table.

"And how long until we can be ready to release another?"

"Three weeks. A month. It takes time," said the scientist. "The process is very—"

"Yeah, yeah. This is bad, you understand? This assignment lost and the one before contaminated. It became an irony virus. Is that any help to me?"

There was a general shuffling.

"What good is it having people acting ironically? Just makes the city look stupid. What's the point of that? And why haven't you found that fridge? Give me a good reason why I should accept your flimsy explanations."

Maddox tried to sort his feelings into words, but it didn't

happen immediately, so his mouth made a variety of shapes and then closed again.

"You find that fridge all right," the mayor said, looking around the table, "and you do whatever needs to be done. Bring in anyone who might have seen it and head hack them here. This has gone too far."

"Yes, it has," said Maddox.

"I would hate for any of you to go the way of Lieberwitz," said the mayor. "He started having second thoughts. So I made sure he didn't have any thoughts at all after that."

There was silence.

PART THREE

chapter

EIGHTY

A raven screeched.

I sat bolt upright, staring the thing in the eye as it perched on the drongle roof. Then it was gone into the night.

The dream about New Seattle lay in my mind, and then was swamped by the cold reality of the drongle.

I sat up and tried to stretch away the cold stiffness in my back. I was unusually thick with sleep. Outside, an outlet of the Quantum Physics Pizza Delivery Company slipped by. It was a chain. They had one in Saratoga, I remembered.

A girl sat opposite, her long hair in straggling curls. She must have gotten in after I fell asleep. There was a small fridge next to her.

I massaged my head as we rumbled through a junction. It felt like I had a hangover. Maybe I had caught something.

New Seattle.

I had not been in this city for eight years. Eight years that had been filled with nothing more memorable than slightly cold food.

I stared out at the gleaming city lights and a massive

Health and Safety sign appeared over the shoulder of the girl, filling the dome with brilliant green light.

"Don't buy indoor houseplants. They look green and luscious in the shop, but will die in weeks," it said.

My life had gone missing since I had last been here, mislaid among too many motels, too many bad memories, and a never-ending succession of nights fogged with the bittersweet taste of mojitos. I had tried to close the door on all that had happened, but that door had never quite shut, and the past had seeped out in a deadly trickle.

Street after street of tall buildings ablaze with lights. I wondered what had possessed me to come back to this city. And then abruptly we juddered to a halt in a line of drongles at a police checkpoint.

The girl had been holding her head and now looked around.

"Thank you for traveling today," said the drongle's tinny voice. "Your lucky beheaded aristocrat is the Duke of Monmouth. Please take the receipt. It is being printed on material that may contain nuts, so if you are allergic, please use the tongs provided." A spool of paper unwound from the machine, and a pair of tongs clattered down through a slot and landed on the floor. Neither the girl nor myself said anything.

A cop pulled open the dome and jabbed his flashlight into our faces. "Out of the drongle," he said, his voice thick with officious boredom. "This looks new," he said. "Since when were there any brand-new drongles in New Seattle?"

"Is there a problem?" I said.

He thrust the flashlight in my face again.

"No problem. Just step out of the drongle. Routine police check to keep Mother New Seattle free from low-life scum."

We climbed out and stood on the sidewalk in the chill of

the night air as more drongles pulled in behind ours and waited in a forlorn line.

It occurred to me that I was wearing a suit that wasn't mine. The thought grew in strangeness, and I suddenly felt overly aware of my body. I checked the pockets and found a brochure from an exhibition about sharp corners. There was also an envelope with two tickets for something. None of these things were mine.

In another pocket were a pile of badly folded photos from a head hack, but it was too dark to make them out. I tried to recall what had happened, but the cop had returned, his cap pulled down improbably low on his head.

"Don't I recognize you?" he said, prodding my chin with the flashlight.

"No," I replied.

"You were through here last night," he said, running the flashlight over my face again. He was so close I could smell the pizza on his breath.

"I was in Portland last night."

Another cop jammed a cold jack pin into the feed at the back of my neck. My headache vaulted, trying to get out near my temples, and cut all my thoughts into small pieces.

"I recognize her, too. You were both through here last night. Is this your fridge?"

"No," I said.

"It's mine," said the woman, but her words lacked weight.

"Hey, he's an ex–New Seattle cop," said the one scrolling through my details on the Handheld Feed Reader.

"That's it," said the other cop. "I knew it was you. We sent you for a hack yesterday."

"I just arrived in this city. Five minutes ago."

"Great story. Let's hear his mood," said the first cop.

It played out as a piece of Motown that had bits missing.

"Guess what? The booths around here are all broken, so we're sending you both off to Head Hack Central. Again."

"Hey! We're not together," said the girl. "I don't know this guy."

"You do so know him," said the cop. He pocketed his flashlight and moved on to the next drongle. "Have a fun evening. Your fridge will be in the Cold Compound. That is, if it's not on the register."

My hands were cuffed and a thin red collar snapped onto my neck. They did the same to the girl. Then we were herded into a four-man cop drongle and after I kicked up a commotion, they went looking for my bag but they came back empty-handed.

A cop clambered in, hauled the hood shut, and sat there with his mustache casting a shadow across his face as we swept through the streets. Several picture screens flickered into life, and the image of a small man with short neat hair and overlarge eyebrows appeared. I felt a visceral dislike of the guy.

"Hi, I'm Dan Cicero, mayor of New Seattle. You might have heard of me. People call me the Mayor of Safety." His eyebrows overpowered the rest of his expression with their sheer bulk. "We have a zero-tolerance policy on danger in this city. If you feel scared or even nervous, call our slightly-on-edge help line, where a counselor will be happy to talk to you about nice things like pet rabbits." His eyebrows eased down to a stop above his eyes.

"Stay safe! Watch out! Stay safe! Watch out for that—" sang the screens. Then there was the drawn-out sound of a long, tortuous crash.

The mayor's face returned.

"And remember, please don't die for no reason. I mean, what's the point? Right?" His face flickered and then froze on the screens.

"Why does he say that?" I said. " 'Don't die for no reason'?"

"It's just a slogan."

"A slogan? But people do die for no reason."

"Hey, this isn't a seminar," said the cop, and he banged a panel with his foot. The picture flickered.

"Right," I said.

Another H and S sign swung by outside.

"Don't ever be tempted to let your girlfriend cut your hair," it proclaimed, sending a bright green swath of light strobing through the dome roof. I looked at the girl again.

"Do you have a headache?" I said. "I have a headache like my head has been in a vice."

"Yeah, so do I."

The cop banged the panel again to try and get the screens working.

"Hey, watch the screens," he said as they came back to life. "It's all about not bumping into tables. You might improve as citizens."

Welcome home, Huck, I thought. *Welcome back to New Seattle.*

chapter EIGHTY-ONE

Mendes went slowly, jabbing his flashlight beam across the walls and through the stale air. It smelled damp, and breathing it seemed like inhaling little bits of death. He headed farther along, dragging the bag with the SEMTEX behind him. Maybe that was why the heavy, dead air also seemed so irredeemably laced with sadness.

He was sweating more now from the fever.

It was hard to know where he was. The building drones had been hacked into so many times, and by so many different groups, that the tunnels they had made through the city wall were haphazard.

He came to another junction and unfolded the huge map so he could see the right section.

He thought he must be near the main gate now. He stopped to listen, but there was nothing but the cold, damp silence. For the first time in a long while, he thought about the place he grew up and how, when he had been a kid, he had gotten such pleasure from simple things like climbing the tree at the back of the house. He had done it so often the branches had worn smooth.

chapter

EIGHTY-TWO

Harsh fluorescent light.

The holding area was a temporary metal cage thrown up around some seating. A man in a suit had been brought in before us and squirmed about with enough audible sighing to fuel a small midwestern town.

A woman with a wild accent was standing at the bars, chewing gum trying to get the cops' attention. "Hey, sometimes you have to take a chance on people, don't you? Otherwise life passes you by and you end up as a quantity surveyor. What's the point of that? I had a cousin who did that. All I'm saying is that people who don't trust anyone else end up with nothing. Come on, let me out of here," she called. But the cops just ignored her, and she kicked the bars.

"Something's wrong," I said to the girl.

"Wrong?" She looked at me. She had brown eyes.

"Yeah. Do you feel as though you've stepped into another life—one that looks like the one you were in before, but with tiny, crucial differences?"

"I feel like I have a headache that could win an award."

"Yeah. That wasn't your fridge, was it?"

"No."

"You think something's wrong?" I said.

"Wrong? No."

The businessman sighed again. He clearly felt being here was the kind of injustice that would require nothing less than a personal apology from God.

A group of cops entered the cage with a flurry of keys. Two of them came over. "You two," said one, and then they herded the girl and me down the corridor with little more than the nod of a head and a grunt.

A line of framed certificates had been screwed carelessly to the wall. One said: "National Police Awards. Longest Stare at a Suspect without Saying Anything."

I tried to pull at the threads of the strange edges that seemed to surround everything, but all I got was a bunch of frayed ends. Our little party reached the head hack rooms and the girl was uncuffed and led into Head Hack One.

The cop took off my cuffs and a nurse led me through a corridor into Head Hack Two. "This way," she said. "Can I get you a glass of wonker?"

"What is wonker?"

"It's like water, but not as good."

She opened the door to the head hack room, and the smell of ammonia hit me so strongly I closed my eyes.

"I'm sorry about the fumes. I dropped a bottle. We've just cleared it up."

"Yeah," I said, as I struggled to see.

"The ether in the solution might make you feel faint. Through here, and we'll see what you have."

"You'll just find a few images of a bar in Portland and not much else," I said, trying to ignore the ammonia-induced tears forming in my eyes as she guided me into the chair and plugged into the feed on the back of my neck.

"Yes, I'm sure. But it's amazing what people store away without knowing, isn't it?"

"Yeah," I said. "It's amazing what you can store away."

While my hands were free I pulled out the head hack photos from my pocket. I felt a frisson of shock. The top one was of Abigail.

chapter

EIGHTY-THREE

The doctor stared at my folder.

"Your records have been deleted. Would you know anything about that?"

"No, I've just arrived in this city." But it was another loose end flailing about, and I didn't like it.

"I see. Are you aware of having any alfalfa allergy?"

"No."

"No? Doesn't make you feel sick? Or make your elbows tend to stick out more than usual?"

He demonstrated.

"Why would it do that?" I said.

"I don't know, but the human body is a remarkable piece of engineering. Type 3-B gel with alfalfa, please, Nurse. Can I check the box marked adverts?" He had turned back to me. "We have one about goose-down pillows at the moment that we can insert quite painlessly. It will play randomly in your mind for no more than a month. You will be paid a fee dependent on your age and social status."

"No, I don't want any adverts."

"Really? Do take a moment to consider this. We pay cash, and the intrusion is minimal. Many people find it life-enhancing."

"No adverts."

The doctor nodded.

I had known people who had come on hard times who had taken every advert going, until they could do nothing more than spend their days watching the endless stream of commercials vying for attention in their mind. It was possible to make a living like that, but only if you didn't want a life.

"Good. Well, sign here, and over here. And fingerprint there. And kiss the paper there, hard." He held the form for me. "Kiss there again," he said pushing it against my face again. "Harder. Kiss harder. As hard as you can. Harder! Even harder! Fine. This is your copy and your spare. I'll staple those to your jacket. There. The hack will take no more than a few seconds. I will not probe any further than twenty-four hours. You have my word on the oath I have sworn to the Medical Council Bear. Fire the head torsion, please, Nurse."

The two plates came forward and clasped my cheeks, holding my skull in an overtight grip.

"And plug into his feed."

I felt the nurse jam in the jack plug and then slop the cold gunge of the gel across my head.

"Head hack in three," said the doctor. "Nice and relaxed. Look at the picture of the lovely puppy. Pretend you're stroking the lovely puppy. Isn't he cute? Two, one. Imagine you're holding the puppy. Fire!"

chapter
EIGHTY-FOUR

S ir!" cried Kahill, breaking into Mendes's office in a
rush. "It's up! We have the system running again. Sir?
We turned the system off and then on again..." He
trailed off but still some words continued to fall from his
mouth. "We got the idea from a girl who works here. She told
us about her... lawnmower?"

But Mendes was gone.

Kahill looked around, as though he might find him hiding
behind the door.

Eventually he picked briefly over the bag and bottles that
were on the desk, then he sat in the chair.

He rocked it back and forth, leafing through the pamphlets by the upturned bag. They were from an herb fair. A
card slipped out from someone called Pulitzer. As he held it at
arm's length between his fingers, the phone rang.

He stared at it for a moment, then picked it up. "Mendes's
phone," he said. "The Pentagon? No, he's not. Can I help, sir?
Really? No, we've not had any problems at all. The computer
is sweet as a moose, sir. Yes, sir. I have the latest list of people

who have gone DST in my hand, sir, and agents are out there intercepting them as we speak. Yes, sir, we've even worked out the settings on the document destroyer. The *document destroyer.* No, sir, the *document—* Oh, it doesn't matter, sir."

He talked for a little longer, but as he was ending the call, an automated voice cut in and berated him for selling towels over the New Seattle phone system and the line went dead.

He put the receiver down in the cradle.

"Sweet as a moose," he said.

chapter EIGHTY-FIVE

I felt my head release from the boards and I forced my eyes open, but all I saw was a blaze of colors.

"Your vision will return in a moment," said the nurse, pulling out the jack plug from my neck feed. "I'll put the picture of the puppy right up in front of you. We've had a little problem. The doctor will explain."

"Mr. Lindbergh. We couldn't get any memories from you from the last twenty-four hours. I've called the engineer and he'll run a test on the equipment. I'm afraid you'll have to wait until we get it fixed. Someone will escort you back to the holding area."

My vision slewed back, and I saw the doctor holding up one of the printouts. It was white except at the very edges.

A cop came in to take me back to the holding area, and I noticed his eyebrows had been stained red. He cuffed me again and shepherded me back down the corridor, unlocked the cage, and motioned me inside. The girl was sitting there already. "Let me guess. Your printouts had nothing on them, too?" I said, still trying to clear my vision.

"The machine was faulty."

"No, something is wrong. And we're in it together."

"Look, I have a spectacularly bad headache, and I'd be grateful if you'd let me wallow in it."

"I've written a hymn!" cried a man, lurching over to us. He had drunk more than enough for an entire stag party. "A fucking hymn, because God forgives everyone, even really nasty people. Listen."

He took out a sheet and began singing in a gravely, late-night, whiskey-sanded growl, to the tune of a hymn that escaped me:

"I'm really sorry.
I've done something incredibly stupid,
But the innate fallibility of the human condition,
Means it's surely not my fault.
Not entirely anyway.
It's just generally a bit of a mess.
Presumably insurance will cover most of it."

Then he staggered toward the bars and collapsed.

"Hey, what's going on in there?" called one of the cops.

I turned back to the girl.

"We need to get out of here."

"We do?"

"That cop at the police check was convinced he saw us both last night, we've both got headaches from hell. I'm wearing a suit that isn't mine and my hair is shorter than I've ever known it. Something is wrong. We're in a world that isn't the one we should be in."

"Honestly, I feel a little tender for this kind of conversation..."

"The machine is fine," a voice called down the corridor.

"Please. They'll start poking further back. I used to work in a Memory Print store. Once you start to reach back more than twenty-four hours, things go wrong quickly. We need to get out."

"The engineer says the machines are fine," said a cop, unlocking the door to the holding area.

"I'm sorry if you have something to hide," said the woman as she got up. "Your past has got you trapped, hasn't it? But that's not my problem."

"They're going to destroy us," I said.

But she just smiled.

chapter
EIGHTY-SIX

A cop led us down the corridor, past the framed certificates, and back to the head hack rooms. Nena walked through the door to room one.

The same nurse met me and ushered me through the corridor that still reeked with ammonia. "Would you like another glass of wonker?" she said.

"It's like water—"

"But not as good. I remember you saying." I said as I grabbed a cloth lying by a bucket. I was guessing they had used it to mop up the spilled ammonia. As she turned, I held it to her face, hoping the solution contained enough ether to knock her out. She tried to scream and then staggered as the fumes overpowered her. Finally she collapsed.

I felt a stinging wave of the vapor wash over me and I crashed against the door. The doctor must have heard, because he came rushing through.

I took him out with one clumsy blow to the head. My fist ached with the impact. My eyes were streaming now, and I found a sink and washed them out as best I could.

Then I searched through the cupboards until I found a new bottle of the ammonia solution. I poured more onto the cloth at arm's length, until I could barely breathe. The ether in the solution began to make me light-headed.

A minute later I was stumbling through the entrance to Head Hack One. Nena was sitting in the chair with the boards clamped onto her cheeks. I lunged at the nurse and pressed the cloth over her face. The doctor made a clumsy attempt to grab me, but I fended him off long enough to see the nurse collapse. Then I knocked him out.

I scanned the head hack unit and pressed the abort controls. Nena fell forward as she was released, springing the jack plug from her neck.

"What's happening?" she said weakly, and I realized she had been in the middle of the hack. I looked at the pictures, but they were all blank, with only a faint blurring at the edges.

"We're getting out of here," I said. "Nothing in your memory still, you see?" I held up the pictures, but her vision was still scrambled.

"You're crazy."

I picked up a knife and put it to her throat.

"No," she said.

I cut off her red collar, and then mine.

I grabbed her hand. "Something is wrong."

"No," she said, trying to stand, but she was still dizzy from the head hack.

"We have to move, now. I was a cop once. I can get us out of here."

"I'm not going."

"Nena . . ."

"How do you know my name?"

I wasn't sure.

There was shouting from the corridor. "Don't you feel anything?"

"No."

"So you want to stay? Is that it?" I said, sensing this all going very wrong. "Okay, you stay. What do I care? I don't even know you." I crashed out of the room. She would have to take her chances.

Ten seconds later, I strode back in. She was still dizzy from the head hack and I knocked her out cold with one gigantic blow. She fell limply to the floor. "The thing is, I do care. I just don't know why."

I pulled the white coat from the doctor and slipped it on. It was tight across the shoulders. I poured more of the ammonia solution over Nena, picked her up, and staggered through the door to the main corridor. A cop stared at me, his mustache obscuring his mouth.

"Dropped bottle of ammonia," I said holding her toward him. "A little fresh air, and she'll be fine."

He grunted and then backed away as he smelled the vapor, and I took this as my cue to move off.

More offices.

And a line of prisoners hanging in sacks from a track in the ceiling. "I'm innocent!" shouted a man at me wildly. "I would never kill anyone in Fresno! Who in their right mind goes to Fresno? No one goes to Fresno." I shouldered past him, found the stairwell, and headed down.

It was two flights to the basement.

When I got there, I found the place was a jumble of dusty service pipes and junk lit by large, naked bulbs. I knelt down and put Nena on the floor. My back ached like hell. Then I moved around until I found the power supply junction box and kicked in the metal safety cage.

The cover on the box was rusty and bent, and sparks spat at me as I pried it away. Then I grabbed an old swivel chair and threw it as hard as I could at the tangle of wiring.

A smattering crack of electricity wound around the room, then the box exploded, sending showers of white-hot sparks flopping onto the floor. I ducked away as they landed like burning matches on my hand.

Smoke curled up, gathering in a thick foul-smelling cloud and I began coughing as another welter of sparks slashed across the room. For a moment, they lit up Nena. She'd staggered to her feet and was staring at me in shock.

Then darkness.

I fumbled my way over to her and found her standing like a statue. I pressed her ammonia-and-ether-soaked sweater to her face until she passed out again.

Why the hell did I care about this girl? What had happened to my life? I lifted her limp body in my arms and carried her up the dark stairwell, ducking into the shadows to avoid some cops.

A smell of burnt wiring knifed through the air. Cops were everywhere, brandishing flashlights in the darkness.

"She needs air. She dropped a bottle of ammonia. She's covered in it," I said, thrusting her toward the nearest cop as we reached the first floor.

"Hey, get her out of here."

The feed readers were all dead at the entrance to the main lobby, and they were too busy stopping people coming in to monitor those going out. I forced my way through.

The lobby was lit by the glow of red emergency lights, but a choir was still singing near the main doors.

"New Seattle Health and Safety," they sang. "Stay safe,

watch out, stay safe, watch out, stay safe, watch out for that—"

"Arrrhhh!" cried a man. "New Seattle Health and Safety. Remember, please don't die for no reason. I mean, what's the point? Right?" I froze, and those last words hung in the air, mocking me.

My mind segued.

And suddenly, it was Abigail's limp, soft body I was holding in my arms.

"She's gone and I couldn't stop it!" I shouted as I held her body. And then I was standing in the lobby of Head Hack Central holding Nena. People stared, keeping their distance.

I staggered out through the main doors into the night air with Nena in my arms. A few stars were out. A bunch of kids were milling with the crowd waiting to take drongle receipts. "Hail a drongle, and I'll give you five dollars," I said.

They all ran madly ahead of me. By the time I had reached the sidewalk, they had one stopped.

"The end of the world is reasonably nigh!" shouted a man on the sidewalk as I lifted Nena into the drongle. "The end of the world is nigh enough for there not to be any point doing big jobs. There might be time to paint the garage, but it's too nigh to bother with the undercoat. The end of the world is pretty nigh. Who wants a sticker?"

I pulled the door closed, muffling the sound, and the drongle juddered off through the traffic. I stared at Nena, lying limp across the seat.

Why did I care about this girl? What had happened to my life? Why did the world seem different but only in the smallest of ways? Why could they find no memories of the last twenty-four hours in my head? Or in Nena's?

I had been back in the city for less than an hour, and

already I had attracted enough trouble to feed a family of badgers for a year.

And then it struck me. It was obvious why they couldn't find any memories.

We had been mind wiped.

chapter
EIGHTY-SEVEN

Wires hung from the drongle panels in shrouds, and the screens were missing.

I stared at Nena, then out at the city.

I tried to work out how much time I had lost, but I had no idea what day it was. My mind skidded about, pulling out useless information and brandishing it in front of me as some sort of displacement activity, so I didn't have to deal with the whole situation.

The drongle lurched to a stop across the street.

"This is South Jefferson Apartments. Please leave the drongle now. Your lucky color today is green. Your lucky thing with a handle is a spade."

I swung open the door and lifted Nena out of the drongle into the chilly night air. I was out of shape and my arms ached like hell as I stumbled awkwardly across the street, sidestepping drongles, and into the apartment block's main entrance.

The door to Gabe's apartment had been kicked in.

"Hello? Marcy? Gabe? Hello? I shouted. The place was empty. I laid Nena onto the sofa and sat down.

Then I went through my pockets and placed everything I had with me on the table. I was intending to examine them, but I suddenly felt drained. A raw emptiness invaded my head and sucked the energy from the rest of my body.

I closed my eyes.

I wouldn't sleep. I would just rest. And only for a moment.

chapter

EIGHTY-EIGHT

The mayor looked at the man as they walked down a corridor. He was bald and wearing a red bow tie.

"You want me to be there during this song by Rusty Ragtail the Safety Squirrel?" the mayor said. They were in part of the main-gate complex of the new city wall.

"Yeah, we thought it would be a nice touch to open the show with you being serenaded by the safety squirrel," said the bald man as a knot of people in outlandish costumes pushed past in a flurry of crackling, shiny material.

"We felt, in terms of marketing, that we'd be presenting a strong image. The two big voices of Health and Safety in New Seattle, together. The cuddly furry animal on one side, representing life and vitality and beauty, and you the mayor on the other representing—you know—whatever it is you represent."

The mayor stopped. " 'Whatever it is I represent?' "

"Yeah. It's all been rehearsed. Please," said the bald man.

"I'm the mayor," said Cicero. "I represent power. I represent this city. Who the fuck are you? I'm not doing this. Get my drongle," he said to the cop following them.

"Please, think about it," said the bald man. "The safety squirrel is very popular. What if it was to run for mayor against you next time?"

"What?"

"Marketing surveys show he's more popular than you. I didn't want to say anything before, but... this way you'll be tapping into his appeal."

"Your drongle is ready to take you to city hall, sir," said the cop.

chapter
EIGHTY-NINE

A raven screeched.

I stood up before I was awake. The world spun and I staggered, griping the sofa arm.

The raven was sitting on the table in front of me. For a moment, my mind was too thick with dizziness to comprehend what it was. And then I watched it hop nonchalantly out of the open door of the apartment. Events came back to me in a jumbled rush.

Nena.

She was still lying there and I felt my shoulders release. Probably I had only been out for a few minutes.

The sudden rush of adrenaline met the remains of my headache, and the two mixed badly. I needed coffee.

I yawned and my eyes ran with sleepy tears as I closed the apartment door and walked to the kitchen. Then I caught sight of my face in the mirror by the door and saw I had short blond hair. I stared. For a second, I had the sensation I was nothing but a tenant in my own body.

I made coffee, hoping I might get something out of Gabe

and Marcy's appliances, but they were all nonspeaking. I recalled how his washing machine had become pretty depressed once because it didn't like going round and round and wanted to be a fridge instead, and they'd had to retire them all to a home someplace because using the kitchen made them too emotional.

I stared out the window, wondering what I thought I would find in New Seattle. A mulch of fading apartment blocks led away into a ramshackle haven of run-down streets, blinking lights, and spewing wood smoke.

Maybe Mending Things with Fire was still out there, serving half-decent mojitos.

When I came back with the coffee, Nena was standing and pointing a gun at me. It was a police-issue weapon, and I guessed she'd found it in the apartment.

"Don't follow me," she said.

"Nena, we've been mind wiped. Take a moment to think about this. Have some coffee and think about it."

"Coffee? If you make any move to follow me at all— *at all*—I fire."

"Listen to me. We've both lost time. I don't even know what day it is. We're mixed up in something together."

"Any move at all. You got that?" And she edged toward the door.

"Nena. Okay, they've taken the memories, but not all the feelings. Look at me. You feel something?"

"No." She didn't move. Her expression didn't change.

"But you haven't left yet. You do feel something, don't you? But you don't know why. This is where the story to find out begins."

She still held the gun on me, but I sensed she lacked the same intensity. I took a step toward her just as the apartment door was kicked open.

As I turned, Nena threw me at the figure and I fell heavily across him. Then she was gone.

"Nena!" I called scrambling after her, but I was dragged back and then felt the cold prod of a gun at the back of my neck.

"Don't even think about moving. You've got some talking to do."

The voice was familiar, and for a moment my mind rifled through my past, scavenging memories of voices from anywhere it could find.

"Gabe?" I said. "Is that you?"

"Yeah, it's Gabe. And who the hell might you be?" he said, still with the gun firmly in my neck.

"It's Huck. Huck Lindbergh."

"Huck?" He turned me over. "It is you! And what is up with your hair?" Then he picked me up off the floor. "Huck!" And he hugged me and started laughing. "I should have guessed. My world turns upside down, and you appear for the first time in eight years. I'm guessing the two things are not a coincidence."

"Gabe," I said. "I'm sorry if I've dragged you into this."

"Don't be. It's good to see you. Eight years. I thought you were only leaving the city to clear your head."

"I know, that was the idea. It just never really happened. And I'm sorry to do this, too, but I have to go."

"Go?"

"I have to find that girl. I'll be back. Five minutes."

"As long as it's less than eight years," he called.

"Yeah," I said, and ran down the stairs.

When I got to the street, there was no sign of her. The drongles rumbled lazily by, and the normality of the scene was overpowering.

I ran a little way down and checked out some of the side

alleys, trying to catch a glimpse of her. Eventually I kicked a pile of garbage in frustration. A kid saw me and shouted: "What's the matter? Lost your fridges?" I turned and stared at him. "Lost without them, are you?" he said as he ran off.

I turned this over in my mind for a moment, connecting it with the fridge in the drongle, but then I dismissed it and headed back to Gabe's apartment.

"You find the woman?" he said.

"No. She was gone."

"Perhaps that's just as well. It looked like she was trying to kill you."

"Yeah, that's pretty much what happened. I tried to per-suade her we knew each other, even though we didn't, exactly. It's a complicated story with some oversize bits missing."

Gabe poured me some more coffee. It was warm rather than hot now, but I was happy with anything that wasn't wonker. That was when I heard him laughing like a three-year-old. "What's so funny?"

"It's good to see you, Huck. I've missed you. And I've missed the chaos that always surrounded you," he said, and finally sat down.

"Yeah. Is Marcy okay?"

"She's away for a couple of days on business. She's ter-rific. She'd love to see you."

Even though I had not seen this man for eight years, I sensed we were picking straight up where we left off, and that was both touching and humbling.

"So, you know what's going on *at all*?" I said.

"No. I've just been released from Head Hack Central and I'm missing a chunk of time, about a day. You know anything about that?"

"Only that I'm missing a chunk of time, too. What's the date?"

"Friday the twenty-ninth."

"Then I'm missing about a day as well." I sipped the coffee. "Head Hack Central wipe your day?"

"Yeah, it's a new directive. It came in three months ago."

"This city is going to hell."

"Yeah. And what about you? How did you end up here?"

"It's a long story. I came around in a drongle with that girl, Nena. But I was wearing different clothes and I had this stuff in the pockets." I pointed to the collection on the table.

"Okay," said Gabe. "Well, now we're getting somewhere. That's one of my suits you're wearing. And one of my shirts. And you've a red patch, see? Right across the chest."

I undid my jacket.

"Red is a restricted color. The cops have the franchise. So I'm guessing that was an arrested stamp that faded in the rain. Looks like they wiped your mind, too, but you came here before we were taken or you wouldn't have that suit."

"You should have been a cop. We could have spent seven years walking the streets of this city together," I said, and I looked at him properly. There were more lines across his face now, and his hair had flecks of gray, but it was unmistakably the same Gabe with his inexhaustible supply of goodwill and patience.

"I'm sorry if I got you into this," I said.

"And I'm just glad that you're here. Real friends are hard to find in this world. I'll make some fresh coffee, and then we'll go through what we know. I'm guessing we have enough here to piece it together."

When the coffee was done, he sat down and I explained exactly what had happened to me. How I had come around in the drongle with Nena and a fridge and a headache the size of Canada, to what had happened at the police checkpoint, how we had taken a trip to Head Hack Central, and how

I had escaped with Nena and brought her back to his apartment.

"Okay," he said, when I had finished. "Nothing fits." Then he began laughing.

"What's so funny?"

"I won't say it's been boring, but it's been quiet. What have we got here?"

We picked over the things from my pockets. An envelope with two tickets to the fireworks that night. A brochure to an herb fair and a pile of head hack photos that had taken a battering.

Among them were several shots of Nena in a drongle, and one of her in a head hack room with a nurse and doctor lying prostrate on the floor.

"Look at this one," I said.

"You think she knocked them out?"

"I wouldn't put it past her."

And then I leafed through the ones of Abigail. "I must have had a long-term head hack. I don't know why they would do that. I'm lucky to be alive." The words resonated and hung in the air as I stared at the picture of Abigail.

"She was a wonderful woman," said Gabe eventually. "These last years have been tough, haven't they?"

"Yeah. I haven't quite sorted them out."

"Sometimes bad things happen." There was a pause. "You want to talk about it?"

"No."

"Sure. Why don't you take a shower? I'll get you another suit. That one appears to have been on fire."

"Yeah, that sounds like a good idea. It's ironic, isn't it? I tried to pretend that the past with Abigail didn't exist, and now here I am having lost the past for real."

"Life does strange things to us. You take a shower. You'll

feel better. I'll do a proper sweep of the apartment. If you're wearing my clothes, then I'm guessing there may be other clues here."

"Thanks, Gabe," I said.

The water felt unbelievably good, and it washed away the remains of my headache. I got dressed in another suit Gabe had found, and felt a lot more human.

"You okay?"

"Yeah, I'm fine. What have you found?"

"You want to talk about Abigail now?"

"No. Is that okay?"

"Yeah, sure, take your time. So what have I found? Well, that's new," he said pointing to a blue bottle on the table.

I picked it up. It was a sample of healing balm.

"It's from a healing fair that's going on downtown at the moment. This map was out, too." He opened it up, and the paper crackled as he flattened it on the table. A red line had been added by hand.

"And you see that?" he said. "I've never drawn on this map, and that route starts from just around the corner and ends up near Seneca. I know that area a little. There's a cop drongle warehouse there. I worked security there a few years back, and even then it was pretty much abandoned."

"This entrance is close by?" I said, pointing to the other end of the red line.

"Five minutes."

chapter

NINETY

The little blue lights of the drongles zipped by in the spitting rain, and across the street an advertising balloon on an apartment block bobbed and swung. We took a turn down an alley that was choked with garbage.

Eyes watched us from dark windows, but the street was deserted. Somewhere far away, a dog was barking. Perhaps at strangers, perhaps out of fear. A coffee table came sidling out a little way down.

"Want to buy an equity fund?" it said.

"No."

"What about an index-linked pension with a stock option? Or a juicy portfolio?"

"No, thanks."

"Okay," it said, and scooted off.

The door to the tube system was painted black and red. And it had vast lettering on the side that said: "New Seattle Police Department. Hookup 489." It looked stark in the night air.

"How do we get in?" I said, running my hand over the door.

"Plug into a feed and it opens automatically if you have clearance. Most of the cops have clearance. There's no way we'll force it."

I looked down the alley and up to a window where a woman watched with folded arms. She turned away and stepped back out of sight when I met her gaze.

The alley smelled of burnt oil.

"So if we can't get in now, how would we have gotten in earlier?"

"Maybe we didn't," said Gabe.

"Okay. So the leads we're left with are the bottle from the herb fair and the cop drongle warehouse near the other end of that route. You want to check out the warehouse first? And then the fair? And if we don't find anything at either, what do you say about heading over to Mending Things with Fire?"

"You still drink mojitos, then?" said Gabe.

"Yeah, some things are never meant to change. And drinking mojitos comes firmly into that category."

"Sure. You mind if we walk? I need to stretch my bad leg."

chapter
NINETY-ONE

For once, I didn't mind walking.

My headache was still hanging on, and the evening had settled into a panorama of stars, whitewashed with a gray haze from the city lights. Around us, advertising balloons bobbed above the buildings, their tether chains occasionally letting out mournful shrieks that pierced the deserted alleys.

The main streets were more packed than usual, and it took Gabe a little while to work out that the fireworks were that night. So we kept to the back alleys, and they were quiet. We talked about Marcy and times past, and the scrapes we had gotten into together. And then, after a pause, Gabe said: "So why did you come back, Huck?"

"I couldn't stop seeing the bad memories. And I thought that if I came back maybe I could start my life again from where it stopped."

Up above, a group of ravens were disturbed from their roost and circled the sky.

"I'm sorry you've had a bad time."

"Yeah. I got stuck trying to pretend that I didn't have a

past. I thought that was the answer. It took me a long time to realize that if you try and fight what's happened you're never going to win, because to fight the past, you have to live there. And it's a sad place to live. The same things happen all the time."

"I guess they do."

"Maybe I was always weak. And that made me vulnerable to events."

"You weren't weak, Huck. You were committed. And that made you vulnerable."

"You think so?"

"I know so. It's all about how you see things, Huck. You can see the world any way you want. That's the choice we all have."

"Perspective," I said, and stopped.

"Yeah, what?"

I realized my legs didn't have their usual tightness and I wondered when that had eased away. "Have you ever come across a place that serves a Fiorentina pizza, but without the egg?"

"No. Why?"

"I don't know. I feel like I've had a Fiorentina pizza, but without the egg."

chapter

NINETY-TWO

The small drongle warehouse office was in chaos.

Strewn piles of papers were scattered over the desk and unopened mail from years before lay like autumn leaves on the floor.

I followed Gabe as he threaded his way through the debris of discarded parts and scattered tools until we got to the main hangar at the back. It was a patchwork of shadows cast by the abandoned drongle shells, old smoke canisters, and piles of boxes.

I kicked a candle, and saw a little circle of them had been laid out on the floor.

"Hello?" I called, but my words stumbled through the dead drongle carcasses and then recoiled. "Anyone?" I called again. Then there was a slit of light over to our left, and I saw a tall object shuffle out from behind a pile of crushed cop drongles.

"Hey!" said the fridge. "You're back! Is the Tiny Eiger with you, because we're missing the top harmony."

"The Tiny Eiger?"

"Yeah! Did you manage to get us any yogurt? You said you'd try."

"Sorry, but we're light on the yogurt," I said.

"Are you feeling all right?" said another fridge, opening its door and spilling shadows out into the mass of the hangar. "Maybe you need some Primula. Processed cheese, straight from the tube. It's a great snack!" And it opened its doors to reveal a tube so flat it looked as if it had been hit repeatedly on an anvil to remove the last of the contents.

"No, thanks," I said.

"I know you wanted us to hide if anyone came by," said the first fridge. "But we've been working out the harmonies to a song about sell-by dates. Do you want to hear it?"

"Not just at the moment. Just wait a minute—"

"Would you like your clothes dried before we're quiet? I feel a spin coming on."

"No."

"Hooot!" said another fridge.

"Okay, look everyone, just chill out a moment."

They all started humming furiously.

"How are we doing?" said another fridge. "Did you want your box back? I've been keeping it safe for you." And it opened its doors to show a wooden box on the bottom shelf.

"Yeah, I meant just everyone calm down, okay?" I said, pulling out the box. It was heavy and it smelled bad. I pried open the lid. "Ah," I cried.

"What?" said Gabe. I showed him and then I put the lid back on and slid it into the fridge.

"Lieberwitz. Poor bastard."

"That explains how we got access through that door."

"Yeah. But how the hell did we get hold of it?"

"Okay, so can you guys tell us what has happened to you over the last day?" said Gabe to the fridges.

"Sure."

"We know all kinds of stuff," added another. "We know the date of the Klondike gold rush. *And* we know the difference between a stoat and a weasel."

"That's useful," said Gabe, "but let's stick to events over the last day."

"Hatchoo," sneezed the other fridge. "Sorry. A peppered steak went bad on the top shelf. Still haven't gotten over it."

"Does anyone have anything that needs drying? I really do feel a spin coming on," said the tumble dryer.

"Maybe later. Just tell us what has happened in the last day. Could you do that now?"

"Sure. Is Nena coming?" said the nearest fridge, and I saw it was a Frost Fox.

"Nena isn't here right now."

"And then we are going to Mexico?" said the other one, moving closer.

"Ah tequila!" the three of them sang. "La! La! La! La-la! La-la! La-la-la! La! La-la! La-la! La! Tequila!"

"Sh," I said. "Let's keep the noise down. Just let us know what has been going on. It's important."

"Oh, I see. Sure," said the Frost Fox. "It was like this. I had a tube of Primula, and the Cold Moose had a pizza, but he wasn't letting on. We all knew, but he kept sticking to his story about having a carrot that was so bendy that you could tie a knot in it."

"Hey, that wasn't a story. I do have an old carrot," said the other fridge.

"Oh, yeah. That's right."

"And some pesto. You forgot my pesto."

"I was coming to the pesto. I was working up to it via the carrot."

"Guys," I said. "I'm guessing the food you each have is not the central part."

"You think?" said the Frost Fox.

"Just bear that in mind as a possibility." I leaned back on a drongle hood. There was just enough light coming from the open doors of the two fridges to throw huge irregular shadows over the roof.

"Sure. Well, the Ice Jumper had an out-of-date chicken fricassee," the Frost Fox went on, "just in case you were wondering. He was pretty protective of it, too, but the Tiny Eiger had racks of test tubes with some sort of virus in them. And that was weird, particularly as he didn't say anything. Anyway, we were holing up in a park, just chilling, and that's when we first met Nena."

The story took a while, particularly as there was a lengthy section about eating the pizza. And a slight holdup while the Cold Moose tried to be sure of the sell-by date. But in the end, the Frost Fox told us everything it knew. I got the whole sequence straight in my head—from the fridges being taken to the Halcyon motel by Nena to them meeting me, to being taken to the cold store by the cops and then being rescued. The Frost Fox described how they had walked to Gabe's apartment and then come here through the big tubes. And then how Nena and I had left with the Tiny Eiger.

"You never said where you were going."

"I really do feel a spin coming on. You sure none of you have anything that needs drying? Not even something small?"

"Not just at the moment," I said, and tried to piece the whole thing together, but there were still bits missing, like where the envelope had come from with the money and why I had blond hair. But the key seemed to be finding out where I had gone with Nena and that fridge.

"You sure you don't know where we went?" I said.

"No."

"But we know where Nena is," said Gabe. "She'll have gone back to her motel. And once the management sees her, they'll call the cops."

"You're right. We need to get over there," I said.

And then a crash, and a flurry of flashlights poked into the office, their beams spilling through the door.

"I heard an owl hooting in here," said a voice.

"Sure you did," said another.

"Let's get out of here," whispered Gabe, and we cajoled the fridges back into the body of the vast hangar, weaving our way through the abandoned carcasses of the cop drongles.

I stopped to look back into the dark of the hangar. They were about thirty yards away—a group of figures in dark orange uniforms and caps were searching among the crates with flashlights.

"Fridge Detail," I said.

And then, abruptly, another man appeared from behind a drongle not two yards away. He stared at me. His hair had been plastered to his forehead by the rain.

"Hello," he said, waving his flashlight in my face. Something bothered me about him. His hair was the same blond color as my own. The same head hack blond.

"The wizard promised me an owl," he said eventually, as he stared.

"What wizard is this?" If this guy shouted for help, we were finished.

"Are you the wizard? The wizard promised me an owl."

"No, I am not the wizard," I said. "Absolutely not."

"He has a sneezing cat."

"I don't have a sneezing cat. Good luck with the wizard, though. It sounds like a great thing to be involved with."

The guy was clearly crazy. And I remembered something about mentally ill patients being shunted onto Fridge Detail to free up more space in the wards. There had been a scandal whipped up by the papers for a bit. I remembered how people pretended to care for a few weeks until the news moved on. The causes people cared about were dictated by fashion, and last year's sufferers were as easily disposable as last year's wardrobe.

He stood there staring. "I thought I heard an owl just now."

"No, there was no owl."

"But I heard it hoot."

"It wasn't an owl."

From behind me, I heard a fridge inexplicably do another impression of an owl.

"There. You see? I should look. Owls are good at hiding."

"There are no owls here." I would have to take him out.

And then, from where the rest of the group was searching in the hangar, a voice shouted. "Huckleberry Lindbergh! Here, now!"

My mind froze. Events slipped sideways.

I glanced around, but Gabe was well ahead with the fridges now.

"Huckleberry Lindbergh!" shouted the voice again. "I will not have members of my Fridge Detail wandering off. We search this place systematically. As a team."

"I'm coming," said the man, staring at me.

And then he backed away and made his way toward the other flashlights.

"Did I hear that right?" Gabe said, appearing out of the darkness.

"Yeah. He was answering to my name. We have to get out of here. Is there a back way?"

"Yeah, through here."

He led us all back through the piles of abandoned drongles to an exit. It was jammed, and when we forced it the noise reverberated through the warehouse like an earthquake. Fifty yards away, I saw the excited flutter of flashlights from the Fridge Detail.

"Quickly, move."

chapter

NINETY-THREE

We hurried down an alley.

A tube from the Prisoner Rapid Removal system ran alongside.

"Hurry," I said to the fridges as they waddled along as best as they could.

They were not the ideal companions in a chase.

"I need the box," I cried to the Frost Fox. I grabbed it from the fridge's bottom shelf and ran ahead to a door into the tube as Gabe cajoled them along.

I plugged in the lead from the head. If this didn't work, we were finished. The Fridge Detail was spilling out of the warehouse, jabbing at the night with their flashlights. I could hear them shouting like a pack of dogs.

Finally the door swung open. The fridges were about twenty yards back now, and the Fridge Detail was gaining fast.

"Hurry," I cried. A shot recoiled off the tube above my head. And then another. "Get to the door," I shouted as their little feet pedaled madly through the mud and debris. The first fridge was there now. And then the tumble dryer. But the Ice Jumper was still five yards back.

I could see the faces now of the closest ones. The detail was strung out in a line.

Gabe grabbed the Ice Jumper and virtually manhandled it inside.

I plugged in.

The door shut and snuffed out the light. Above our heads, a huge metal eye hung from a track in the roof.

"Let's go," I said, and we began walking off in single file along the tube. The fridges opened their doors and the little slices of light sank into the distance, barely finding the wall. A thin trickle of oil ran along the floor, making the going slippery.

Shouting and shots outside the door.

But anything else was lost in the noise of the grating roar of machinery above as the track clonked into life. A screen flickered ten yards away, and a man appeared.

"You have been arrested by the New Seattle State Police," he said, his voice just audible over the track, "a force that is dedicated to your well-being. You should feel proud to have been arrested by one of the top-four state police departments on the Western Seaboard Area, as voted for by the readers of *Happiness, Money, and Golf* magazine." He held up a copy. "And maybe that's because New Seattle P.D. officers have some of the finest mustaches anywhere. A mustache is more than just facial hair. It represents our commitment to justice for the people of New Seattle. It represents our belief in human rights for all people all around the world. And the other thing is, you can use it to do this trick with a cocktail stick and an olive."

We walked on.

The soft slits of light from the fridges fell in thin columns, struggling to illuminate the gloom, which was studded with a fog of falling particles vibrated into the air by the shaking track.

The noise was deafening. When it finally fell silent, my ears rang, as though some part of the noise had gotten inside my head and now needed to be released. Far off in the distance, we heard someone shouting, and then the sound of a drill.

We came to an intersection and disturbed a scattering of rats that ran off unhappily down the slippery metal into the darkness. Gabe unfolded the map.

We took a left. The track kicked into life again. The atmosphere was damp and alien.

And then, ahead, the light from the fridges caught the shape of a body prostrate on the floor. I nodded to Gabe and we approached cautiously. Gabe kicked it gently.

Then he kicked it harder.

The man squirmed in fright and sprang to a crouch.

"Don't shoot!" he cried, his words clanking about the tube as he shielded his eyes. "Are you the cops?"

"No."

"You going to get me out of here? I can't get out. And now I'm lost."

"Yeah, we'll get you out. Keep walking." He had a heel missing from one shoe so he bobbed up and down.

"I ain't seen anyone. Just heard shouting now and again. Far away, but I could never find it. Couldn't get any of these doors open. This place gives me the spooks. You guys are my angels, though. I thought I was going to die down here. Those your fridges?" His words rang and clattered around the tube, mixing with the clanking roar of teeth over our heads.

"Yeah."

"Nice. I've always liked fridges. Any of them got anything to eat?"

"I've got some Primula," said the one. "You want some?"

"Sure."

"Hey, just keep moving."

"But he wants some Primula. Here."

The fridge opened its door wide and the man took the tube. He tried to squeeze it out into his mouth as our column began moving again, holding it above his head as he bobbed up and down.

We came to a junction and Gabe pulled out the map and traced a route to the Halcyon. We went right. And then left to an area where the track didn't seem as if it was in use yet. Sheaves of wires hung down in sad tentacles that fell across our way every now and again, so we had to sweep them aside.

The guy had gone quiet, and I watched his figure bob up and down as the wind howled across the metal, rattling a loose wire forlornly on the outside. After another five minutes, we came to a door.

I took out the box and plugged in the head and it swung open. The guy looked into the box.

"You guys are angels," he said staring at the head. "If there's anything I can do for you, let me know." And then he swallowed, stepped through, and hobbled off down the alley.

"Are we crazy to let him go?"

"He might go to the cops," said Gabe, "but I doubt it."

chapter
NINETY-FOUR

The Halcyon motel was in a decaying, decrepit, frankly-couldn't-give-a-damn part of town. Most of the buildings around here were an advert for single-story hell.

The door from the tube opened in an alley around the corner.

We left the fridges there and walked to the corner.

Across the street was a Health and Safety screen, flashing that you should only go on vacation if you didn't mind throwing all your standards out of the window. Otherwise, you should stay at home where ALL YOUR NICE THINGS ARE. The last words were in capitals.

We headed down the street in the evening gloom, but as we got closer, a bunch of cop drongles slithered around the corner and came to a flamboyant halt right outside the Halcyon. A muddle of security vehicles had already gathered under the glow of arc lamps. More cops from Security Detail piled out carrying laser-sighted guns.

"I'd say we've found her," Gabe said. "But so has everyone else."

chapter

· NINETY-FIVE

Nena had already taken a shower. The bathroom was disgusting, and the plumbing sounded like a snarling dog, desperate to get off the leash. But the water had eased her headache.

She sat on her floor, drinking what was left of the whiskey and wondering why she had checked in here in the first place.

Red streaks dripped from the walls, and the room was littered with spent smoke canisters. There was a collection of empty bottles on the desk marked: Osteopath Urgent Response Unit Massage Oil. And a large torn picture of a puppy had been left lying near the bed, along with a wallet.

It was from someone in police marketing and its contents were mostly missing.

There was also a hole in the ceiling and someone had gone through her stuff. But there wasn't much to take.

She thought about reporting it to the management, but presumably they knew the cops had been here. And anyway, she was too tired. She poured herself another whiskey and wondered about the guy who had pulled her from Head Hack Central. He'd been interesting, but not interesting enough to get mixed up with.

She took the whiskey over to the bed and found a picture on the bedside table. When she held it to the light, she found it was a head hack printout of her in a drongle.

On the back was a note from someone, saying she had been mind wiped and if she wanted to know what had happened, she should come to the address below.

She turned this idea over in her head.

Clearly she had been arrested and lost some time, but she was too tired now to chase after answers. And maybe she should just get out of here anyway. Too much had happened.

After a few hours of sleep, she'd make for the state line and put this all behind her.

She lay down.

chapter

NINETY-SIX

The explosion threw her off the bed.

Smoke clouded the room. And then black figures burst toward her, prodding at everything with red laser sights that crisscrossed the air but found only scattered clothes, a sad, sagging bed, and the prone body of a girl on the floor.

They fell on her in a tumbling, wild scrum.

She was turned face upward and searched as the smoke began to coalesce and drip down the suits of the detail. Someone with a huge plume of feathers stuck to his helmet loomed over her.

He bent down, thrust a jack plug into her feed, and then scrolled through her details on a Handheld Feed Reader. He played her mood. It was a bit of happy Motown that jarred with the atmosphere.

He pulled out the plug, and the jerk reignited her headache before leaving a cold trail through her skull.

Two members of the detail barged forward and dragged her out by the heels, over the filthy carpet and then outside over the cracked tarmac of the litter-strewn parking lot that smarted under the harsh, artificial glare of the arc lights. The area was alive with cops, standing around drinking coffee and eating doughnuts.

She had already been sucked out of life and into the system.

Another member of the Security Detail placed a machine on her chest, but he was abruptly dragged away, leaving the machine to clatter onto the ground.

After a moment, another cop knelt down next to her. "Shh!" he said, taking off his helmet and holding his finger to his lips. It was the guy from the drongle.

"Maybe I did feel something," she said, "but it was hard to tell. So don't count on it."

chapter
NINETY-SEVEN

Sky Malbranque was lost.

The Fridge Detail had been let into the Prisoner Rapid Removal system ten minutes earlier.

The cop they found in a pastry shop couldn't see how anyone could have gotten in there, let alone with some fridges, but he had been tired and wanted to get home. And having five overly excited people from a Fridge Detail gabbling away had just gotten too much for him.

And now, Sky Malbranque wandered brandishing his flashlight at the walls with awe, as though he were Lord Carnarvon entering the tomb of Tutankhamen.

At each junction, Sky Malbranque listened for the hoot of an owl. "Owl?" he called into the darkness. "Are you there?"

He wandered on, footsteps echoing from the metal.

"Hi! I'm Dan Cicero, mayor of New Seattle. You might have heard of me," said the voice, reverberating into life on a screen a little way down the tunnel. "People call me the Mayor of Safety." The picture froze. Sky Malbranque watched, his head tilted to one side.

"Are you the wizard?" he said. And then after a while, when nothing happened, he took off his orange coat and covered the screen. "Dead man," he said.

And then he froze. He was sure he heard a hoot echoing faintly down the tube.

He scurried after the noise and eventually saw slits of light.

"Hey," said the Frost Fox as he approached. "Want to hear a song about sell-by dates? We've been working on the harmonies."

"I heard a hoot," said Malbranque.

"Yeah, that's the Ice Jumper. He likes to hoot."

The fridge did another owl hoot.

Malbranque stared wide-eyed, then walked over and patted it. "The wizard said he would get me an owl. I'm going to look after you," he said. "I've never had an owl before."

"I'm not actually an owl," said the Ice Jumper.

"You must be," said Malbranque. "I heard you hooting. You are the most beautiful owl I have ever seen. What do owls eat?"

"Yogurt," said the fridge. "And milk and hummus."

"Then I shall get you some. Would you like to come with me, owl?"

"Yes," said the fridge. "I would like that."

And Malbranque led the fridge out into the alley.

"Bye, everyone," called the Ice Jumper.

"See you!" said the tumble dryer.

"Yeah, catch you later," said the Frost Fox and the Cold Moose.

And they watched as Sky Malbranque led the fridge off by the hand.

"Der! Der! Der! Boom! Boom! Boom! Boom!" he hummed in a vague approximation of *Thus Spake Zarathustra*.

And the fridge joined in.

chapter

NINETY-EIGHT

"Hey! Get some cuffs and a collar on that girl, then bag her and track her out of here," called a cop across the lot. "We have another target located, so let's move, people!"

"You felt something?" I said.

"You think you can read me? Is that why you're here?" she replied as Gabe helped me stuff her feet into a sack and pull it up to her chin.

"I'm here because we're in this together."

Another member of the Security Detail came over, hauling yards of heavy chain. He wound it around her and then attached a massive hook at the top, near her neck.

Then he left.

Police drongles were beginning to pull out now, and everywhere people were packing equipment. We dragged Nena right through them all, weaving through cops whose uniforms were covered in red streaks.

We were close to the corner to the alley when a member

of the detail stepped out in front of us. A massive plume of feathers sprouted from his helmet.

Other cops closed around us.

I could see the door to the Rapid Removal system behind him.

The one with the plumes removed his helmet.

"She's not going that way," he said. His face was running in lines of red sweat. "She's going special delivery! Put her in the drongle. She's going for the mother of all head hacks."

A group of cops took her from us and dragged her across the lot into a waiting drongle. I felt my heart pump wildly.

They shouted the address into the horn.

It was on Twenty-third Avenue.

chapter

NINETY-NINE

Across the lot, we searched for an empty cop drongle. "We have to stop this. That kind of head hack will kill her," I hissed to Gabe.

"We'll get her out of there. We'll think of something."

"Where are you headed?" said another cop, catching me as I opened a drongle hood.

"Twenty-third Avenue," I said.

"Great. Hey, Harry. This one's going to Twenty-third, over here."

They clambered in and closed the door.

"Your lucky boxing stance today is southpaw," said the drongle, "and your lucky light industry is the manufacture of nickel/steel bearings. For Health and Safety reasons, don't die for no reason. What's the point? Right?"

"Don't die for no reason," I said. "What kind of a slogan is that for a city?"

"Yeah, I preferred the old one: 'Live life and eat more of the creamy center,'" said the cop called Harry.

"That wasn't a slogan. That was an advert you had

implanted," the other cop said. He had a pockmarked nose.

"Was it?"

"Yeah. It was for cookies. Don't you remember? You had it planted because you wanted some extra cash."

"Oh. Well it was good, whatever it was. You didn't have that one?"

"No, implanted adverts are bad for you. I read about it," the one with the pockmarked nose said, shaking his head.

"They say everything is bad for you. Even food is bad for you, if you believe some things you read," Harry replied.

"What sort of food?"

"All food."

"How can all food be bad for you?"

"That's what they said. All food contains stuff in it that is bad for you."

"So what was the advice?"

"Make sure you select a reclinable chair from Randolf's," Harry said.

"What?"

"Make sure you—oh, no. That's another advert I had implanted. I'm getting mixed up."

"Your mind has gone. I could get more sense from a badger." The cop with the pockmarked nose shook his head again.

The drongle crept forward as the crowd heading for the fireworks began to build up further.

"This thing is too slow," I said, feeling powerless.

"What the hell was that?" said Harry, and he pointed to the sidewalk where the crowd was panicking.

A yellow blur gleamed in the evening lights, and there was a muted explosion as it hit the sidewalk. People began to scream as our drongle finally moved on.

"It's a melon," said the cop with the pockmarked nose. "Someone's dropping melons from the roof again."

"Oh, yeah," said Harry and sat back in his seat.

The cops chattered on inanely for the rest of the journey but I tuned it all out, willing us through the traffic.

I felt raw emotion for Nena. She was someone that I knew, and yet had not met. I was no longer clinging on to the past with every fiber in my body, and she was the reason. I was willing to take a chance on the future. And I hadn't done that for years.

We slid in through a set of gates and into a massive lot.

"Thank you for traveling in this police drongle. I hope you are able to make the world a safer place today. And please take a few minutes to sneer at the Chicago safety squirrel. It's a piece of crap compared to Rusty Ragtail."

I swung back the door and stepped out. The night was clear. Above rose a massive, gray building.

It was city hall.

chapter
ONE HUNDRED

As we approached the entrance, a gigantic picture of the mayor stared down smiling. Underneath were the words: "Stay safe for Mother New Seattle!"

We followed the other cops inside.

"Huck, think rationally about this. If we get caught now, we're in an ocean of trouble," said Gabe.

"I'm getting her out of there."

"I know. I'm just saying don't let your heart rule your head, okay?"

"Okay."

The whole building was sleek and faceless, as though nothing that happened here would stick. Security was checking everyone in.

"There she is," I said. Ahead, Nena was being dragged down a corridor. But first, we had to get past security. A cop with a smoke canister tucked into the back of his belt was standing just in front of us. I pulled the tag and then pushed him into the waiting line.

A red plume sprouted from his back and he fell, taking out another cop holding a riot shield.

It caused enough chaos for us both to slip into the heart of the building. We headed down the corridor, passing offices until we came to an internal lobby with a receptionist sitting behind the desk. "Which floor for the head hack rooms?" I said.

The girl looked up vaguely from painting her nails, then focused on something that clearly wasn't us.

"Hi," she said. "My name is Monica and this is city hall. How can I help you have a safe day today?"

"Hi. We're looking for the head hack rooms. What floor would they be?"

"Would you like to speak to someone about our range of safety leaflets?"

"No thanks. We just need to know the floor."

She had pretty, procelain features, as though she spent most of her days sitting here away from the sun, wrapped up in her own world.

"Top floor," she said vaguely, and it occurred to me the thousand-yard stare didn't actually originate from shell-shocked troops; it was something they picked up from watching receptionists who had been interrupted while painting their nails.

I felt a tightness in my throat as we stepped into the elevator.

"We were good at this once," I said. "We broke in on hoods, prostitutes, and every kind of low-life scum this city has produced. Do we still have it in us?"

"You never forget, Huck."

"No?"

"No. There are some things you never forget."

"Yeah, you're right about that," I agreed.

The elevator doors opened and we stepped out on the top floor. People in white coats were wandering around. I tried the first door. It was a science laboratory. "My mistake," I said as the people looked up. "What the hell was that?"

"That's the place where they've been making the virus the fridge was storing. Right here in city hall."

A little farther down we came to the head hack rooms. The corridor was busy, so we tried not to look out of place and we peered cautiously through the small windows. In one, there were five cops and about the same number of technicians. Nena was already strapped into a head hack chair. I edged the door open a touch so we could hear what was going on.

"Where is my fridge with the test tubes?" A man dressed in a tuxedo had his face pressed up close to Nena's. "You had it in your motel room. Did you steal it from here?"

"Do you see that? That's the mayor of this city. No wonder the place has gone to hell," I whispered to Gabe.

"Your records say you haven't been mind wiped, so you can't pull that one. You know where it is. Look at me. I'm the mayor. Don't mess with me."

I checked that the small red cop gun was loaded.

And I thought, *look in their eyes; that always gives away who's going to freeze, who's going to run, and who's going to get himself killed.*

"Head hack her," said the mayor, "and dig as deep as you like. Find out why she decided to do this. And who helped her. And hey, little girl, don't die for no reason. What's the point? Right?"

"No!" cried Nena as the machine kicked into life and her head was clasped between the boards.

I looked into Gabe's eyes. "You never forget," I said, and then we burst through the door.

"Freeze!" I shouted and the cops stood, unshaken but immobile, staring. A flutter of pictures was printing out from the machine. I swept my gaze around as they stood nonchalantly.

"What is this? April Fool?" said the mayor.

"Turn it off," I said, approaching the technician by the control panel as Gabe covered the cops.

"Leave it running," said the mayor.

I let off a round next to the guy's head. "Turn it off," I said quietly. He nervously shut the machine down. The noise vibrated away, and pictures from the hack continued to print out methodically in the silence.

"You think you can mess with me?" said the mayor, and his eyebrows became agitated. "Do you know what happens to people who mess with me?"

"Huck," said Nena as she came around and her head was released from the boards.

The cops stared.

"Get her out of there," I said.

"You're finished. How the hell do you think I stay safe?" said the mayor.

The door slammed back and I spun around as a horde of cops flooded through. I aimed the gun, but my finger hovered over the trigger.

A scuffle of bodies took me down and they ripped the gun from my hand.

"Who the hell are these clowns?" said the mayor, brushing down his tuxedo with his hands. "Head hack them all and find out who is trying to upset my operation. And dig so deep there's nothing of them left. I've had enough of this. Now, I have to get over to the celebrations. Give me a report later," he said and left with a small entourage.

The cops manhandled us all into head hack chairs. Gabe

had been knocked out cold and sat limply, his head hanging forward. I looked at Nena. We were going to die or come out as vegetables, and live a waking death.

"This is not the end, Huck. Tell me this isn't the end. Lie to me if you have to," she said.

"I don't need to lie," I said as they slopped cold gunk over my hair.

"Really?"

"Really. Safe journey, Nena. Don't be scared."

"You mean you're not scared?"

"No."

"No, you're not. I can see it in your eyes."

And then the gel ran down and blurred my vision.

I had come back to this city looking for a switch to start my life again, but all I had ever needed to do was open my eyes. My future had always been here, waiting for me to take part, but I'd chosen not to see it.

The machines began to fire up, and my thoughts blurred.

I had been free to see the world any way I chose. And now I chose to see it full of shadows and magic. And love for this girl I would not see again.

I had finally come home.

Then my mind tingled and flamed as though it was filled with fireflies.

Images ran amok as if disturbed by a soft breeze. Pictures of Nena, one after the other, spun through my mind, vibrant and sharp.

And then the machine began to claw further back and my life started to open out before me, spinning back through the years at Memory Print, bars, and motels and faces and voices.

And then through the years with Abigail. And as the memories streamed through me, I saw that our time together had been a complete thing. And that the love she had had for me still ran through my body like a white light.

And then the pain began to grow. Images were sucked from my consciousness too fast to comprehend as the machine clawed at my past with a fury that was tearing out my very essence. In the distance, a darkness rose, its power beyond anything I could comprehend. I fought it, standing my ground, but I could feel its menace crush my soul to a tight incandescent ball.

Then darkness.

I fell forward.

After a minute, I opened my eyes and saw the blurred outline of cops strewn about the floor.

"My name's Maddox," said a voice. "We don't have much time."

chapter

ONE HUNDRED AND ONE

I managed to turn my head and, through the streaming head hack gel, saw that Gabe and Nena were both still moving.

"They're tranquilized. I can't start killing cops. I've had too many years in the force," said Maddox as he started to unstrap Gabe.

Behind him a cop stirred and raised his gun. I tried to speak, but my mouth was dry. It was all happening in a horrible slow motion.

"Even if the force has gone to hell," said Maddox. He still didn't see the danger.

Then there was a crash as a window smashed. A flying object came sailing in and caught the cop on the head. He dropped the gun and it clattered across the floor as he slumped down, knocked out cold.

Maddox turned.

The cop had been hit by a small dog. I tried to focus. The dog got to its feet, shook itself, then sat panting happily.

"Right," said Maddox. "A dog. Huh." He finished undoing the straps holding us to the chairs. "We have very little time."

He helped us all to our feet, then led us out of the room, and into the corridor. It was deserted. The three of us were all weak and stumbled along like wounded soldiers. "Evacuate the building," said an alarm coolly. "Leave in an orderly manner."

Maddox opened the door to the first lab. It was empty. He threw in a grenade and then hurried us away. The thing exploded, shaking the walls and bringing down the ceiling tiles.

"There is a small fire, but it is under control. As a precaution, please evacuate the building," said the alarm.

We passed the next one and he did the same thing. Another huge explosion.

We reached the stairwell and hobbled down, flight after flight, until we reached ground level. The lobby was in chaos and we shouldered our way through the crowd. The girl at reception was still painting her nails as people crushed against her desk.

We hustled our way through the scrum of technicians and cops until we were outside.

Smoke poured from the roof of the building.

"Who the hell are you, Maddox?" I said.

"Doesn't matter. Get the hell out of here. Your records will all be cleaned up over the next few weeks. Stay low until then. Take a cop drongle from over there. Go."

Applause.

The six-foot furry squirrel had just finished singing the song to the mayor.

"Ladies and gentlemen," said the bald marketing man, "I give you Rusty Ragtail the Safety Squirrel." There was a huge cheer and the squirrel came to the front of the stage to accept more applause. And bunches of flowers.

"I hope you enjoyed that. And I hope you like the new city wall!" said the marketing man.

The crowd cheered inanely.

"But remember, what you see behind me isn't just a wall. It's a symbol! It's a statement from everyone in this city! And you know what it says? It says, 'This is New Seattle. The city of safety. A special place. And whoever you are—whatever creed or nationality, however far you have traveled to get here—go away! Get the hell out of here!'"

The crowd applauded, but the sound was more polite and obedient this time.

"Let's hear it again for Rusty Ragtail the Safety Squirrel," added the marketing man, and another huge cheer allowed him to move on. "Now we come to the official opening, and I'm proud to be able to ask our very own mayor, Dan Cicero, to cut the ribbon on this historic evening."

"Thank you," said the mayor. "I feel privileged and humbled to be standing here on the cusp of such big changes in this remarkable city of ours. New Seattle is a city like no other. And I think it's right, on an occasion like this, for us all to take a moment to give thanks that we don't live in Chicago. And so, it gives me enormous pleasure to declare this new city wall open."

But as he cut the ribbon, an explosion rocked the other side of the city, and a fireball rose into the night sky.

chapter

ONE HUNDRED AND THREE

The cop drongle shuddered and the sky above us glowed red, reflecting off the drongle shell in a myriad of shapes.

"Who are you, Huck?" said Nena as she looked at me.

"You know who I am."

"No. I know what I feel, but I don't know who you are."

"He drinks too many mojitos, gets irritated when he sees sculptures made of rusting metal displayed in a woodland, or someone in a jazz trio wearing a hat. And he cares like hell about you," said Gabe.

"As you can tell, this man knows me pretty well."

"So that's it? That's all I get?"

"For the moment. And what about you. Who are you?"

"I'm Nena."

"Yeah?"

"That's it. That's all *you* get. I'm just me." And she leaned against my shoulder and closed her eyes. "I'm just a girl from a small town someplace."

The drongle slipped smoothly through the streets. The

checkpoints were stalling huge lines of traffic after the explosion, but the cop drongle just sailed through and we continued on until we reached a jammed interchange. The drongle took a sharp left and squeezed down an alley that was thick with Dumpsters as we wove our way toward Gabe's apartment and away from the traffic.

"Looks like you made it," said Gabe. "Welcome back to New Seattle. It's a hell of a city."

"Yeah, it's a hell of a city."

The drongle came out on Main Street and we could only inch forward. It was the kind of traffic I remembered from the New Seattle Festival of Traffic, when an area of the New Seattle streets was purposely gridlocked in celebration of St. Ryan the Late who, theologians claimed, would have been at the Last Supper had he not been held up.

The drongles were stuck solid, fender-to-fender, in a giant smorgasbord of traffic as people tried to get to the celebrations. Ours lurched and stumbled slowly up onto the sidewalk, forcing the crowd to scatter as we bumbled a little farther.

Finally we came to a stop with one wheel slewed up onto the sidewalk, and a dribble of blue liquid cascaded down the inside of the drongle shell.

"This is South Jefferson Apartments. Please leave the drongle now. Your lucky thirteenth-century heretics are the French Cathars. Please take the receipt that is being printed. It may contain traces of dead fox." Then the drongle began printing out yards of receipt.

We were still a block from Gabe's apartment, but I popped the hood, helping Nena out onto a sidewalk as the entire drongle filled with paper.

Ahead, all we could see were a sea of little blue domes

and, above, the pinpoint white lights of the tall buildings and the advertising balloons melding with a sky rich with stars.

And the three of us walked through the evening night air, feeling properly alive.

ONE HUNDRED AND FOUR

Gabe made coffee, and I sat on the sofa. Nena was leaning on me, half asleep.

"So, you should just be in time," said Gabe.

"In time for what?" There was a playfulness in his voice.

"The party," Gabe replied. "You have two tickets."

"I think we might give it a miss. We're pretty tired."

"Hold on. What kind of attitude is that? And you haven't even seen what I have for Nena yet."

"What is it?" she said, opening her eyes sleepily.

Gabe held up a white ballgown he'd had behind his back. It rustled and cracked with chiffon. "It's Marcy's. I'm guessing you're the same size, and she'd want you to have it. This is a special day."

"Gabe!" I said.

"Oh, it's beautiful," said Nena, standing up.

"And since you've ruined all my other suits, you might as well ruin my tuxedo as well," he said, and held that up with his other hand.

"It's so beautiful," said Nena, holding the dress up to herself. "Why don't we go? Have you really got tickets?"

"Yeah," I said, finding the envelope from among the things on the table. "VIP tickets. Gabe, I've ruined your apartment, most of your clothes, and very nearly your life. And still you offer me more stuff?"

"That's what friends are for, Huck. Now, get this girl to the party."

Nena looked stunning.

Her hair hung down in straggling curls and the dress rustled as we walked through the evening under the rafts of stars. Above us, another massive Health and Safety sign declared: "Don't go into a room and then forget what it was you went there for. What's the point of that?"

The sidewalk was thick with people and, as we got closer, I held her around the waist as this great swarm of humanity swept us on. It seemed like the whole city was here. A group of men with furiously large blond wigs a little to our right were carrying cans of drink and cheering randomly at pretty much everything they saw.

"Brilliant lamppost! Just brilliant!" cried one. And they all cheered. "That metally thing there? Awesome!" cried another. And they all cheered again.

We hustled our way left, weaving our way past rosy faces until we could see the security cordon thrown up amid a festival of flags and banners and streamers.

Around us, women in lavish dresses with their hair swept

up in beehive hairstyles, and men in sharp suits and bow ties that refused to sit flat, held each other arm-in-arm. We waited in line for the VIP area. The security personnel were all dressed in black-and-white uniforms, looking like large, overofficious badgers.

They were plugging into everyone's feed, but they were only checking their moods with a Handheld Feed Reader. A couple in front of us both had pretty somber moods, and they were both guided to a first-aid tent on our right.

We reached the barrier.

The woman was young and had an easygoing air about her. She inserted my tickets into a machine. It bathed them in red light and then played a happy little chord. She waved a jack plug at me.

"Just need to check your mood, sir." I twisted my head so she could plug in. After a moment, I heard a piece of Handel's *Messiah*. "That's great," she said, and then plugged into the feed on Nena's neck. Her mood translated as a massively upbeat big-band number.

"Glad you're both in such good moods this evening. One of the happiest couples we've had. I'm sure you'll have an awesome time. Enjoy the party. I hear the Lodge of Maculfry is very cool. It's a full hoot tonight."

"Thank you," I said as we walked through the cordon and into a long snaking tunnel of white canvas that opened out onto an area that had been decorated with twirls of ivy, palm trees in pots, burning torches and wild streamers, and enough party lights to rival the stars. Turf had been rolled out onto the road, a wooden floor had been laid, and there were tables piled high with food and a full orchestra playing sweeping music.

Everywhere waiters with drinks trays were swanning effortlessly about, among the women in party dresses and the men in smart suits, buzzing around tables stacked with champagne glasses.

"This is so perfect," said Nena, holding onto me.

"Shadows and magic."

"And music and dancing. *And* champagne."

And as we stepped together out into this unreal landscape, the arcing explosion of fireworks cast a melting flame across the sky, leaving it thick with falling sparks and plumes of smoke.

N ena stood by the edge of a fountain to watch the fireworks explode above in rafts of silver trails as I wove
my way over to one of the tables laid out with bottles
of champagne.

A man sat on a step near the table. His jacket was torn
and rolled in dust, and his hair poked up in wild, uncared-for
peaks.

"He didn't get interrupted. He just got stuck," he said,
looking at his reflection in a bottle of champagne and then up
at me. "Coleridge. He got stuck. He claimed that the poem
Kubla Khan came to him in an opium-induced dream, and
that he never finished it because he was interrupted by a person from the village of Porlock who came around for tea."

"Right."

"But really he just got stuck. What do you think he meant
by 'floating hair'?"

"Who?"

"Coleridge."

"I've no idea. You okay?" I poured some champagne into a couple of glasses.

"I have a fever, but it's nothing. Can I ask you something? Have you ever done anything stupid?"

"Yeah, sure," I said.

"Then you're lucky."

"Lucky? What do you mean?"

"I never did. I was always the good kid. Always doing the right thing."

"Well, you didn't miss out on anything, believe me. Nice meeting you. Enjoy the party."

But the man grabbed my jacket as I tried to pass so that I spilled a little of the champagne.

"You don't understand," he said, looking into my eyes. "All those years at Philadelphia High, at Harvard, at the Pentagon, I did the sensible thing—because I was *responsible.*"

"All right. Take it easy."

"And now I'm going to do something stupid."

"Fine. You do it."

"Yeah, I'm going to do it." He let go of my jacket and walked off uncertainly. I watched him go and found that a waiter was already topping off the glasses.

"Allow me, sir."

"Champagne!" I said to Nena as I returned under an umbrella of sparks scattering across the sky.

"I love champagne. We should toast."

"Sure, what to?"

"To forgotten friends," she said.

"Good choice. To forgotten friends."

Awesome," said the mayor, stepping onto the stage, as the sky dripped golden trails.

I held Nena close.

"Thank you! Just to let you know, there has been some trouble over at city hall, but it's nothing to worry about. But we are looking for someone. And that's anyone who is not in a good mood! Seriously, if anyone is feeling unwell, or they have a dip in their mood, we do have first-aid tents around the perimeter, all equipped with friendly Labrador puppies that you can stroke. But now we come to the moment for blessing the wall. We are very honored to have the Lodge of Maculfry with us today!"

Lights flooded the stage to reveal a mass of people dressed in black robes, each wearing a pointy black hat that must have been three feet high.

"This is Maculfry Hoot number 364. It is an authorized hoot under the laws of hooting. Silence for the hoot!" called a man. He wore a purple hat adorned with lights that flashed in time to his words.

The crowd noise dropped.

The beat of a single large drum. And all the people with the hats began swaying slightly.

"Mac-ul-fry! Mac-ul-fry!" shouted the man at the front. "Mac-ullllll-freeeeee! Hoot!"

"Hoooooooooot!" they answered, drawing out the word as small white lights blazed from their hats.

Then silence.

After a while a single man in the crowd jumped and shouted: "hoot!"

Then a few more began randomly jumping in the air and also crying "hoot." The lights on their hats flashed each time they jumped, so you could pick out who it was.

This went on for around five minutes.

And then all the people on the stage leaped into the air and simultaneously shouted: "Hoot!"

And then knelt.

"May this wall be blessed with all good things," said the man at the front with the purple lights flashing on his hat. "May all those it stops getting in and out be blessed with happiness." He motioned them to all stand up, and they all shook each other's hands. Then he turned to the crowd again. "And that concludes this hoot."

Cheers from the crowd and a certain amount of clapping.

"You might like to know we shall be hooting again in two weeks time at the opening of Congress," he said.

The orchestra began to play again.

"Well, that was relatively insane," I said.

"Yeah, but kind of cute as well. Shall we dance?" Nena said.

"Yeah."

"New Seattle Health and Safety!" sang the choir on the

stage. "Stay safe! Watch out! Stay safe! Watch out! Stay safe! Watch out for that—"

"Arrrrrrrrrr!" sang a woman in a warbling opera singer's soprano.

"Stay safe for Mother New Seattle!" they sang on chirpily to the strains of the orchestra. "Stay safe for Mother New Seattle! Do not die for no reason! Unless it's absolutely unavoidable!"

And as we danced to these extraordinary lyrics, in the middle of the square amid a sprinkling of other couples under the shadow of the main gate as rafts of fireworks began to explode over us again, I realized that the slogan didn't bother me anymore. Sometimes people do die for no reason. And it's just the way the world is.

And then we were taken up by the atmosphere as we glided amid the fairy lights, getting lost in the music and the magic of it all.

And there was nothing else that mattered.

In Porlock, there was still no sign of Mendes, and nearly all of the other operatives had gone home now, their eyes red with tiredness.

But Kahill stayed.

The latest printout from the computer showed a major DST alert from near the city wall main gate.

Perhaps the machine was not working entirely accurately, but the alert was massive—the largest he'd ever seen.

He tried to contact the agents again, but the communications system was down now.

It insisted he was selling towels.

He walked up the fire escape steps onto the roof and was momentarily surprised to find that it was dark. When he reached the parapet, he saw the blaze of lights and realized it was the night of the fireworks display.

"If you do this, then we're finished, and Mendes will kill me," he said, staring out. "Whoever you are, don't do this thing."

chapter

ONE HUNDRED AND NINE

The orchestra came to the end of the piece as another volley of fireworks drenched the sky in streams of silver.

We held each other, oblivious that the music was gone, still cocooned in a haze of well-being. Eventually, Nena pulled away and grabbed another couple of glasses of champagne and some canapés from a waiter and handed them to me as the lights dimmed and the stage was flooded with red smoke.

"Is this processed cheese?" I said as I tried one of the canapés.

"Could be."

"One of the fridges had some today. It was obviously my destiny to try some."

"You believe in destiny?"

There was a wild unexpected crack, and a deep booming shudder. The surrounding buildings felt like they all shuffled a bit to the left.

"Just when it comes to processed cheese," I said uncertainly.

A sweeping circle of huge birds, disturbed by the sound, came flying across the sky in a loop.

A flurry of fireworks exploded in a mass of abrupt sparks. And the letters on the city gate blazed into light. "Good night! Stay safe! Do not die for no reason! What's the point? Right?"

Then the fairy lights around the square blinked.

Darkness.

Someone screamed uncertainly.

And the wall shivered.

From the parapet, a butterfly of masonry fell in a shadowy arc, dropping in slow motion before exploding on the ground.

"The end of the world is nigh!" called a voice in the silence.

And then the massive bulk of the wall fell, leaning in the darkness until there was a heartrending implosion that rumbled on and on, spilling the heavy scent of lavender and ginseng out among the clouds of choking dust.

And as the sound echoed away, the void was filled with screams, and cries, and moans of people in agony.

Sparks belted up from frayed electrical cables, and a broken water main scudded thick trunks of water toward us like runaway fountains. More waves of choking dust fell in a huge engulfing cloud, and mad, bleating sirens began to wail.

Chaos gathered momentum in the darkness amid the wall of heart-agonizing moans of people crushed and dying. And I felt the world gathering itself up ready to brace against the terror and fear that had already been released.

I scrambled through the dark.

"Nena," I called. "Nena!"

The crowd broke into a wave, and came hurtling over the square as one like a swirling beast, trampling everything.

"Huck," I heard her call somewhere, and her voice was desperate.

A mass of bodies. Eddying pools of people riven with panic, churning through the square like a tsunami of fear.

"Huck," she called. And as I crawled toward her voice I saw her lying on the floor, in the moment before another wave of people swamped over the two of us. There was a massive blow to my ribs. And then nothing.

Silence.

Utter silence.

I picked myself slowly off the ground. "Nena!" I called.

"Huck," she cried. I staggered to where she lay, aware that the square was deserted. "Are you all right?"

"My ribs ache. What's happened? Where is everyone?"

"I don't know. It doesn't matter," I said, and lifted her into my arms. "You're going to be all right. We'll find someone."

"Do you think we're dead?" she said.

"We're certainly . . . alone."

"No, you're not alone," said a voice. "And you're not dead. We pulled you out. We felt that it was not your time." It was a man dressed in black standing a few feet away. Through the dark, I could just make out that he was wearing sunglasses.

"Come, you'll both be safe now. We don't have champagne here, but we do have pizza."

EPILOGUE
FIVE MONTHS LATER

We looked out across the city from the hill in the park. A tree grew there, its branches forking shadows onto the grass, and its leaves spraying a cloud of maple green above our heads. Down below, people walked dogs and fretted over young toddlers who were running slightly faster than they had the capability to control.

It had been a close-run thing for the park, teetering on the edge of oblivion as it slowly decayed into another patch of wasteland, but a group of citizens had come together and resolved to repair the paths, plant the beds, and sweep away the litter that had accumulated over too many years.

We were sprawled out on a rug after a picnic, feeling the breeze on our faces. And listening to the swifts wheeling overhead with their soft screeches.

"I've had to wait too long to meet Nena. And is this a Fiorentina without the egg?" said Marcy, waving a piece of pizza.

"Yeah, it's a new thing we discovered."

"So how did you manage to end up in Mexico with the fridges?"

"We had some help," I said.

"There's something you're not telling us."

"Yeah, but it involves the Heisenberg uncertainty principle."

"What the hell are you talking about?"

There was an open feel about this city now that I really liked. Even the mustaches on the cops seem less obtrusive. "I made a promise to keep it quiet to someone with sunglasses. I like this city now."

"It's changed somehow," said Marcy. "The ravens have all gone, too. You notice that?"

I lay with my back on the grass of a hill and stared up at the clouds as Nena rolled on top of me.

"So, we are home now?" she said, and I caught the expression in her eyes.

"Yeah," I said, "we're home." Her face smiled against the gently drifting clouds.

Many people had died when the wall came down, crushed in the scrum of the panicking crowd. It had brought out a wave of national sympathy, and an outpouring of public grief that seemed to have helped heal the city itself. The wall had been removed, and the scar planted with a park. So now the city was encircled in a ring of green.

The mayor was among those who had died.

I looked at Nena and realized how good it felt to lie here with her so close.

"We're definitely home," I said, aware of ground under my back as her weight lay on top of me.

"Good," she said. "I've never had a home before. I'm definitely having more champagne then." And she rolled away.

And the four of us spent the afternoon there, basking in the pleasure of one another's company, drinking and watching the sun float down into the bay, making the sky ripple through a blush of colors.

And then, toward dusk, we packed up the picnic and prepared to wander back down the hill in the warm evening air. But just for a moment we all stood at the top of the hill under that big maple tree, looking out across the city, and I put my arms around Nena. Then Gabe's gentle voice carried on the breeze. And after a moment I realized he was reciting the speech that was supposed to have been made by Chief Seattle.

" 'Tribe follows tribe, and nation follows nation, like the waves of the sea. It is the order of nature, and regret is useless.

" 'Every hillside, every valley, every plain and grove, has been hallowed by some sad or happy event in days long vanished. Even the rocks, which seem to be dumb and dead as the swelter of the sun along the silent shore, thrill with memories of stirring events connected with the lives of my people.

" 'And when your children's children think themselves alone in the field, the store, the shop, upon the highway, or in the silence of the pathless woods, they will not be alone. In all the earth there is no place dedicated to solitude. At night when the streets of your cities and villages are silent and you think them deserted, they will throng with the returning hosts that once filled them and still love this beautiful land.' "

And the four of us walked down toward the city.

about the author

TIM SCOTT lives in England. He writes for radio and tele-
vision and won a BAFTA in 2003. This is his second novel.